The Triplet's Odyssey

Tome I : Celtic Origins

Marcelle Chapleau and Paul Corriveau

MARPA Productions

Edition
MARPA Productions
686, McIver
Bury (Quebec)
J0B 1J0
Tel.: 819-872-3765
Marpa.productions@gmail.com
Cover Pages Art Work: Martin Corriveau

Legal Deposit for Library and Archives Canada, 2016
Dépôt légal — Bibliothèque et Archives nationales du Québec, 2016

Available from: Amazon.com and other retail outlets

Available on Kindle and other retail outlets

Printed by CreateSpace, An Amazon.com Company

ISBN: 978-2-9816425-2-3
ISBN (ePub): 978-2-9816425-3-0

To be published:

The Triplet's Odyssey

- *Tome 2: The Sacrificed...*

Warning:

This book describes certain events that have taken place, areas that exist, and displays vivid characters. However, it remains a work of fiction and therefore does not claim to be exact.

About the Author

Marcelle and Paul, "MARPA," are two grandparents and co-authors of this Odyssey. Each, in their own way has evolved in the context of their career: Marcelle as a nurse, Paul as a military officer, consultant, historian, and both as a trainer, coach, mentor... Their professional and personal experiences contribute to their writings. Their travels and interactions within different cultures and their ongoing apprenticeship, as their odyssey, serve as the backdrop to the story.

Dedicated to our children Isabelle and Martin,
To their spouses, Loan and Paul,
And to our dear grandchildren:
Maxim, Marcus, Lili Rose and Jolan.
You do not cease to blossom and amaze us.

Our gratitude goes to our collaborators and friends for their encouragement and their comments. Our special thanks to Martin Corriveau, our son, for the cover art work; to Joy Valade, for her co-operation in the translation of the French version: Odyssée des Triplés Tome 1: Origine celtique; and to Suzanne Léger and her team at "Effet Boomerang," a Publishing Agency, for the cover pages' graphics.

Table of Content

Prologue

It is Pheas, my own personal guide, an elf of great beauty who notified me of the upcoming prophecy. This prophecy dates to over ten thousand years, to the days of the Atlantes. I'm sixteen at the time. Pheas has guided me since my childhood. According to him, I must prepare myself for I am part of the collateral damages of a universal event that is to take place early in the next century.

I confess that I took it lightly. At sixteen, I have other fish to fry: my Secondary School studies, my escapades with my girlfriends and my buddies, my babysitting for four families to facilitate my outings. We are not rich; we are still five children at home at this stage of my life. I don't pay much attention to the prophecy. Why should I care?

Pheas contacted me again on my eighteenth birthday. At that time, I listened to him more carefully. His message was more specific. I took note and kept the information in my heart preciously. Pheas did not bring up the subject of the prophecy until I turned fifty-three years old. Then he really applied more pressure. This time he is more insistent and factual: my daughter Marion will be the bearer of triplets. These triplets have a mission, a special destiny. They are to undergo an odyssey leading up to the liberation of mankind. I, and my spouse, have a role to play in the adventure. We are to support and prepare them.

I was stunned. Actually, my legs went numb and I fell to the floor, dismayed, incredulous. I was frightened and overwhelmed by the task facing Thomas and me. How can we be the grandparents of the triplets so expected for centuries? According to Pheas, the Gods don't make a mistake, they have prepared their coming. The triplets have been identified. They bear the mark, the birth mark that identifies them as the only triplets with the genetic chain required to complete the mission sanctioned by the gods. Pheas does not spare me. He adds more. My heart is shattered. I ache. I waver. I hesitate. I want to push away the cup he presents me. I can hardly believe the message he delivers. Why me? Why my family? My children…

--- OOO ---

I am fifty-four years old. The triplets are here. All of them are healthy and rosy like burgeoning rose buds. Hilarious delight lingers in the Corribus family. I stand aside a few moments. I look at them all. They are in happiness; I am in my pain. They are in sharing; I am in my solitude. They are planning and forecasting the future; my future is already all mapped out. Will I have enough moral strength to get through this? They will need us. I will be there. Thomas, my life companion for some forty years and I will be there.

Pheas promised. He will guide me. I must not fear. True, he never abandoned me. He always told me the truth, the greater one, the only truth, the one that inhabits me since I was but a child. I repeat it to myself: Louise, your intuition connects you with the Universe, listen to it.

These children have so much to give. They are supported by the Light. They will be the softening balm on my wounded motherly heart. I accept the entire educational challenge that is presented to us. Yes, I have the courage of the ram. Like him, I will climb the mountain of rocks and finally reach the much-coveted summit.

Engage! Engage! I hear myself shouting with enthusiasm, surrounded by my brother and my friends in an attack against our neighbours. We were playing cowboys, we were the good guys and they were the bandits. We were ten years old. Now, I am fifty-four. I keep, deep inside myself, the same dynamism, the same propensity to win.

--- OOO ---

The Accident

"Madam! Madam! Madam! Wake up! Wake up!" Three medical responders insist; they need to verify if there is any state of consciousness or not.

The ambulance crew, present at the plane crash site, insistently stimulates the half-conscious lady. She is still breathing despite her serious injuries. The pulse at the level of her neck is weak, but present. Everyone hastens to prepare her for transportation to the nearest hospital. The crew members settle her down on a stretcher; carefully and methodically they install an immobilizing collar around her neck and then attach straps to her chest and pelvis to keep her still during the transportation to the medical centre in Maniwaki that awaits.

Quickly, a nurse administers a saline solution to keep her vein open in case of necessity. She checks her pupils. They react to light so well that a possibility of bleeding to the brain is excluded for the moment.

Finally, Marion is quickly plugged to a cardio scope immediately upon entering the ambulance vehicle.

"Hurry, it's urgent!" Orders the medical attendant to the driver…

The pilot and the second passenger are dead. Their necks were broken on impact. The documents identify the second passenger as being Marc Corribus, husband of the lady, as her name and that of Corribus are included on her documents.

"They were so young and probably parents" express one of the paramedics … saddened by this mess…

The paramedics took little time to reach the site of the accident. The repeated distress calls from the pilot of the Cessna "Mayday! Mayday! Mayday!" was captured by the Trenton Rescue Centre and transmitted to the emergency and police services of the Maniwaki region.

The three passengers, lifelong friends, were performing a recreational flight to admire the fall colours in the Laurentians.

The survivor, a blond woman with green eyes and fair complexion suffers with multiple injuries. She is rushed to the hospital located less than thirty kilometres from the crash site.

The woman does not feel her limbs. She travels back in time. She does not remember the accident. She believes she is somewhere else, with no point of reference. She hears the people around her, however, she does not recognize the voices. She drifts into a nightmare.

She remains in a semi-conscious state.

--- OOO ---

The medical staff in Maniwaki provided immediate care and rapidly transferred Marion to the Polytrauma Centre of Ottawa where her condition was stabilized.

Time goes by and the medical tests provide little hope for recovery. Marion remains hospitalized. She cannot return home. Her physical state requires too much medical attention. Meanwhile, the children continue to attend their classes under the supervision of their grandparents.

Three months have lapsed since the accident.

Marion and her parents organize her transfer to the specialized trauma centre in Sherbrooke, within the Eastern Townships of the Province of Quebec. The Centre is sponsored by a reputed team of sports medicine physicians. Marion becomes a case study for them. The arrangements are beneficial to all concerned. The displacements are much easier. As for the children, they are acclimating to their new school, and their maternal grandparent's lifestyle. Often, tension and opposition require negotiations and the management of teeth grinding. The process is slow but effective.

Louise and Thomas assume responsibility for the education and well-being of the Corribus triplets: Cedric, William and Sofia. They are only nine years old and undergo so much suffering!

--- OOO ---

Throughout the year following the terrible accident, Marion sees her children as often as possible. The medical staff, at the physiotherapist request, regularly provide an armchair equipped with a headrest and appropriate supports for her arms and legs in order to keep them in functional position.

"I can't go on like this," says Sofia with tears in her eyes. "I don't like seeing my mother pinned to a hospital bed. Besides, she can't move her arms or her legs. Grandma, please, tell me this is a nightmare I am living. Tell me mom will be back very soon and I will return to Ottawa with my brothers. I want to go back and be with my friends."

Sofia bursts into tears in the arms of her grandmother. Louise knows the ultimate outcome of this catastrophic event. Both feel their personal emotions growing. The two boys are with their mother in the adjoining room. They talk about the activities at school, at home with their grandparents. They observe their mother, Marion, increasingly pensive… They are unable to fuel their mother's morale.

Louise hugs Sofia tenderly and remains silent. This silence best conveys all the pain and wrenching of this heart already scarred by human suffering. She holds her in her arms for as long as Sofia so desires.

Suddenly Sofia pulls away from her grandmother's arms and softly says in Louise's ears: "Why do I have flashes of this nightmare in my head? I used to have a similar nightmare when I was little. I remember I would wake up in tears and soaked wet with perspiration. I would call out for help and mom would come to help me go back to sleep."

"My beautiful little princess, I have no answer to give you at this time. Perhaps you have this ability to see into the future! I do not know. What I do know, though, is that you and your two brothers, you're courageous to live this tragedy."

Louise keeps stroking Sofia's hair, half blond, half-reddish, dishevelled hair, but still, so cute with her little mischievous face. Now, she lost a little of her zest for life; time will heal matters!

Getting over her great sorrow, Sofia confides to her grandmother that she noticed that her brothers have been acting strange for some time now.

"You know grandma, William weeps profusely every night and he comes in my bed as he did with Mom and Dad when we were at home in Ottawa. I confess: it makes me feel sad to see him like that. I do not know what to do. One evening, he said to me that he could no longer stand to see mom in this state, that if she died, he would follow her, that he too would die. I'm afraid he may do something crazy, Grandma…" "I also noticed that Cedric does not act normal. He does not cry, he does not speak. He writes pages and pages in his notebook and certainly does not want to share them with me or anyone else. He scares me more than William. He normally keeps nothing to himself. Usually, he is very energetic and expressive when he speaks. We even had to stop him in order to be able to get a word in. Now, he says nothing."

"Hum! Breathes, Grandma. This is very serious. I thank you for the information. I will pass it on to your grandpa. He has an excellent connection with the two boys. Meanwhile, let me know if something special happens with your brothers."

Grandma continues: "With all these events since the accident, I confess, my beautiful princess, that I have a head full of cobwebs. I am taking over, my dear; it is not your responsibility to have an eye and even two on your brothers' behaviours. Your mother gave us this responsibility and I humbly admit that I have let it slip away a little. I will let your grandpa know. I'll fill him in on the situation. We are with you three and especially with your mother Marion. We love you all so much. Is it alright with you, my beautiful Sofia? How about we go see your mother?"

"Thank you, grandma, with all my heart. I knew you could do something for us three. I feel I am alone. Why us? Why is this happening to us? I'll be ten years old soon. That is too much. I am not capable of living all this at the same time."

Sofia bursts into tears again: her little body trembling like a leaf in autumn. Time stands still for grandma and her. Nothing else exists except them two…

"*What a fate! What is in store for them?*" thinks, grandma.

--- OOO ---

For months now, Marion desperately tries to move her legs, her arms, without success. Yet, she remains hopeful. All the interveners of the medical circle support and encourage this determined and courageous woman. Marion cannot and will not give up. She wants to heal and retrieve her three children, Cedric, William and Sofia, fatherless now for almost a year.

One evening while Cedric, William and Sofia are with their mother and the grandparents are in the hospital cafeteria, Marion babbles some words through her teeth.

"What are you saying mom," asks William, approaching her carefully? He places his little hand on that of his mother, still inert since the accident despite all the physical therapy efforts.

"I was muttering, it's true. I saw myself again at age eleven in Denmark with an international organization for children."

"What? You went to Denmark, the land of Vikings!" questions Cedric, curious to learn more.

"You never told us about that trip, insists Sofia. Did you leave for long? With whom did you go? Grandma and grandpa let you go at eleven? C'mon it's too dangerous to go so far without one's mother and father!"

Marion laughs and tears run down her whitish face, still little coloured for quite some time. "True, I did not tell you of that period of my childhood life." Marion takes a deep breath and continues: "I represented Canada through the CISV organization. The Children International Summer Village is sponsored by the United Nations. We were 52 children if I remember correctly; thirteen countries were represented in my group. We left in teams of two boys and two girls per country, accompanied by two adults, a man and a woman."

"It was in July 1986, let out grandpa on entering the room. I remember it like it was yesterday. Heck, we were so happy for you, however, very worried as far as we were concerned. Is that not so, Louise?"

"Indeed, it was! I did not sleep a wink in the first five days after your departure."

"Is that true, Marion asks her parents? I thought you were above all those fears and terrors that other parents were voicing."

"We never admitted it to you before you left. It would have spoiled your stay in Denmark," answers grandma, looking at her with so much love that her spectacles fog up. Marion remains pensive for a moment. The look she bestows on Louise is that of admiration and kindness for her mother.

"You know mom, it was at that time that I realized that I was different from the other girls and boys. I perceived things with disconcerting clarity. In fact, at that time, I refused to believe in my intuitive and premonition abilities."

On hearing these confidences, Sofia approaches her mother and whispers softly in her ear: "I think I'm like you are mom. I have weird dreams. I see things that happen later on. I am not able to keep this to myself. I share it with my brothers who tell me they are just like me."

Marion frowns on hearing these revelations. She reflects: "*Where were we Marc and I, not to know such things of our kids? The daily living, alas! It has taken hold of our family life making way for routine to settle in.*" Marion, this time weeps of grief, regret, sorrow. Sofia, close beside her, notices it, "Mom, what's wrong? Have I said something that hurts you? Why are you crying so much?" Sofia wipes the tears off the sweet face of her mother Marion.

Choking, Marion manages to say to her three children: "I regret not having been there more for you three. I thought I had plenty of time ahead of me; life itself has a brutal way of telling me otherwise." Marion closes her eyes and visualizes herself at work, at home, with the homework, lessons, appointments here and there, shopping, sports events, etc. Fortunately, there were Friday nights to relax with a good family movie and some popcorn. She smiles tenderly.

"You can still see us together, watching TV, popcorn in hand, asks Sofia." "Truly Sofia, you are gratified by the Gods," says Marion, tenderly. Louise and Thomas observe, speechless and moved.

--- OOO ---

Time goes by. Unfortunately, fate persists! From pneumonia to urinary tract infection, to difficulty in breathing, Marion finds that her vitality is slipping away. She requests the presence of the whole medical unit. She wants to get to the bottom of it.

Shortly after, the medical team come to her bedside. Everyone is present around her. Marion speaks to the head of service: "Doctor, tell me what are my chances of recovering at least 50% of my motor skills and what are my chances of going home to be with my children. I have been with you for many months now and I reckon that not much is improving… I need to know, to set the record straight…" she insists, determined to do find out what lays ahead for her.

The specialists look at one another: they admire this woman who never complained. With a common accord, they deliver their prognosis: “You barely have a few weeks left, two months at most,” they admit to this fighter in an emotional voice.

“I do not hear you very well,” insists Marion, her eyes full of water and short of breath. “We are sorry; there is nothing we can do. Your body is deteriorating every day,” they add, lowering their eyes before this stare that yet demands a miracle. “Already, your survival to this day defies all our experiences and the scenarios we anticipated.”

The Promise

Time has elapsed further.

With difficulty and her heart bruised with emotion, Marion asks her specialist, a neurosurgeon, to send for her children, her mother and her father as quickly as possible. Dr. Faubert, taking her right hand deformed by muscular inactivity, says: "Madam, I will take care of it personally. Your children will be here with their grandparents shortly." The members of medical staff present, are overwhelmed with tangible emotion as they exit this fighting woman's room.

Tears flow profusely from Marion's green eyes. She cannot control this source of tears that flow like a river in spring. Her arms can't allow it. They have been disabled since the terrible accident. Her arms with which she loved to encircle her companion in this life and her three children... Her hands, inaccessible, do not offer the discretion so desired. They can no longer serve as a screen to conceal her pain.

Her face streaming, remains exposed. Marion is at the mercy of all eyes. Thankfully she has this private hospital room where she can be within herself, with her emotions and moods. Right now the emotions are upsetting her core.

She senses the expiry date.

Her sorrow and heartbreak flow freely down her cheeks. Her tears fall continuously on her pillow, in this multiple trauma recovery bed. With a cry from the heart Marion implores her grandpa Noel: "*You, who in 1997, warned me of the great joy of an encounter with the man who was to become my life companion on earth, where are you now? I need your help so much. Please, bring me some of your great serenity. That's how mom described you. She would tell me you were the wisdom incarnated. My body makes me suffer so much but it is nothing compared with my state of mind. I am compelled to leave everything behind, to abandon everything, even what I hold most precious on earth: my triplets*!"

Marion has difficulty breathing. She keeps her eyes half-closed. Suddenly her spirit unwinds, her features relax and her plump lips open to let a few words through: "*I knew you were here to accompany me in this final journey. Gracias! grandpa Noel. Even if I never knew you in my lifetime, I feel you in my heart and it calms me and makes me feel very good. I feel more relaxed within myself, which is not the easiest thing in my case! I now know you'll be there when I have to cross the last moments.*"

Marion remains in a hypnotic state. She sees herself with Louise, her mother. She hears Louise telling her that she is part of a special lineage of women with special gifts. For more than forty generations, these women have been available to mend God's will. Deep inside herself, she now knows that Sofia will undergo much upheaval in her lifetime. She is chosen amongst many humans to accomplish a mission of liberation.

"Phew! I feel far away already! I can barely breathe in this life! I'm speaking to you, grandpa, because I know that you hear me and you listen to me. Life is weird! I, who refused to believe in all my gifts, in all my ultra-sensory abilities, I now see myself pinned to a hospital bed, forced to live off from others!"

Marion turns her head on the pillow wet with tears. She grimaces and continues to speak to her maternal grandfather. "*The worst part grandpa is to realize that I have little time to live here on earth! I will never return to live in Ottawa with my dear children!*"

Marion, calmly, plunges back into her emotions. Tears begin to flow again, gently, like a little stream in the springtime. Her pillow, like a sacred receptacle, absorbs her suffering, her sorrows, her memories; impassive witnesses to her dying moments.

Louise, withdrawn in her personal meditative space, perceives that her life is tumbling down like an avalanche triggered by a thunderbolt. She now faces the obvious: she and her Thomas will be responsible for these three special children. They are to prepare and accompany them in their immense mission in life.

Louise is amazed, Pheas was right. "*The secret portion of the dream is now happening. I could not speak about it. God, I feel lonely.*"

She's been living this dream since the accident. She, too, hoped. She naively hoped that the messenger was wrong! Yet she knew! She had never been deceived by her guide. She was suffering and now it was time to live the outcome of this nasty nightmare. What to make of all this? She knows it is her and Thomas, who will take responsibility for the education of their three grandchildren. They will have to see to the preparations for Cedric, William and Sofia's mission which will lead them towards their destiny which is impossible to determine or believe for the moment. They must respond to a prophecy and achieve it in spite of everything…

--- OOO ---

On arriving at the hospital, Thomas, Louise, Cedric, William and Sofia are greeted and escorted to Marion's room by a department nurse.

Midnight has struck, service changes are completed. The floor hallways are gloomy, silent. Diffused lighting, originating from reduced electric lights, offers a bleak feature. Only the oily or dry coughing of inpatients punctuate the silence.

Sofia, William and Cedric have settled around their mother's bed. All three are in tears. They can hardly focus on their mother's words. With much effort and courage, Marion speaks to them softly, quietly, her eyes filled with tears, emotion. It is totally heartbreaking.

She suddenly becomes very pensive. "*How weird life is, I had such great plans for my three little darlings and here I am, my life is slipping away... I defer to you, Lord, Creator of the whole Universe and I place my adored children in the custody of my beloved parents. I know that You will guide them well and I give You thank.*"

Coming round, with difficulty, Marion addresses her mother, Louise and her father, Thomas, as well as Cedric, William and Sofia. Marion insists that her parents take her children by the hands and that together they listen to what she has to say and bequeath them: "Dad, mom … take care of my children." She coughs with difficulty. "Help them to live with dignity … according to our family tradition."

Marion pauses for a moment and catches her breath. One can hear her laboured breathing, warning of that final moment of life on Earth. "Cedric… William… Sofia… I entrust you to the unconditional love of your grandpa and grandma … to their ability to take care of you … to teach you all the skills you will need to know … and have … to perform in this life … that is yours… I know … that you have a very special destiny to carry… You have a mission… You are part of a prophecy… Grandma will explain it all to you … when you're ready to hear it…"

Marion catches her breath more than once before pursuing: "My children … promise me that you … will listen to grandma and grandpa … that you will do what it takes … to carry out the prophecy…" Marion continues with superhuman effort. "Great challenges await you … promise me … promise to do whatever it takes…"

Marion looks at each of her children intensely and insists with the last efforts that life gives her in these so precious minutes: "Promise me … promise to act … in line with the prophecy … tell me … promise so that I may go in peace… Phew! I feel I'm departing... I'll be there … in your heart, whenever … you need … my … thought… I … love … you ... remember … our … star."

Marion and her spouse, both good sailors, had explained their children how to observe the sky and recognize the stars and specifically the one that will bring their family thinking together, the one that is their rallying point. Cedric, William and Sofia remember the Polaris star, or North Star, known as the "Alpha Ursae Minoris." They have observed it as a family during evenings. They have observed those small white flames on this immense deep blue carpeting of the night.

The children look at one another and nod. Their face is bathed in tears and their nose running. "Promise, mom." Hic up the children in unison.

Cedric, William and Sofia are in a kind of hypnotic state. They are just so in shock that their head sways automatically.

The tears continue to inundate Marion's already soggy pillow.

Heavily, Marion's gaze follows these precious children she gave birth to almost ten years ago, she knows that many challenges await them in order to fulfill the prophecy. She remembers her conversation with her mother. She was told in a dream of her pregnancy and the birth of the triplets.

With difficulty, Marion articulates her last words: "There is peace in death … to make it happen… I must make peace … with life … my life … and that of others…"

Marion's eyes level out. Her breathing is choppy, faltered with apnea. For a moment, she sees her life … her birth … her mother's and father's supporting arms … her friends from school … her passage through the Canadian Armed Forces … her first meeting with her life companion, Mark that she so loved … the surprise of her triplets … their family trips … the children's school and sports activities … her future projects as a woman… She hears a murmur that reminds her of Louise's voice, this murmur again crosses her mind. It is with these words that she will leave earth: "*It is through women that society will come to establish peace in the human heart. These words are so sweet to my ear now that I know Sofia's destiny. I have contributed to the blossoming of this luminous flower. She will guide her brothers and all the other humans."*

Marion withdraws from her earthly reality. She neither hears nor sees anything. All her senses are departing one by one.

Together, the three children let go of their grandparents' hands to stand around their mother's bed. They cannot speak. Only the sobbing cuts the silence. They are ravaged with emotion.

Cedric holds his mother's right hand giving the impression of wanting to loosen it and keep it preciously for himself. William is glued to his beloved mother's head. He drools all his pain over Marion's white cheeks. As for Sofia, she is curled on the edge of the hospital bed, hugging her mother's waist while her left ear rests on her mother's breast… When she was unhappy, she would seek this position and hear her mother's heart beat in unison with hers and watch miracles happen.

She barely hears Marion's heart beats. She is distraught… She shakes her mother… She implores… She cries… Time stands still…

The silence that follows this outburst of tears, screams and punches on the bed enables Marion to close her eyes, breathe more and more deeply and slowly. She takes one last breath on this earth and leaves in peace. In a last supreme effort, Marion opens her eyes. They are wide, intense with love. In turn she looks at Cedric, William and finally rest on Sofia.

Marion closes her eyes slowly. The silver cord breaks!

Marion is gone. The body is inert, peaceful. She is free at last. Marion's life has left for other heavens while through the windows one can already see life settling into the Spring.

The children embrace their mother everywhere they can, non-stop. They cannot leave her. It's too much. It's as if the floor of the hospital room gave way under their feet…

The nurse who had been requested by grandma discreetly withdraw after disconnecting the devices so as to release the body and thus allow unhindered contact.

Distress cries resound from Marion Valroy's room, tearing screams of pain, abandonment and despair.

William, clinging to his mother, remains in a hypnotic state. He has difficulty breathing! "He's having an asthma attack!" says Grandma, calling the nurses back to rescue her grandson.

He is immediately taken to the hospital emergency for treatment. Cedric and Sofia follow their grandparents like robots. They are emotionally stressed.

Grandpa and grandma envision the immense challenge before them. Despite their age, they know that these children, these triplets must live several bereavements: they lost their father and their mother, their home in Ottawa, their school environment, their friends, their sports community. "Phew! Where and by what do we start?"

Ming and Patrick

Time goes by and the triplets are recovering slowly and with difficulty from the mourning of their mother and their father. Everything is so disrupted in their head and in their heart. Yet, they know they are safe. They are protected and loved with grandpa and grandma. Thomas and Louise support them discreetly. They know the children must absorb, digest and live the loss of their parents. They, themselves, also need to grieve the departure of Marion and Mark.

One morning, Louise wakes up and shakes Thomas vigorously. "Thomas, I have received a suggestion from Pheas, my guide. Let's plant a tree and dedicate it to the memory of Marion and Mark. I'm sure the children will appreciate." "That's awesome, replies Thomas. I agree. Let's see their reaction at breakfast."

Good Humor prevails when grandma demands attention and states: "Children, what would you say if we planted a tree in memory of your parents?" The children look at Louise with wide eyes then at one another. "We will place an inscription; William says suddenly, thrilled by the idea."

Cedric and Sofia, enthusiastic, support the idea and suggest that they do the choosing. The same day, the family goes to the regional tree nursery. Grandma is no stranger to the owner and presents him the project. Moved, the latter speaks with the children in order to better understand their desire. The choice is difficult. However, after several suggestions, the children agree to choose a beautiful flowering hawthorn of two metres high and of good girth.

“Look at the beautiful white flowers. They are star-shaped; they look like they have a sun between their petals.” “Yes, it’s true Cedric. I’m so happy answers Sofia, I will be able to talk to mom and dad through our tree.”

Thomas addresses the children: “I am impressed with your choice; this tree is called the tree of righteousness. Its energy is powerful and said to nourish the heart.” “Could we plant it in the centre of the Zen garden, asks William emotionally?”

Thomas looks at Louise with tenderness and gratitude. “The garden is my favourite place. Every morning I go there to pray and watch the sun rise. Marion and Mark can accompany me!”

--- OOO ---

Summer is here. Although they arrived at school in mid-session, the Corribus children completed their current school year with success. Their mind was not on studies. However, thanks to the understanding and collaboration of their teachers, they rank amongst the top 15 of the class. Many students were very encouraging to them. They helped them understand the Quebec school system which is somewhat different from the one in Ontario.

Grandpa and grandma, ever present, had to deal with behavioural setbacks on the part of their grandchildren. With calm and good humour, they faced countless emotional storms. Today is one of those days. With his report card in hand, William states in anger and with a determined look on his face “I am not returning to this school in September, I do not like the guys and girls in my class,” he adds, rushing into his bedroom in the basement of the house. He slams the bedroom door so loudly that the walls of grandpa’s office shake. *“Well! Now is the time when we make it or break it, thinks grandpa.”*

Grandpa heads for his grandson’s bedroom. William is the most rebellious yet the most sensitive and the most curious of the three. On entering the room, he observes William filling three suitcases: one with clothing, one with his dinosaur toys and another with comic books. He notes that William is not forgetting the piece of broken rosary beads that his mother Marion used to hang in their car for protection and that he had retrieved after the funeral ceremony.

Grandpa, as he faces the crying and heartbreaking moans, thinks back to his son Patrick. He remembers him in the same situation several years back. It was the same scenario. "William, are you preparing to leave? Where have you decided to move to?" asks grandpa with great tenderness and love? "I hope you are not asking me to drive you to the provincial bus like your Uncle Patrick did when he was your age. He was so angry with your grandma that he did not want to speak to her again..." William looks at his grandpa in awe...

"At that time, I asked him to answer two questions on a white sheet of paper. The sheet was divided in half with a line in pencil. On one side was the question, 'what do you gain?' and on the other half 'what do you lose?' when you leave home." Grandpa thinks back to that scenario and giggles. "I laugh at it now, but I must tell you that at that time grandma did not find it funny at all... It's so funny, yet so serious, but I cannot stop myself from laughing. Excuse me, William, you were saying?"

The story told by his grandpa drew William's attention. Coming back to his reality, William asks his grandfather: "What did Patrick do grandpa?" William holds his emotions back in check. He sits down on his bed. The suitcases are on the floor, half-closed and higgledy-piggledy. He looks at his grandpa right in the eye.

"He never lowers his eyes that one, no more than the other two for that matter... " thinks, grandpa.

His uncle Patrick is pure gold. Everything he does, William tries to imitate. He is his idol now. Patrick has a positive influence on his nephews and niece. Seeing grandpa on the brink of answering, William hastens to ask: "Did he leave? What did he write on his sheet of paper?"

Grandpa's presence calms Will, as his brother calls him. In fact, William breathes easier. This little man with tousled brown curls and brown irises crowned with green is prone to asthma attacks when he is upset, or when, of course, he has flu-like symptoms. Nevertheless, grandpa believes he has a delightful way of ribbing. "*He is a clown that one; he is the inventor of situations. His imagination is overflowing as a volcano in fusion.*"

"You ask your uncle Patrick tomorrow, he will be here along with Ming, your favourite aunt," answers grandpa affectionately. "In fact, they are coming to help us develop a training program in line with your mission. You remember... your mother spoke to you three about a mission when she was in the hospital..."

William moves his head in an affirmative way. He remains distant for a moment then shakes himself up a little so as to be attentive to what his grandfather has to tell him. "Will you be there with us? Grandma and I, we are very happy to have Patrick and Ming visit us. We know that they have your success at heart in every respect. Patrick promised your mother to look after you three in their absence, especially in the context of your school and extracurricular activities. Together, Patrick, Ming, grandma and myself, we are there to help you three to potentiate, activate those gifts you have and which are just waiting to blossom."

"I'm not sure he grasped my whole sales pitch ... well, we will see!" Thinks, grandpa.

William listens intently to his grandpa. Indeed, he does not seize everything that his grandfather says, but he nods as a sign that he is listening and slowly says, his eyes filled with water: "Grandpa, you know I've been having trouble to concentrate lately and I don't want to look foolish in front of my new friends. Mom had begun to take steps in Ottawa for the school system to help me in this regard. I don't like being laughed at." "Let me reassure you straight away, William. We pursued the same procedures with the school board, and this year you will have a computer for your written French. In addition, we will see what we can do to increase your concentration and your attention. Patrick believes that archery and martial arts would be interesting paths to begin with for you three."

"Archery! Martial Arts! ... Yes! That would be fantastic! I want to start as soon as possible." A sparkle shone in William's eyes, a new desire to participate and play has been triggered. "We'll wait until your uncle Patrick arrives and we'll talk about it, OK William?" says calmly grandpa.

"OK, I'll put my luggage back where it belongs." He remains silent for a moment and then adds painfully, with sobs in his throat: "It's hard you know grandpa ... without mom and dad..." He sniffs and wipes his runny nose on the left sleeve of his jacket... "William, here, take these paper tissues... Come on, blow your nose, a good blow and you will feel better afterwards. I'm so sorry, continue, I stopped you with my remark." "I think of them often. I search for them in my memory and I wouldn't want their image to fade forever..."

William takes a deep breath, blows his nose with the paper tissue that his grandpa had just given him. He approaches his grandpa Thomas of whom he is particularly fond. Grandpa hugs him tenderly in his arms and says: "When you're sad and you have a hard time talking about it, come see me whatever the time of day or night. Understood?" adds grandpa, looking him straight in the eyes with so much love.

William grabs his grandfather Thomas and embraces him on both cheeks making a noise with his mouth. In a flash, grandpa sees his daughter Marion bursting with the same emotion and making the same noise when she was happy with the conversation she just had with him. More so, when they were alone together while Louise was working on her evening shift as a nurse.

"Don't worry William, you will keep the image of your mother and your father in your memory until your own departure, your death, it's magic. I can still remember my own mother's face and she passed away a long time ago." "Ah! Thank you, grandpa. I am happy now. It makes me feel good." William, reassured, rushes up the stair leaving his grandpa with his thoughts.

--- OOO ---

The triplets are ready. They are waiting for their Uncle Patrick and Aunt Ming. They should arrive soon.

"Yippee! There they are!" shouts Sofia, always on the watch, very present to anything that happens. Her grandpa Thomas calls her his mobile scanner. She is a very crafty and clever little minx. Sofia knows how to quickly take the vibratory pulse of the environment, of situations and of people. Her hair, golden as autumn leaves, is normally cleverly dishevelled, and her hazel eyes sparkle with vivacity. For Thomas, Sofia is a real treasure, a sunray in his environment. Many times, she acts like a Jack in the Box.

The boys arrive in a whirlwind, breathless. They were playing soccer in the field neighbouring the house. "Hi everybody" shouts Patrick, coming out of his car, a red Mazda that he and Ming particularly enjoy.

Ming follows with a bunch of treats for the triplets. She herself relishes chocolates and every flavour of sweets. She loves to spoil her nephews and niece. It's so funny to see them enjoy what she brings. It's her great pleasure. "Wow! All three of you appear to be in really good shape," continues Patrick lifting Sofia in the air. He twirls her left and right. She screams at the top of her voice. She bursts into laughter. She is so happy… "Uncle Patrick, you are so much fun. I want you to come see us more often. I always look forward to seeing you both. You bring us a breath of fresh air."

"Wow! You make proses now, my beautiful Sofia. That's right, go on! Boys like that. Ha! Ha! Ha!" Says Patrick kidding and giving her a kiss on both cheeks. Sofia blushes hearing this joke.

Cedric and William rush to their uncle and hit him with friendly punches. Patrick loves these physical contacts. He practises martial arts since his adolescence. A professional soldier, he trains every day and remains a gym rat. His good physical condition is primordial in his line of work. He is methodical and disciplined so much so that several athletes either consult him or train with him before their martial art competitions. The children see him as a G.I. Joe. Patrick laughs at the image the children stick him with.

Patrick, Cedric and William shove one another, roll over on the ground and push each other. Cedric and William try to press their uncle's shoulders to the ground. It's euphoria.

Grandpa and grandma find that it was about time Patrick arrived to allow the boys to release the steam inside them.

"So, kids, you are on your Summer holidays… Two months before you get back to school. You lucky guys … we are so happy to see you three… We love you so much, you are like our children. You know you can count on us to support you, help you… You are our family… Family is important!" Patrick adds enthusiastically.

Cedric very seriously looks at Patrick: "Why is it not you that keeps us instead of grandpa and grandma? We would be living in Ottawa and we would have kept our friends. It would have been easier for everyone."

"Wow! I know that Cedric is the most serious one of the three, thinks grandpa. *He very often raises existential issues. However, this time it is really serious."*

Cedric has large azure-blue eyes. He is open to questions and intelligent responses. Generally, when he is thinking, he tilts his head slightly to the right. Then, when he is ready to give an answer or make a comment, he shakes his head and makes his light-brown hair wave, all this embellished with smiling lips. His gaze is honest and jovial. At times, he can also marvel at a ladybug falling from a twig of grass.

A silence settles amongst the family members. Everyone looks at one another and no one dares say a word. One can feel the unease discomfort with Cedric. His nonverbal speaks loudly, he can't express it in any other way. This is the first time he expresses himself to others since his mother died. To date, he has been writing pages and pages without ever sharing them. This is his first cry from the heart, from his troubled soul.

Patrick looks at him with affection, takes him in his strong arms and hugs him tenderly against his athletic chest until Cedric burst into tears. Cedric struggles, he does not want to pass for a wimp. He has the pride of a strong ten-year-old. Patrick knows. He holds him to his chest while massaging his back close to the nape to help him relax.

For a few minutes, Cedric gives vent to his emotions, his anger and his tears. He sobs. Finally, Cedric calms down and his tension relaxes.

William and Sofia are speechless. They don't move. They are stunned by their brother's behaviour. Cedric is always the one who reassures them in difficult times. He behaves as the eldest in the trilogy. It's weird, but it's like that! William and Sofia look at one another and find that they feel the same way... "Astonishing!" They say at the same time. Cedric questions in an abrupt voice: "What is astonishing?" He thinks that his brother William and his sister Sofia are making fun of him. He frees himself from Patrick's embrace to approach them. He looks at them and notices that their gaze expresses surprise.

They simply can't get over what they have just witnessed. "What is it that astonishes you? My behaviour surprises you?" Grandpa and grandma do not recognize Cedric's tone of voice. He speaks with anger and appears ready to jump on his siblings.

"Wow! Wait before drawing conclusions," retorts William who does not appreciate his brother's tone.

"William and I just noticed that we think the same thing at the same time," indicates Sofia, moving her head as a signal to Cedric that he may have gone a little too far in his emotional behaviour.

"I recognize my brother when he speaks with his arms up in the air... Finally, he is his usual self..." thinks Sofia.

"What! You think that I usually have my arms up in the air when I talk," replies, Cedric? ... Oops! He just realized that he too can hear the thoughts of others.

"What's happening?" The triplets ask the question simultaneously, looking at grandpa, grandma, Patrick and Ming who are laughing their heads off and giving each other pats on the back.

Grandma seizes the opportunity to speak. "This is the beginning of your apprenticeship. You will have to be patient and discreet with your school friends. They may not understand and be uncomfortable with some of your gifts. I will take the time to tell you later. For the moment, we are happy that you, Cedric, have freed yourself from a load that seemed to weigh on your chest and prevented you from being yourself. Am I right? I glimpse a little truth deep down," asks grandma very gently.

"It made me feel good," says Cedric, as he touches his heart with both hands. "I am particularly grateful to Patrick who held me at the right time." Cedric looks at everyone before rushing into the arms of his brother and sister. "Thank you everyone... I really have more space right here in my chest, I had the impression I was suffocating ever since mom died..."

Silence...

Cedric looks down and intimately enfolds William and Sofia in his arms. *"I can't believe this is happening to us, the Corribus family,"* he thinks to himself, as he considers their respective irises, one greenish brown and the other hazelnut.

"You see, it's happening again. William and I can hear you thinking," says Sofia happily.

"The more you progress through your learning, the more you will develop the many gifts that we humans had a very long time ago. Then, we could use quite a host of gifts every day. It was normal for humans to communicate by telepathy." Grandpa smiles as he advances towards them.

"My father always laughs in silence," thinks Patrick smiling.

“We heard you Uncle Patrick” say the triplets together. “It’ll be amusing amongst us,” interject all three. They are already making scenarios.

“Careful, there are rules and I want to ensure that you comply with them,” intervenes Ming, who had not said a word since the beginning of their chatting. “Grandma will explain these to you at the end of the day, for the moment, let’s have fun together. It’s the beginning of school holiday, enjoy it. Later, it will be back to school and new challenges await you in several areas.”

Grandpa and grandma leave the room to let them play and enjoy themselves. The children run away jostling with Ming and Patrick.

“Louise, I feel like we are in Ottawa and Marion and Marc will arrive from work soon,” says Thomas, raising his eyebrows.

Fond memories float back to their memory. The death of their daughter and son-in-law has created a great void in their heart and in their family unit. Looking at her partner with affection and heading for the kitchen, grandma mentions: “Cedric is more reserved when it comes to demonstrating his feelings. William is a ball of fire, and Sofia, on the other hand, always scans people before taking any action or uttering a word. It is important to note that and take it into consideration during their training and education programs.”

She maintains her gaze on Thomas, who understands her message. They have been living together for over forty years now.

Telepathically, they tell themselves that they have much to learn from their grandchildren. The few family gatherings every year, either in Ottawa or at the paternal home in the Eastern Townships, are not enough to thoroughly get to know these children of their late daughter Marion and their son-in-law, Mark. This plane crash was truly tragic.

“We will have to observe them discreetly and coach them with much care, gentleness, openness and patience,” says Louise, looking Thomas in the eye while he tenderly rocks her in his arms.

--- OOO ---

The meal takes place in joy. Ming and Patrick recount the adventures of their recent trip to Bali. That is why the children had not heard from them. They normally communicate with their godparents through Skype on a weekly basis.

During dessert, William turns to Patrick: “Uncle Patrick, grandpa said that when you were my age you wanted to leave home because you were angry at grandma. He said he also made you write something on a piece of paper. What did you write on that paper?”

Surprised, Patrick looks at his father, his eyebrows a question mark. Thomas raises his shoulders while opening his hands. His face indicates that the answer belongs to Patrick. Before answering Patrick turns to Louise and smiles tenderly.

William insists: “What is it you wrote?”

“Your grandpa must have had a good reason to talk about that event. What happened?” Asks, Patrick.

William rapidly describes grandpa’s interventions with his suitcases and comes back with the question: “Grandpa said he asked you to tell him what you would win and what you would lose if you were to leave home. Now, tell us what is it you wrote?”

Patrick smiles and looks intensely at him. He asks: “You, William, what would you have answered that question?” “Hey! Why do you answer me with a question?” “Because your answer would certainly be different from mine.”

“Perhaps. However what was it you wrote?” “What I wrote is on a piece of paper grandma gave me when I got married. It is in my personal note book. Here is what I propose to you: You, you answer the question on a piece of paper and when I return, I will bring my answer and we will compare notes. What do you think?"

William looks at his Uncle incredulous, eyes wide open and mouth opened. Patrick keeps smiling at him and opens his hands, meaning to say: "well what?" Resigned, William says in front of everyone: "It's not just! I just asked a question. Uncle Patrick, you tricked me!"

"Really? Rather I think that what I propose is equitable. If we exchange our answers, we are both gaining. Otherwise it is unfair for me…" William looks at his Uncle, frowning: "OK, I'll do it then you will show me your answer."

--- OOO ---

Weeks are rolling by and the triplet's training is progressing at a fast pace. The month of August is just about gone. Already the leaves begin to lose their greenery. It really feels like the beginning of the school year.

The preparations for school are well underway; the clothes are placed on their respective chair in their room. The two boys sleep in the same environment, a pale blue bedroom with two single beds. They share the bedside table that separates the beds.

William has installed all his dinosaurs on the ledge along the wall. He looks at them and aligns them when he goes to bed. He is happy, these are his fetishes. He has ten of them that he assembled himself or with the help of his father Marc. It is with him that William learned to work with a Lego plan: one step at a time.

As for Cedric, he placed his computer on a small table that grandma put at his disposal for his research on the marine world. He aspires to become a marine biologist. He already knows so much about the world of water and its inhabitants. Furthermore, Cedric swims like a fish. It's impressive to hear him speak of his research and discoveries. He knows how to communicate his enthusiasm. It's one of his assets. For him, to talk about his research or his findings is very easy, however, to talk about his feelings or to confide in somebody is something else… Marion, his mother, knew how to get him to talk. Now that she is no longer here, he is withdrawing within himself. Now, it is how he protects himself.

Sofia, on the other hand, has the largest room. That is convenient for her, she has a lot of personal items that were entrusted to her by her mother when the family left Ottawa to live in the Eastern Townships. All these objects are of great value to her and her brothers. For now, she keeps them all in her sunset yellow room. Through them she connects with her mother and father's presence. Often, her brothers drop in, especially when they are in a nostalgic mood. They touch the fetish objects, slip them between their fingers and sniff a scarf or two that belonged to either their father or their mother. They remain like that for a good while, silent, and then they leave happy and satisfied. They are always very grateful to their sister Sofia for respecting their privacy.

Confidences

One day, Sofia talks to her brothers about the dreams that she has since Marion's death. She does not dare talk to grandma about them. She does not feel quite at ease to do so. However, she needs to share her anguish. She must discuss her dreams with her brothers. She has a profound need to do so. She asks Cedric and William to join her in her room; she wants to share an important secret with them.

Solemnly, she invites her brothers to sit beside her on the bed: Cedric to her right and William to her left. Then, placing her arms on their shoulders, she says while hugging them affectionately: "I love you my brothers!" The two boys, bent over, look at each other and telepathically communicate: *"What is she going to announce to us with such a serious introduction."*

Sofia, although she is the same age as her brothers, considers herself as the older sister responsible for Cedric and William. This attitude sometimes peeves them. Sofia, takes time to breathe, she does not wish to upset her brothers. She continues in a friendly tone: "I urge you to keep the promise we made to mom before she died. I don't know if the dreams that I've been having for some time now have a direct link with mom's death..." Come on sis get to the point," intervenes William. "Just listen, I'm getting there," taking a deep breath Sofia continues: "I'm having more and more dreams in which I see someone who seems to be a high priestess of ancient times. She is dressed in beautiful clothes that I am not familiar with; clothes I've never seen in magazines or on TV. In every dream, each time, she invites me to follow her. I see strange paths full of ambushes, wars, castles, scary monsters, sometimes there are streets paved with roses them I am in a room with slimy walls, other times I see characters that seem to come out of horror movies, and when I wake up, I'm afraid. I'm truly afraid of being alone… I don't understand what that means to me."

Cedric stares at his sister: "But! wait a second Sofia! I too have weird dreams. It is scary. When I talked to William about them, I found out he also had dreams like mine. Those dreams are practically the same dreams you have." "What? You both have dreams also!" asks Sofia.

Cedric pursues: "Yes! Can you imagine? Your dreams, they are almost the same as ours. I think we should talk to grandpa and grandma about this. I am sure there is a link with what mom told us before she passed away. Remember, she spoke to us about some prophecy in which we would be involved." William says: "Me, in my dream there is also an old man with a very long beard and dressed in white and often I wake up while I'm fighting." "Me too, I am fighting most of the time," mentions Cedric. "The lady in my dream often speaks with an old man," adds Sofia.

Cedric pauses, looks at his brother and both embrace their sister. Cedric declares: "Yes we will honour our promise, sister. Nonetheless, what impresses me is that we have the same dreams and that we are always fighting in them. I do not understand what that means." "Me neither, I do not understand," says William. "It is hard to accept everything that we have seen in our dreams. What does it mean? What is the message given to us," questions, Sofia? "Is it mom trying to tell us something," demands, William?

"We should talk to our grandparents," continues Cedric. "I think they could help us understand and reassure us. As Dad often used to say: 'the more information you have on a topic, the more you can control and remove the fear that inhabits you,' what do you think?"

"Yes, that's right, I remember, he would repeat that phrase especially when I was afraid in the dark," adds William. "Dad reassured me by making me see the forms that were detailed on my bedroom wall. I would realize that it was just tree limbs outside that formed shadows on the wall facing my bed. You remember, Sofia, I would scream and it woke you." "Yea! I would tell you to go to see dad. He would know what to say to you and what to do to reassure you" "And that's what I did all the time. Dad would accompany me back and help me to see what was real and what was imaginary." "I think it's a good idea to go tell all of this to grandpa and Grandma," conclude Cedric. The triplets leave Sofia's bedroom and rush to their grandparents.

--- OOO ---

The children are waiting for their grandpa. They are seated in the lounge reading comic books. All three enjoy silently browsing the fantastic stories provided in the comic books, or BD as their uncle Patrick calls them. Grandfather Thomas and Uncle Patrick are fond of comic strips, particularly those of a historical nature. "By Jove, children, what is happening for you to be so quiet," questions Thomas on entering the reading room?

All three drop their comic books and rush to their grandfather: "Grandpa, you told us that it is normal to dream because dreams are necessary to relieve stress or pressure, isn't that so," asks Cedric? "Yes, and grandma has often said we play all the characters of our dreams, depending on the dream," adds Sofia. "However, all three of us are having the same dreams and almost repeatedly," adds William. "That! that is not normal."

"Just a minute children, not all at the same time. Yes, dreams are essential and inform us in their own way. However, I would like to understand what is going on and what is troubling you. Come, let's go into the kitchen with grandma and tell us what you have to say, but one at a time."

Quickly the children settle down, then in turn, tell their grandparents about the dreams they are experiencing. Grandpa Thomas, his hands crossed with forefingers pressed to his lips and elbows resting on the arms of his armchair, listens attentively. Grandma, leaning slightly forward observes each individual child giving the version of her or his dreams. She focuses on the feelings, the body language of the youths. Her sixth sense is on alert.

"Hum! Very interesting," says grandpa. "You know my children, Freud would say 'The dream is the royal path of the unconscious mind' and a specialist in the analysis of dreams, a man named Christian Genest, adds that it is also "the quickest way to initiate the change in our life for a permanent and physical development."

"Wait, don't panic let me explain, I can see in your face that these words went over your heads." The children keep looking at their grandpa. "I have told you before that from antiquity to the Middle Ages, in all the great civilizations such as Egypt, Assyrians, Babylonians, Greeks, Romans, the Indies, China, in short, everywhere, dreams and their interpretation were regarded with great respect… In the Middle Ages the people of the Church had a lot of difficulty with these people who interpreted dreams and they organized themselves, especially with the inquisition, to persecute all those who interpreted dreams. These people were considered as witches at the service of evil. It is only since the early 1900s, particularly with Freud, that the analysis of dreams has again become more important. Today, experts consider dreams as means available to us to know ourselves better, to channel our energies or to find answers to what concerns us."

Grandpa looks at the children and teasing asks: "You're not planning to burn me like they did with witches in the middle Ages I hope? If so, I will stop," says grandpa smiling. "Well, no," answers Sofia with a knowing smile! "What I'd like to know is what this dream means and why all three of us have the same dream and why this dream is recurrent."

"Good questions, Sofia. To answer you, here is what I know on the subject: it is said that our brain is ten thousand times more powerful than the most sophisticated computer that exists to this day and it registers numerous elements, most of the time without our knowledge. Impressive don't you think?" "Hum! Hum!" nod the children. Grandpa continues: "our brain is associated to our intellect, which itself works with what it hears, observes, experiments in our current life on earth. However, our intuition works at the level of the spirit and can thus call on notions heard, observed, experienced in previous lives."

"For the past year, you have been working very hard at the physical, emotional and mental level. Your instructors, Ming, Patrick, grandma and I, are making you live experiences always to properly prepare you for a mission that will become clearer over time. However, your intuition is also working to prepare you. Through your intuition, your soul also communicates with the cells of your physical body and it can trigger energies that can serve to prepare you for this mission. You are triplets, and not identical, that is true, however, you are very interrelated." The children remain attentive yet wondering what their grandpa is really saying.

"Is your subconscious preparing you for the work you must do together? I do not know; however, I think it's possible. Then again, my interpretation of your dreams may be very different than grandma's interpretation, or yours… So, I will not try to interpret it for you."

"What! All this to say you will not help us! I don't believe it," says Cedric frustrated. "Hear me Cedric. Try to understand what I am saying. What I find awesome and it impresses me is that you started to talk about your dreams amongst yourselves. More important, you are sharing your feelings… What my intuition tells me is that I should encourage you to continue to share your feelings and as well, to try to grasp, individually and together, what message the dream provides about yourself and about your team as a triplet." Grandpa looks at each one and concludes: "What do you think?"

The children shrug their shoulders while looking at their grandfather and open their hands hoping for more information. "I am sure that with time it will become clear," says grandpa. "It is as though your individual guides are working together to also collaborate in your preparation. Do not be afraid, have trust in each other."

"Yes, trust one another," intervenes grandma, "do not be afraid to fear, to be uncertain and to have questions. As your grandpa so often says, questions are like little rocks in our shoes, we have to remove them by asking and by discussing otherwise they are likely to haunt us and cause us harm. If your dream recurs, it may be to alert you of something important. It is certainly to help you. Talk about it with your guides, ask them to help you."

The children exchange and share their concerns with their grandparents until late as it often happens when they are passionate about the topic on hand. Cedric, Sofia and William agree to note and discuss their dreams amongst themselves and with their grandparents when needed.

Louise and Thomas point out that it is now time for them to go to bed. Everyone heads to her or his bedroom, wondering what learning the night reserves them.

--- OOO ---

The Apprenticeship

Three weeks later, it's Saturday morning, a beautiful fall day. Ming and Patrick are present and when grandpa makes a spectacular appearance the group burst out laughing. "Not very far from the place where I grew up, there was a craftsman whose specialty was to manufacture armour. This man was an artist and an excellent gunsmith. However he was as serious as a pope," says Thomas solemnly as he advances solemnly towards Ming, Patrick, Cedric, William and Sofia.

Grandpa in all his knight attire, his breastplate with cushioned leather adorned with metal plates, his helmet also in metal, clad with leather and presenting a visor, in his right hand a sword measuring at least one metre...

"Pops, you look like a knight overfilling his armour, both in terms of years as by the size," says Patrick. "What are you doing? It's not Halloween yet as far as I know! ... I didn't know you kept that costume. I used it so often to play with my friends. I thought it was time-worn and that you had put it in the trash."

"I want to try it on," requests William, enthusiastic and so much more cheerful ever since his godmother and godfather are there once a month to train them in the martial arts. Cedric rushes upon grandpa and checks whether all the paraphernalia is real. "Wow! It's all real! Not junk!" concludes Cedric while looking at Patrick and his sister Sofia.

"Yeah, I made it myself," says grandpa proudly. Ming questions the reasons for so much pleasure around metal objects.

"You know that I'm here with Patrick to give you lessons in hand to hand combat. You must master the sword, the broadsword, the club, the knife and the slingshot for sure. Nonetheless, your most versatile and most precious weapon is your body."

Ming speaks with assurance, determination and control. Her ancestors were combatants in Vietnam. She herself, during her childhood, lived for more than ten years, in an educational institution specialized in martial arts, she went through a kind of sport and study program!

Sofia is astonished, surprised and her open mouth shows bewilderment. Sofia looks at Ming as though she does not know her. She approaches Ming and says: "Aunt Ming, I've always seen you in leather boots, high heels, short skirts, hair blowing in the wind and black leather jacket. How can you talk about weapons and fighting?"

"You are not at the end of your surprises, beautiful little princess," says grandpa laughing and thinking she did not believe he could still wear his knight equipment. He expected a reaction from Sofia, but not that much. Grandma, who just came out of the house on hearing the cries of joy and amazement, comes to her granddaughter's rescue: "Thomas, it's not because of you that she is amazed, it's because of Ming who is showing her another facet of herself. She cannot believe that a woman can be a savvy warrior, equipped and trained without, however, being a murderer." She continues as she approaches Sofia: "It's possible my dear, wait, you will soon understand that all these teachings have a purpose and that you will need them in due course."

Sofia thinks back to everything that her grandparents told them by the fire on a starry night. *"Really! I shall have to make use of all this," she thinks? "It's frightening. In what have we embarked? What's the meaning of all that?"* She clings to her grandma as a lifeline, then heads towards the others. She promises herself to look at, scans and notes in her mind the most information possible.

The weekend unfolds filled with activities of all kinds. The children complete training with knives. Sofia is introduced to the sword, one adapted to her size, of course. She becomes rapidly very skillful, enough to defeat her brother Cedric, who is having more difficulty in wielding the sword. He is working harder than his brother and sister with the sword.

Patrick and grandpa watch them.

Ming notes that Cedric is the thinker of the group, while William and Sofia have natural coordination and physical engagement skills.

The coaches take notes and decide amongst themselves of a training strategy for each child. They must succeed in a short time, as their first commitment will take place during their twelfth year…

Two years is very short to complete their physical, emotional, mental and spiritual training. Fortunately, these children are blessed by the Gods. They are provided with special gifts that they must also learn and master. "Phew! The task is enormous! Nevertheless, the work is worth the effort," thinks grandpa.

Louise, Ming, Thomas and Patrick are aware of the importance of their mandate to prepare these triplets to fulfill the prophecy. Do they have any doubts?

These children are human. The trainers do not forget. They expect many challenges. Anything can happen. They rely on their intuition and the advice of their respective guides as well as what they have received themselves as teaching from their respective instructors.

At the moment, they are working to develop self-confidence and team spirit and cohesion in these children. In a short time, they need to learn how to use their body, be mentally alert, use their gift to their advantage and learn to cooperate with each other. Their creativity and coherence will be the key to their success and that of their mission.

School resumes its pace and the triplets learn to share with the other students from the school in their village. They mix with new friends. This year there are two new students who come from Africa: Peter and Jocelyn. The two boys quickly become friends with Cedric, William and Sofia, of course. Sofia attracts particularly Jocelyn's attention. As for Peter, he is a year younger than the other four.

The Nightmare

For several nights, Sofia dreams of a scary and monstrous character. To overcome her fear, she clutches to her heart the picture of her parents, the one she preciously keeps in her paper work chest. She keeps this chest on the bedside table. Every night before falling asleep, she goes through this ritual, it's important. She contacts her parents by means of this picture. For her, it is as though they are alive and protect her.

One night, while Sofia was deeply asleep, she raises her upper body and sits in the middle of her bed in a panic. She screams. Her shouts awaken the whole family.

Her nightmare is so real that grandpa and grandma come running quickly, racing down the stairway two steps at a time. Sofia is bathed in sweat; her brothers are already at her bedside. They are trying to wake her, impossible.

She screams louder, she wriggles under her blankets, she utters incomprehensible words. She appears hypnotized, her body and eye contact are void. "Louise, look after the boys while I take care of Sofia," orders grandpa. "Sofia, it is grandpa, what do you see? Whom do you see?" asks the latter in a firm and assured tone of voice while standing in front of her.

Sofia's hair is dishevelled, she looks frightened, her eyes wide open, her skin white as a new layer of snow in December. Grandpa notes that she is really scared and must be brought back to reality. "He is there, he is there, and he is talking to me. He is saying words to me, I do not understand. He is appalling. I am afraid. He is trying to touch me, to take me by force,

HAAAAAAAAA! I'm afraaaaiiiid! I don't want to see him any longer."

"Sofia, where is he," grandpa demands firmly? "There! there, in my window. He is staring at me with his green crocodile eyes, haaaaaaaaa!" Grandpa moves towards the window then opens it wide and commands with authority and conviction: "Whoever you are, you are not welcome in this house. I order you to get out of here and to leave my granddaughter alone. I forbid you to come back. You are banned from Sofia's bedroom and from this property. GET OUT YOU HEAR! AND IMMEDIATELY! I order you to leave her."

Grandpa's tone is so resounding that the boys hid in Grandma's dressing gown as she stood with them by the door. "Sofia, did he leave?" asks grandpa assertively.

Sofia drops on her pillow. She trembles in every limb. She looks around to see if the monstrous character is still there, in her room by the window. "No, I do not see him, she answers feebly," half reassured.

Grandpa takes her in his arms, cradling her tenderly, slowly, so she catches her breath. Sofia calms down. Her heart rate slows. She stands up, moves away from grandpa's arms, looks at him with astonishment and says, her eyes inquiring: "What happened to me? Why are you all here around me? Cedric, William, grandma and you, grandpa, why are you holding me in your arms? What stupidity did I do for you all to be here looking at me like that," she asks with surprise?

"Don't you remember anything," questions William, stunned by all his sister's questions? "Come on! You were shouting! You were struggling and you were wriggling like a snake in the field." "It's unbelievable; we did not come to see you in the middle of the night to have a picnic. You really don't remember anything?" insists Cedric with a flabbergasted look on his face.

"All right, boys, I'll take care of it," intervenes grandpa. "I will remind her of a few specific facts so that she recovers her memory."

Grandma is concerned that this character is a nondescript individual with great supernatural power. Her guide has warned her of an evil presence lurking around Sofia. "*I must take care of this,*" thinks, Grandma. "What must you take care of grandma?" Question at the same time Cedric and William? "Do you know this monster that scares our sister?"

"*Of course, they can read my mind,*" reflects grandma, trapped yet proud of their capacities of execution and learning. "I'm just speculating, that's all. Whew! Buff!" Her mouth ajar forms into a balloon as to blow out steam.

Grandpa looks at her and sends her a message by thought in German. (A means they agreed to use to evade detection of their thoughts by the children.)

"Are you alright, Sofia," asks grandma immediately so to veer the conversation? "I'm a little shocked," she says. "Where am I?" After a moment's hesitation, she shakes her head and answers: "Ah yes, in my bed, with all of you."

"I will ask you a few questions and we'll see afterwards if you remember the nightmare that made us all get up in the middle of the night, OK," mentions grandpa looking into her eyes. "Firstly, do you have any recollection of the character in your nightmare and secondly, can you describe him to us?"

Sofia reflects and after a few moments, opens her eyes wide to better identify the character. Her two brothers are now sitting next to her on the edge of the bed, so as not to miss a word of the anticipated story. "Well! Is it coming?" insists William? "Who is in your head? What colour is he? How big is he? Does he have an enormous head?" "Hurry up to describe him to us," insists Cedric even more.

Grandpa cuts in to tame the impatience of his grandchildren: "Children, wait, she just came back from her nightmare. Please give her space to breathe…"

"I'm getting there," Sofia hurries to say at the insistence of her brothers. "His face was dark, some sort of a greenish black, with vertical pupils such as those of a crocodile... His skin was like the skin of a reptile and his teeth, yak they were sharp and slated like those of sharks. He was grunting... He was running after me, and he wanted to grab me, to touch me, to put his paws on me... BRRRR, God I was scared..." she says with a shudder.

"You can say that again," William laughs! "Oops! Excuse me. That came out by itself."

"Very funny brother," says Cedric. Then turning to his sister: "Continue Sofia, do not worry about him, you know how he likes to make silly jokes when he is overly stressed." He looks at his brother with an air of disagreement. His eyes speak volumes. William understands. He repositions himself on the bed and says: "OK sis, that monster must have been really scary. I believe you. In your place, I would certainly have panicked."

"I do not know what he wanted from me, but he really was trying to speak to me." Sofia is silent for a few minutes as if trying to remember the words the monster said. Sofia resumes, frightened: "All I remember is that he was grunting," The boys are speechless. They stare at one another. They are really scared.

"*We must pick up the pieces*," the grandparents communicate to one another telepathically. The time to explain to the triplets has come. "I'll make you a good cup of hot chocolate," grandma says to Sofia. "Yes grandma, it will do me good," Sofia is starting to relax and move more naturally in her bed. Her grandpa helps her slip out of bed.

"We want some also" throw in the brothers, frightened. "We will examine all this tomorrow morning. Luckily, it's the weekend." Grandpa hastens to add: "thankfully we did not let our crocodile tears come out, isn't it, children? That is not a silly joke, my beautiful Sofia." He looks at Sofia smilingly and, "pouf!!!", the whole family bursts out laughing. It eases the stress. Laughter is the best way to soothe tense members.

The hot chocolate episode completed, everyone goes back to bed. Only grandma remains standing next to her fetish articles in the meditation room. She tries to enter into communication with her guide. Intuitively, she hears the message: "VIGILANCE, VIGILANCE." She understands the message! That's enough to be able to proceed!

Fortunately, they all fell asleep, even Sofia, who is holding the photo of her parents to her heart. The boys are wrapped in their blankets up to the neck. They are sleeping, they are resting. Grandma thinks about the message: "*We need to act with great caution. I will contact Ming and Patrick so that we can accelerate the learning process. The children must be able to defend themselves against the forces of darkness. What happened tonight is a signal that we must press on the gas pedal.*"

"The children must acquire the greatest autonomy and confidence possible. We must review the training plan. The training program must be conducted in several stages. They must learn to orient themselves in any terrain with the use of a compass, reading the bark of trees, and reading the stars. They need to know how to recognize edible plants, track down animal tracks, sniff the wind, determine the time without a wristwatch, count steps with the help of a rope, observe nature, etc. As well, they must learn how to communicate with the trees, know how to ask them good questions and wait for their answers. Of course, all these items will not be taught in one single weekend. Come on! It would be interesting for the children if from time to time some of their friends could participate in some activities. Yeah! Yeah! This is a great idea."

"Tomorrow morning, I will contact Jocelyn and Peter's parents, their African friends. It would be nice if they could participate in the orientation activities. They can come for the weekend and we will bring them with us. Yes! That way, the learning will be done in pleasure and play. Every now and then, we can have a picnic or go camping. Yeah, thinks grandma, it will be very nice! We will begin by sleeping out this weekend. We will go to visit our friends, Lise and Michel, who live on a small farm, near Mont Mégantic. The children will sleep in the tepee which is set up in the woods near their home."

"I will ask Lise to send for Francis, her nephew of the same age so that he takes part in the training with Cedric, William, Sofia, Jocelyn and Peter. That way we can group the children in teams of two... Well! That's enough little hamster it is now time to sleep. Stop working. I'm going back to bed and try to sleep. Tomorrow is another day."

--- OOO ---

Team Spirit

Autumn is already in full progress. The rain season is more present. Grandpa and grandma believe that the coming weekend will be an excellent time to bring the children to Lise and Michel's home and have them live their orientation field experiment.

It is Saturday morning. The wind is cool; the humus of dead leaves on the ground is intoxicating. The sun is shining.

"Now is the time to put into practise everything you have learned in orientation: compass, map reading and ground interpretation," says grandpa. "I do not want to be with you," says William, looking at his sister as if she had leprosy. "I want to take on the challenge in the woods with Francis, my weekend buddy."

Sofia looks at him with evil eyes. Grandpa interrupts the conversation between Sofia and William which is degenerating into a few rude words. He separates them and walks towards Jocelyn saying: "Jocelyn, would you mind sharing your experience with Sofia, even though she is a girl," he asks? He looks at his grandson who is being fussy this morning and gives him a glance in a sign of bad faith!

"With pleasure," replies Jocelyn immediately, delighted with the course of events. He could not have hoped for a better duo than this! "And you, Sofia, what do you say?" Grandpas asks while looking at her.

She bends her head and looks at her grandpa and the others, and tells them, in frustration: "I rise to the challenge with Jocelyn, not without suspecting a maneuver from all the rest of you, because I am the only girl amongst all of you. Wait to see what you will see. Come, Jocelyn, let's win this adventure." She pulls on his arm and leads him towards the path at the edge of the woods.

"Wow Sis! Don't take it like that, it's Jocelyn who asked to be with you and it's good timing, because William prefers to go through the experiment with Francis," hastens to say Cedric. He adds: "Jocelyn did not know how to ask you. We suggested that William chooses and his choice was not a very difficult one. He told us repeatedly that since we are always together at grandpa and grandma's home, this would allow him to talk with his buddy that he sees only now and then."

A silence settles in. Grandpa and grandma look at one another and nod to signal they were not aware of what was afoot. "You could have been clear amongst yourselves," grandpa says to his grandchildren. "We will talk about this at home. For now, let's focus on our goal."

"Grandpa I want to say something," says Sofia. "Yes Sofia."

"Thank you, grandpa. William, I'm sorry to have judged you without being aware of all the details," says Sofia, moving towards her brother. Then, turning to Jocelyn, in an unequivocal tone, continues: "And you, Jocelyn, why did not you address me directly to let me know that you wanted to share the exercise with me? You can talk to me even though I'm a girl," she concludes with irony.

The five boys look at each other and with an accomplice look in their eyes, they all say: "*Ah! Girls. It's so complicated.*"

Grandpa requests the attention of the six youths undergoing training. He reminds them of the reason for this exercise. "As I told you, the purpose of this exercise is to develop your confidence and your ability to move around in unknown territory with a compass and a map." "OK, let's return to the actual exercise. It's simple; you'll be in teams of two. Your challenge is to complete eight azimuths as quickly as possible. Each team will have an adult accompanying them. These accompanists do not have the right to help you; they follow you, that's all. If there is an emergency, they will react accordingly. The important thing for us is to see how you will react to the unknown. Cedric and Pierre, you will leave with Louise and Lise, Sofia and Jocelyn, you will be with Michel; as for you, William and Francis, it is me who accompanies you."

Everyone nod their heads showing their understanding. "We will leave you at a specific location where you will find a chest. Inside, you will find a map and the instructions to get to another chest. In the chest, there is also a card that you both must sign. The same scenario will be repeated for the six other chests. Remember the two of you must always sign the card. At the end of the exercise, you should be back at your starting point. Any questions?"

There is no question? "As I told you, the winning team is the one that will take the least time to complete the circuit. Again, the accompanists are there to encourage you and not to disclose anything to you. Is that clear?"

They all stare at one another grinning and with a pounce, rush to the woods, yelling: "Yeah! Hooray! We will be the winners, shout each participant, already taking their momentum towards the wooded area."

*"W*ait!" shouts grandpa in the direction of the group! "You must wait for the departure signal and the location of the first chest where you need to go. When you get to your starting chest, your accompanists will call me and it is I who will give the signal. Your accompanists and I have adjusted our watches." "Do you have all the items you need to complete your mission? Now wait, no kidding, your accompanists are not your age!"

The six youths burst out laughing and retrieve the older persons and in unison: "Let us not forget our 'old-timers' …" *"Terrific, it is very promising!"* Thinks grandma, grandpa, Lise and Michel.

Several episodes occur in the woods: detours, unexpected slipping on wet leaves, cries of joy and animated discussions within the duos and many more. The children return complete the exercise astounded and delighted with their findings.

After dinner, everyone, sit on logs around a roaring fire prepared by Michel in his field. They all share their experience of working as a duo, being observed by the accompanists, trusting themselves and trusting each another.

Cedric draws everyone's attention: "You should have seen grandma when we went through a thick grove. Her foot crashed the ribcage of a dead deer covered with leaves." "Puah! What a smell and to hear your Grandma's yell! You guys must have heard it; she was so load. And the flies, millions of them began flying around us. You should also have seen Lise trying to find her way around the area," interrupts Pierre.

"Don't forget the maggots," says Louise. "I hate maggots. Yak! I almost vomited. That why I didn't hesitate going into the creek nearby. Normally I try not to get wet. But this time I had to wash that dirt off my boots." Grandma shivers and the kids laugh out loud at seeing the disdain in her mimic.

"We got Michel to run. Jocelyn and I, we did it on purpose. We could hear him bitching and swearing." Sofia continues: "however we had the scare of our life when he slipped on a wet tree covered with moss... We thought he'd hurt himself... Ouf ! It's a good thing we did not have to carry him." "You would have deserved to do it," said Michel to himself as he drops some wood on the flames.

"Wow Michel! I heard you!" says Sofia. "You can't be serious? We would have had to stop the exercise and call on everyone to come and help carry you." "Careful young people! I'm not big, I'm just well endowed and much stronger than the average." Michel looks at everyone with a twinkle in his eye.

Thomas cuts in: "OK! OK kids! Shouldn't we talk about Francis and William ... especially when they heard that noise near the swamp?" "Yeah! That beaver hitting the water with its tail … really it surprised us…" says Francis. "You almost jumped into my arms," laughs William. "You took some time to get your wits back," adds grandpa. "However, that Beaver Dam really helped us remain dry" "Yeah! That dam is very well made. It is impressive."

Grandpa continues: "The winners of the race have earned a special prize; they each receive an I-Tune card for their iPod. The winners are Sofia and Jocelyn… Here are your prizes… Your time was recorded by your accompanist Michel. Everything was done by the book. Let us congratulate them all together." "Hurray! Hurray! Hurray!"

They all stand and embrace while continuing to tell their personal adventure. Sofia and Jocelyn look at each other from the corner of the eye. They lived their first experience together. They smile with complicity! A sparkle in Jocelyn's eyes already signals his interest towards Sofia. "We are happy and proud of you all. You have managed to trust one another and to work together. Congratulations," says grandma. "Come on! Let's all have a snack together. It is well deserved…"

The snack completed the six youths head to the tepee where they will spend the night, together, lying in sleeping bags. The tepee is huge, there is room for everyone. Michel has built a solid wood base to reduce the humidity. The children are ecstatic.

Chuky, Lise and Michel's dog, a brown Border collie, are now assured of a place amongst the young campers. During the exercise, he remained tied near the house. He was not allowed to follow the group in the woods for obvious reasons. Tonight, however, inside the tepee, it's a celebration for the dog with the children.

Summer Solstice and Stonehenge

Three years have lapsed since the family tragedy. Sofia, Cedric and William will soon be twelve years of age. The collective and individual training to date has been very fruitful. The triplets are much stronger, more confident and more powerful to the astonishment of their uncle Patrick. Ming had mentioned that one should not rely on their young age, because it has been shown that youths, when well trained, can achieve results far beyond the expectations of adults.

Time really flies. Soon the children will embark on their first mission. The Corribus triplets will turn twelve years old next June. They must continue to develop their skills and an unwavering trust in themselves and with each. This will be crucial for their survival and the success of their ultimate mission.

--- OOO ---

It is 5:00 A.M. The starry night is slowly fading away. The Sun has yet to rise. The golden light on the horizon forecasts a sunny day. A day where the sun propels its energy to enlighten us, to warm and keep alive all living beings on this bluish planet.

Pops, as this is how Patrick and Ming call him amongst themselves, is sitting cross-legged on his meditation chair. He sits facing the window, amongst his books, his mystical characters and his totemic animals.

He enjoys seeing the sun rise. He loves to watch it. He likes to communicate with his “guides”; these beings of light that are ever present. They are there to help him make the right decisions. He consults with them daily.

Pops is a professional consultant in corporate strategic planning. He regularly works with women and men who direct or manage businesses and organizations. Many of these managers, like him, engage in morning meditation or rituals that are like his. Some have been Yoga practitioners for several years. The meditation practice is efficient! It works!

--- OOO ---

Lately, pops has been experiencing adrenaline when transmitting knowledge. The three children are now at the age of establishing their values, their beliefs and their future friendships. They want to be listened to, to put forward their ideas, their suggestions and above all, they want to acquire their autonomy. Wow! What a challenge it is for the grandparents!

Pops has taught and coached young people of the age of the triplets in hockey teams, archery and martial arts, such as karate, judo and wrestling. He knows how much the children's energy must be channelled in this beginning of preadolescence. At twelve, one overflows with vitality and creativity, and especially, one seeks to assert herself or himself.

--- OOO ---

One afternoon, the children are examining artifacts in pops' library. They are intrigued by a photo showing a magnificent sunrise on an archaeological site. William, always curious asks: "Grandpa, what is this photo?" "This is the site of Stonehenge[1] in England," answers grandpa. "And this picture was taken on June

---

[1] Stonehenge, whose name is said to mean "Hanging Stones," is a megalithic monument consisting of a set of structures built between 2800 and 1100 BC, from the Neolithic to the Bronze Age. The site shows traces of living 8000 BC and a course of study dating from 3500 BC. The entire site is inscribed on the UNESCO World Heritage list.

21, such as the day of your birthday. On that day, it is the moment of the summer solstice."

"Summer solstice!" Repeats William, with a look of curiosity. "Yes. Since immemorial times," continues pops, "several cultures celebrate the Summer solstice, the longest day. They celebrate as well the Winter solstice, the shortest day. For example, Stonehenge in England that you see in the picture, gives rise to celebrations every year. Stonehenge and its enormous blocks of stone arranged in a circle, keeps the secret as to its origin and use. Many researchers agree that its construction dates from the Neolithic period, nearly 5,000 years ago, well before the coming of the Celtic and Roman people."

"The Celtic?" questions Sofia?

For three years, already she's titillated by dreams and readings. She hears conversations between her grandparents regarding this people. She is attentive to her grandpa's words. "Yes, the Celtic! They are also called the Celts. It is a great nation of conquerors. Their warriors are acknowledged as very strong and courageous men. Their story is very interesting and somewhere in our western evolution they played a very important role. Someday, I will tell you their story…"

"They do not know that…" thinks grandpa. "We don't know what," asks in earnest William, in search of an answer. "Nothing! Nothing for now," replies grandpa, surprising himself at thinking of what lies ahead for them. Phew!

"Now where was I," Pops asks the children. "You have to tell us the story of the Celts," says Sofia, interested in the subject. "That's it! Yes! You must tell us their story, I am anxious to hear it," says Cedric, always in search of stories to nurture his imagination.

"I will talk to you about the Celts later. For now, I will continue on the subject of Stonehenge. Is that OK, Cedric and Sofia?" "Yes! Of course, grandpa," answer the two, looking disappointed.

After looking at his grandchildren, pops resumes: "Most people are certain that Stonehenge was originally built as a sacred place for ceremonial and religious rituals. It is very likely that the first architects were sun worshippers since the axis that divides Stonehenge and aligns itself on its entry is basically oriented towards the sunrise in summer... In Ireland, there is a monument called Newgrange[2], a monument built nearly 1000 years before Stonehenge. However, this monument was directed towards the sunrise in winter."

The children are sitting in the lotus position with their elbows on their knees. Their chin rests in their hands. They are very attentive and gaze at pops to encourage him to continue.

"Both sites are very intriguing and many researchers are trying to understand why they are there and what purpose they served. Many legends and traditions confer it a mystery. The site has certainly been witness to the evolution of the people of the region and has most likely lived many rituals, especially with Celtic druids." "Druids as those in the historical comic strip, Vae Victis, that you have in your library," questions, Cedric?

"Yes, however, Stonehenge dates from long before the Caesar period which corresponds to the adventures of Vae Victis. The British astronomer, Gerald Stanley Hawkins, voiced a theory in the 1960s that Stonehenge was an astronomical observatory and a calendar. He believed that the ancient people used the monument to anticipate, to predict the major astronomical phenomena. This theory is still prevalent today, although there are a certain number of uncertainties. Many experts doubt that the builders of Stonehenge had the ability to predict numerous

---

[2] The site, built around 3200 BC, consists of a large circular mound in the centre of which lies a mortuary chamber which is accessed by a very long covered corridor. The exterior wall of the tumulus is flanked by monumental stones on which it is possible to observe spiral drawings and a few triskells. Each year (according to the observation of Sir Norman Lockyer in 1909), the day of the winter solstice (December 21), at 9:17 a.m.

astronomical events offered by this theory. Therefore, Stonehenge remains intriguing and raises so many questions for which we still do not have answers."

"Wow! Will we go to visit these places," ask the children in chorus? "It is possible, answers grandpa. One last interesting point about the Summer solstice: during the period of the festivities of the summer solstice, several nations took advantage of this moment to renew their warning systems provided by the bonfires. Back then, a large stake system was arranged on the hills along the land and maritime access routes. When they were lighted, these fires allowed the rapid warning and reporting of the arrival of the enemy or of a significant threat."

"Grandpa," intervenes Cedric, "at school we were told that in Quebec the celebration of the Saint-Jean every Summer, offered this opportunity to evaluate the system. Numerous fires marked out the St.-Lawrence River from Gaspé to Quebec City as a warning system." Sofia adds proudly: "Why yes, grandpa, and to avoid any false alarm everyone burned the fires at the same time." "They say it was beautiful as everyone started the fires at the same time that is when the bells rang at 6:00 P.M. That time was important because this allowed to verify the warning system during the day and at night," exclaims William, the warrior spirit of the group. He adds with a laugh, "I remember, because for that specific course, I was attentive, I wasn't in the moon."

"OK, enough for today, children, go play outside."

Grandpa remains pensive, especially since he almost revealed too soon to his three grandchildren their mission on Earth. "*They must be fed by the spoonful, gently, tenderly, using the right words. I know the time is near, however, with the help of Louise and her great diplomacy, we will get there.*"

Grandpa leaves his library that the children baptized very lovingly: "the library of mysteries." Grandpa knows that it contains many well-hidden and well-kept secrets and that his grandchildren would like to know more about his books and more so, his books of spells. That will be done in due course. He is not ready to disclose them and they themselves are not ready for them…

The section at the far-right side of the large wall bookcase is forbidden. They must not touch any of these books. It is a treasure of mystery! Grandpa will reveal a part of it when the time comes…

--- OOO ---

Louise and her Guide

Louise has known since her childhood that she possesses exceptional mental faculties. Her father named Noel after the day he was born (December 25, 1900) was a person that acted according to his beliefs in peace, justice and love. He was gifted with a very strong intuition. Her mother, Antoinette, three years younger, was also a strong believer in peace and love. She was known for her generosity and as a soft-spoken, humble and yet a very determined and loving mother. Together they raised their daughter with strong moral and family values. Louise, born in 1946, is recognized amongst her friends as a white witch. Although very discreet about her abilities, one must recognize Louise's intuition and her capacity to feel people and read situations.

At school, she would predict forthcoming events; she could see the auric vibrational fields of all her classmates. She could also see the colours of their chakras and those of their subtle body. She was different from the other girls. With the help of her father and her mother, who themselves were already considered wise; grandma lived her difference with much joy, enthusiasm and discretion.

Andrew, her sole brother, was her privileged playmate. Together, they would see and converse with beings living under their back porch; goblins, fairies and elves. These elementals were magnificent. They played in and protected all the flowers and plants in their garden. They were their personal playmates. There was no restriction. All friendly blows were allowed; all the adventures were grandiose.

Her personal guide, Pheas, an elf of great beauty, with silver skin and eyes golden as the sun, with red lips and a nose slightly turned up, has accompanied her since that period of her childhood. It is he, in a dream, who advised her of her career options, of her future. He is of great stature. He is impressive. When she sees him in a dream he is wearing a golden suit, chiselled across his chest. He adorns a bluish cape made of light leather that covers him from the shoulders to the ground. A lightweight brown fur collar embellishes this cape. The fur undulates in the wind. However, it is mostly his hair that retains Louise's attention. It is pearly with silvery highlights. His ears are pointed and barely deviated from his head. Pheas is very precious. He regularly advises her on decisions to be taken. Although as a teenager she often resisted his advice, she considers him as her mentor.

One day in a dream, around the age of 18, Pheas, the elf guide, warns her that she will have to spiritually guide triplets that will be her three grandchildren.

"You will complete another cycle of learning and evolution with a soul you knew in other lives. With this man, you will have two children, a boy and a girl, and the girl, in time, will give birth to triplets."

"These triplets, a girl and two boys, shall have a great mission in life: that of accomplishing a very ancient prophecy. They shall bear a sign, a birthmark on the neck, in the region of the seventh cervical vertebra. This mark, formless in appearance, will be sensed through vibration by you, your companion and the otherwise entities they will encounter. The mark reflects a stylized beetle. These triplets will be born at the Summer solstice, in the year 2000, the time of year when the light is brightest, a day of great power."

This revelation has had a great impact on Louise ever since that day. She keeps this secret in her heart until the said prophecy is to be fulfilled.

--- OOO ---

Thomas, the promised companion calls Louise "Princess," a title well deserved. She carries this name perfectly. Always very elegant and sober in her attire, she embodies a natural charm. The white hair, braided at the back of her head, the blue almond shaped eyes, the well-defined and smiling lips; all about her conveys charm and confidence. She is welcoming, cheerful, playful and attentive to others. Grandma loves to laugh. Every occasion is an opportunity to joke and spread her infectious laugh. She loves and enjoys the company of people. However, she regularly takes time for meditation and appeasement. She cherishes reading next to a cozy fire during the Winter. In Summer, she also appreciates relaxing under her favourite apple tree, or walking in her garden smelling the perfume of flowers while listening to the birds.

Louise accompanies Thomas in his travels wherever Earth is willing to disclose its secrets. Curiosity, introspection and unconditional acceptance are omnipresent in these two lovers.

--- OOO ---

The triplets are there. Louise and Thomas are now grandparents. At birth, they identified the mark on the neck of their grandchildren; it confirmed that they are the children of the New World. Since then, both are regularly in communication with their respective guide. Pheas warned Louise that these children would live with her and her spouse during a turbulent period which would last over ten years. During that time, Louise and Thomas would be constantly guided to prepare the triplets for their lifetime mission.

Life with the grandparents is now more stable. School, sports, special training, in short the routine is well in place. One day while the three of them were playing in the field near the property, a woman came to the front door. This woman was looking for a particular person in the village. When grandma opened the door, she immediately felt a discomfort in her plexus.

"I am looking for Marie Hurtubise, an old friend. I was told that I could speak to you as you have been living here in the region for a long time." The woman, a tall redhead with large emerald-green eyes, slender body and a smile nonetheless engaging, continues to question her about the region and the surrounding area for a good fifteen minutes. The more she talks, the more she arouses grandma's suspicion. Her bonhomie does not ring true.

"We do not know of any Mary Hurtubise in the village. Whomever informed you misled you in suggesting that we had all the answers to other people's questions." The woman thanks Louise walks and to her car. She opens the door to her black car and looking at grandpa and grandma with an icy stare, says in a deliberate tone of voice: "Thank you for your concern and your trouble."

While slowly leaving the property, she casts an inquisitive glance towards the field next door where the three children are playing. Grandma, who notices her movement of the head, expresses her concern to Thomas. He, too, has detected deceit and duplicity with this visitor.

"Let's be vigilant," says grandma, throwing loving eyes towards the children who are indulging themselves to their heart's content in the field next door. "Thomas, we must make sure that the children know how to detect individuals who may cause them problems," adds Louise. "Also, they must know how to protect themselves from such individuals by warning one another."

--- OOO ---

Louise is patiently waiting for the triplets in the library of mysteries where she has summoned the children for 4:00 P.M. this Friday afternoon. Sofia is the first to show up: "How are your telepathy practices progressing," asks grandma.

Sofia answers: "Am I the first to arrive? Really! Boys, you can't rely on them," adds Sofia, while Cedric and William enter the room. "Careful sis," replies William immediately, "we hear your cerebral verbiage continuously since returning from our expedition in the woods with grandpa." "Bla, Bla, Bla," continues

Cedric, laughing and grinning from ear to ear. "Enough boys!" says grandma, throwing them an affectionate wink.

"I saw you Grandma," says Sofia, "and I feel wronged in my status of being a girl. Hum! I will remember this; you are my brothers' accomplice." "Come on, it is not all that serious," replies grandma, taking her granddaughter by the waist. She adds, looking very serious at the boys: "I invite you to apologize to your sister, she does not deserve that. She is always punctual and I also recommend that you remember this great quality because you will greatly need it one day."

The boys do not like to apologize, especially when it is imposed. They move towards their sister standing next to the large library and together, say: "OK, we apologize Sofia we also apologize for dropping you at the edge of the forest. We were eager to find grandpa who was moving further away into the woods."

Sofia makes them a pout and looking them straight in the eyes, she says sarcastically: "Anyway, I've heard all your conversations. Grandma, you want to know the status on our progressions with telepathy. Well, I can tell you that in my case, it's going well. I even feel embarrassed sometimes, at school, especially when I hear all the thoughts of others, it's a real cacophony." "We totally agree with her. It's so tiring that I block my mind not to grasp everything that is thought around me," agrees Cedric, moving towards his sister that he likes to tease from time to time. "*She rises to the bait so easily,*" he thinks.

"Stop thinking that I easily take the bait to your teasing," Sofia retorts, raising her voice and shoving him in the corner of the room.

"Phew, children! That's enough. Let me tell you how to defend yourselves against the thoughts and indiscretions of each other's mind rather than jostle one another." Grandma continues: "It is precisely for this purpose that I wanted to see you. You need blocking mechanisms to help you select conversations and thoughts you want to follow. You also need to protect yourself against intrusions in your own thoughts. Others may do that, especially individuals with the same gifts as you. I want to show you these blocking techniques and I encourage you to practise them amongst yourselves and with others such at school or at sport. Grandpa and I will also practise with you."

Grandma then directs the children to their respective cushion. "For three years now, you have been under our responsibility, grandpa's and mine," says grandma. "You have learned much, studied a lot, given considerable efforts, individually, together and collectively with your friends. You really got going in every subject and skill that we presented to you." Looking at each of them in turn, she asks them point-blank: "What have you retained from the exercises to accentuate your gift of telepathy?"

Cedric, William and Sofia merely answer her: "We are confronted with knowing enough to understand many things but not enough to sort out the information that comes to us from everyone around us." "OK, I see where you're at," replies grandma, thrilled by their ability to assess themselves. "I believe it is now time to give you some pointers to protect yourself from intrusive communications amongst yourselves and with others."

"You do remember that to establish a contact between you and others, you must not be tense; you must be calm and optimistic." "Grandma, even if we don't always do that, the contact is made anyway," says Cedric. The other two nod to confirm that: yes, that's right.

"By what I hear, I can see that your gift is so natural and your reception executed with such incredible ease that the only thing left for you to practise and integrate is to build yourself a protection around you. With that you will be able to remain in touch with the reality in your environment and, at the same time, select only the snatches of conversation that are of interest to you. What do you think about that?" questions grandma.

"Will the people notice this little trick," asks William, ready to give it a try as soon as possible? "Yes! William is right. We are not 100% sure of this trick. How do we test it?" replies Sofia. "It's easy, you just have to try it..." says Cedric, he hesitates a moment and adds: "Why not try it now amongst ourselves?"

“Congratulations!” Grandma says, smiling. She was hoping that one of her grandchildren would suggest it. “So, let’s take our places, it takes an emitter and a receiver, therefore we will start with Cedric and William and I will be with Sofia. Afterwards, we will change partners.”

The practice lasted more than an hour. The partner changes gave very instructive and pertinent results. “I believe you’re ready to brush up on your learning in a new context. I will tell you about it tomorrow with the help of grandpa, Ming and Patrick who will be with us this weekend.” “Yeah!” exclaim Cedric. “It always ends in fun with Ming and Patrick. We work hard but we also play hard with them.”

The Leather Book

The whole family is gathered in the library of mysteries. Grandpa and grandma are waiting for the right moment to begin. They must discuss the next phase of the children's training. Sofia, William and Cedric are curious to know the next steps. Ming and Patrick are seated with them in the middle of the room, legs crossed like samurais.

"I would just love to accompany them on their next adventure," thinks Patrick, intrigued by the challenges they must face. "What?" exclaims William, "I heard you thinking uncle Patrick. What are you thinking about when you mention their next adventure?"

Grandpa, Grandma, Ming, Cedric and Sofia look at each other surprised. They heard William question Patrick about a possible adventure and they are waiting for his response.

Patrick slowly rises from his Samurai position and looking at his father and his mother, he tells them: "Well now, pops and mom, I believe it is time to fill them in on their next stage of life as teenagers, says Patrick, shaking his head slightly to the left. Sorry! I let it slip a few minutes ago while thinking about the inter-dimensional journey that Cedric, William and Sofia will have to live soon."

Ming and Patrick are aware of the challenges awaiting their niece and nephews during the next eight years. The children are speechless. They are dumbfounded; they do not move a muscle. They are looking at grandpa and grandma with eyes wide, and their mouth open to mosquitoes. After some hesitation, they shake their head; they swallow their saliva and recover from their emotions. Cedric rises, unbinding his numb legs. He speaks, stammering and holding his breath. He looks at his grandpa in the eye and asks breathlessly: "Fill us in! Inter-dimensional journey! What is this story about filling us in? Filling us in about what? Of whom? And especially of why?

Cedric is still breathing with restraint. William and Sofia slowly rise and join Cedric to affirm their solidarity with their brother, with the Corribus clan. All three await bravely, united. What will their grandparents reveal?

Grandpa looks at grandma intensely. They consult one another through their eyes. They know they need to clarify the situation. They need to reveal a part of what they know of the children's mission.

Grandpa slowly heads towards the far right end of his library and retrieves the mysterious book that the children have been devouring with their eyes since they have been living with their grandparents. They all observe grandpa's movement. He stops in front of a beautiful picture of a General. The picture shows the general in deep reflection, seated, in a splendid military uniform with his medals on the left-hand side of his chest close to the heart. The medals recount the feats of arms experienced by the General during the 1914–1918 War and the 1939–1945 War in Europe. This general is very significant for grandpa. He considers him a mentor. The general's posture reflects a man in reflection, pondering over the situation. With the forefinger of his right hand touching the ring finger of his left hand, the general appears to be saying "and secondly" while giving an explanation. This photo inspires and appeases grandpa when he must reflect on a situation or an impasse. In fact, right now he really needs to think before speaking.

The children are waiting for explanations. Patrick sits back down near Ming. As for Grandma, she goes over to grandpa in order to support him in his revelations. The triplets are holding hands and form a solid united trio.

--- OOO ---

Thomas and Louise now face their grandchildren. Ming and Patrick, standing back, support them. The moment is very serious.

"My children," begins grandpa, "I was not planning to tell you about this today, nevertheless, I know it is important that we make you more and more aware of what we know to prepare you to live different events that are forthcoming for you. Are you ready to hear what we know?" Grandpa stands straight as an oak tree, grandma beside him, solidary. "*Yes!" say Cedric, William and Sofia together, holding hands and their feet well planted in the light-blue carpet of the library.*

Given the offensive attitude of his three grandchildren, grandpa realizes the importance of relaxing the atmosphere. He asks Cedric, William and Sofia to kindly sit beside Ming and Patrick. Likewise, he prompts grandma to do the same. As everyone settles in, he takes a deep breath, asks his guide to support him, then sits before his family. He looks each of the children successively in their eyes. As a first step, with them, he goes over their story from their birth to the death of their mother and father. When he speaks of their last moments with their mother Marion, he asks the children: "What did you promise your mother before she passed away?"

The children look at one another intensely and Sofia beckons Cedric to answer. "We promised to follow your instructions, grandpa, grandma, Ming and you Patrick and to accept the training that would prepare us for our mission in life to fulfill a prophecy." Then Cedric adds intensely: "we know absolutely nothing of that prophecy."

The nonverbal support of Sofia and William for Cedric's words is very eloquent.

"Thank you, Cedric," says grandpa, bending his head towards his chest. "Grandma will reveal the actual prophecy in due course. For now, let's stick with the preparations and the training you had to assimilate at the cost of constant effort. We understand that the three years you have just spent in the company of Ming, Patrick, grandma and I as your instructors and coaches were most demanding. Your progress in telepathy, your skills in martial arts and combat techniques, the protection techniques against potential mental intrusion and all the other disciplines that we are working on with you are all essential for your life during the next few years and beyond. We are impressed with your attitude and the quality of your work."

The children straighten up on their cushions with pride. They were not expecting congratulations! "Hum," smiles grandpa, looking at them wobble on their cushions! "Can I continue or are you tired of listening to me?" "No, no, it's alright, answers William," who is usually the one that least tolerates a constant position. "Then I will continue, it won't take much longer."

Picking up his chain of thought, he adds: "You have learned to respect and control your curiosity; you work very well together; you focus on solutions; you are very effective in looking at difficulties as a challenge; you have a lot of physical stamina, endurance; plus, you are brave and determined. In short, you've proved equal, no; I would rather say, you have performed beyond our expectations."

Grandpa looks at them affectionately. He regards these triplets, not like superheroes, but as teenagers that are very courageous and trustful in their instructors. "Thank you for trusting us," says grandma gently, leaning towards the three children.

"I want to point out that we have a lot of fun making you work together," interjects Patrick with a teasing smile. "Ming and I came to you three to fulfill our promise towards Marion. We promised her we would help prepare you to keep a clear head in front of any possible situations. In fact, we want to give you all the physical, emotional and mental tools you need. But more important, we want to get you to trust yourself and to trust one another. I would hope that we have fulfilled a part of our promise."

William, who has not spoken much since the beginning of the meeting, says loudly and clearly: "You didn't fail, uncle Patrick, especially, I remember the time my fingers got caught in my sling shot and I almost threw my projectile in Sofia's legs." "Yeah! You almost injured me," she says, recollecting the moment when she had to jump so as to avoid the rock as big as an egg. "And all our wrestling matches, sword and dagger techniques, judo projections, karate katas were not to standards and so on," says Cedric, remembering the bruises on his arms and legs that took forever to heal.

"Yes!" says Cedric, "I believe you have passed the test for best instructors in the area. We understood that nothing is achieved without repeated and sustained efforts. Like you say, 'the only place where we have success before work is in the dictionary.'" "I can't believe I went through all these learning obstacles. Fortunately, we had our friends, Jocelyn, Peter and Francis to change the tempo and to relax with us," states, William.

"Yeah, however, when we were lost in the Mont Megantic Park, we were not that relaxed," continues Cedric. "Especially when it started to rain. We could not see anything and we could hear all kinds of noises we did not recognize. We got lost despite all the safety precautions you had given us before our departure. Fear almost took over. We started talking and arguing loudly amongst ourselves. I took over to calm us down, you remember Sofia, you wanted to turn back with Jocelyn. William, you interfered with, of course, the support of your buddy Francis. Things turned sour. It was a disaster. After several minutes of disputes, we came to realize that it was just a game and we had to make the situation less alarming for us to realize that we would get nowhere by remaining stuck in a stressful mindset." They can laugh about it now. That night in the mountain, however, they did not find it funny at all, no, not at all.

"How about if we get back to our subject, as you say so well grandpa, what is the revelation," questions Sofia, who has not lost a thread of the conversation and who remembers fully the reason for their presence at the centre of the blue carpet?

"Thanks Sofia" says grandpa looking at her with affection. "The revelation will be given to you in two parts. You see this book of mysteries that I am holding in my hands with utmost respect, it contains two items that we must give you before an important meeting with three magical guides. We are currently in early May and grandma and I have been told to give you a part of the revelation. We must give you an item, a very precious item. This item will belong to you alone. You will get another item later, that is, once you have learned to use effectively the first one.

Grandpa noticed the children's look when he mentioned the word "magic," particularly that of Cedric, the most curious of the three. "Yes, Cedric, I am ahead of you, your eyes speak volumes when I said magic. As for you two, William and Sofia, you'll be thrilled when I reveal the identity of this mysterious guide."

Grandpa opens his book gently taking care not to prolong the mystery with the children. The book is thick. As soon as it is open, it reveals a cavity within the pages. It is hollow but not empty. Inside the cavity are two small velvet pouches, one is black and one is magenta. This book, with a dark brown leather binding displays an Egyptian symbol engraved in black and gold. It's a decoy. Never, would one have thought of such a subterfuge.

"It was necessary to protect the two items in question in this false book. A marvellous idea, don't you think?" asks grandpa smiling? "Does all the section on the right-hand side of the library hide similar books with a false identity," asks Sofia? Eager to see for herself, Sofia rises. However, grandpa asks her to kindly sit back down.

"Grandma will continue giving you explanations on the item in question," concludes grandpa, stepping back to make way for his wife. "Ming and Patrick, have you anything else to add," asks Louise, looking at them intently? "*I need your help, magic is your field.* She thinks in German while looking at her son.

"It's OK, mom," answers Patrick, smiling and looking at his mother to let her know that she may take over. "The children are ready. They are ready to get into action." He adds: "Perhaps you hesitate to take action, mom, because as soon as you do, they must grow up in spite of themselves and that's not what you are hoping for at this time, is it not?"

Louise looks at him oddly. She does not want to admit it to herself. She has a mission to accomplish. Yes, it will be done, except that this mission will snatch the children from her motherly arms. This moment is the most difficult part to live. Since she has been responsible for them, along with Thomas, she has tried to hold off the moment when she must reveal them their magical guide, their new mentor. Watching them grow up so fast, learning new concepts almost every day, especially at a rapid pace, and seeing them depart more and more frequently from the paternal home, create a void in her heart.

"Mom, are you here," questions Ming, raising her head towards her? "Yes, yes, I'm here, I just wanted to tell the children that..." "We have been following your train of thought, Grandma," states, Sofia. "We will always be here beside you, the best grandma of all. Your motherly arms will always support us in difficult times." "Your love is essential for us," says Cedric, wiping a tear beading at the corner of his left eye. All three get up and tenderly hug their grandma and after a few moments, they regain their place at the centre of the blue carpet.

"I am very moved... Thank you for your show of affection towards me. I am happy to realize that you can express your feelings with ease.... That is a great gift to me. I am very grateful to have children like you with me. You are proving to me that, what you have learned throughout the last three years, it is not only the brain that has absorbed notions but also your heart has grown with your head... Keep this attitude amongst you and with others. This is precious."

Three Pins

Louise moves towards the three children and asks them to stand up. They position themselves with Cedric to the right of Sofia and William to her left.

Thomas withdraws the black velvet pouch from the book and hands it to Grandma. Louise is moved. The children look at her intrigued. Then silently, she pulls three jewels out of the precious black velvet pouch, three bronze pins in the shape of a dragonfly.

"So much mystery for three small pins," whispers William, disappointed. "I expected a precious stone or a piece of gold or anything else, but not a dragonfly jewel." "May I tell you a story, William?" Louise looks intently at her grandson, the most rebellious of the three? Still serious, she asks: "do you trust me?" "Yeah grandma, I am listening. "

William rubs his nose with the forefinger of his right-hand. He looks at his sister and brother who throw him a fiery look. "What? Bronze dragonflies, that's for girls," replies, William.

"All right, children," cuts in Grandma. "I will tell you the origin of these dragonflies. I have a guide, a magnificent elf. Pheas is his name. During our last conversation, he entrusted me with gifts for you three. They are these dragonflies. These pins are pure magic and they will always be accessible to you. They must be used in the event of exceptional travel needs. I see many questions emerging in your eyes. Wait, I'm not done, you will ask your questions when I am finished."

"You will need to carry these pins at all times. You will be the only ones able to activate them. Your dragonflies are individually personalized to you and you need to tame their power. That requires a lot of trust." Louise looks intensely at Sofia, then Cedric and as she sustains William's stare, she continues: "Do you now grasp the importance of trust? The trust you must develop between you three and with your own guides? You will need it." "You are intriguing, grandma," interrupts Cedric. "Yeah!" adds Sofia, in complete agreement with her brother.

As for William, he remains mute, silent, he is waiting for more.

Grandma continues to reveal more of the message to them. They note particularly the most important portion: "To activate the process of transformation, because there will be a transformation, you must pronounce three words discreetly, with confidence and conviction, without hesitation, 'Dragonfly! Dragonfly! Dragonfly!' while tapping gently on your pin three times with your right hand. It is obvious that you will wear your pins on your clothing in a discreet manner every day. As soon as you have spoken these words, something very special will happen and an enormous yellow dragon will appear to you, as by magic, pouf! And there he is."

"Me, seeing a Dragon! I don't believe it! Protests William. 'Your personal dragon,' grandma keeps on saying, 'will greet you and will be at your service, as your mentor and your instructor for the years to come.'

'Grandma, wait you are going too fast,' says Cedric with his hand up. 'I told you to hear me out first,' interject Grandma. 'But Grandma…' says Sofia… 'Please hear me out,' insists grandma with her hand commanding the children to stop. 'You need to hear and understand the whole picture before questioning' says grandma looking intensely at each of the children to ease their questions. She continues slowly: 'Initially, these dragons will help you perfect your ability to communicate by telepathy. They will be invisible to other humans. Only the bearers of natural gifts will have the opportunity to see them. This gift of the gods is given to you with love. Be true to your mount.'

'What! We are going to ride them?' William eyes are wide with surprise. Speechless he awaits further explanations from his grandma? 'This is fantastic,' says Patrick, 'you who always wanted to play with real dinosaurs. You're going to have one for you alone.'

'C'mon, uncle Patrick, it's impossible. I can't see dragons; they are only in our imaginary! I'm no longer a kid!' 'You'll see, William, the imaginary can translate into reality,' replies Ming, while placing her hands on her nephew's shoulders.

'Just like that! We will each have a yellow dragon,' exclaims Cedric, eager to know what follows! 'That's wonderful.'

As for Sofia, she seems fearful, stunned. She has not spoken a single word since grandma told them that all three of them would have a dragon at their service. She pinches herself to make sure she is here. Is this another crazy dream to which she has been confronted for some time now? '*This is pure invention,*' thinks Sofia, while looking at her astonished brothers.

Grandma hears their reflections and notices their astonishment. She continues talking to them. She approaches them and successively hooks, with delicacy and solemnity, a dragonfly on Cedric's chest, on William's and finally on Sofia's chest. The children let themselves be decorated with these pieces of bronze. They look up to their Grandma, and then, in succession, they look at grandpa, Ming and Patrick. Their smiles are contagious.

Cedric, William and Sofia are speechless. They are stunned, not a single word is spoken. Suddenly, William awakens from his inertia. He bravely announces to grandma and to all others around him as he moves his hands towards the pin: 'I will not wear this pin on my chest every day. It's out of the question. I refuse. I will never be the laughingstock of my friends at school. Cedric, can you see me with this pin on my school sweater or t-shirt? Never! I will never give in to this masquerade. I withdraw from the race. I will not be part of it. The prophecy is not for me.'

William stops struggling with the pin and takes a defiant stance. His body remains as straight as an iron bar; his fists are clenched, his arms interlocked and his look determined.

'Relax, William,' says Patrick, while advancing towards him. 'We understand your astonishment and your concern about what the others could think at school... Let grandma explain the usefulness of this pin as her personal guide told her to do; then you will be in a position to judge and decide if you still want to refuse to wear this piece of bronze as you say. Does this suit you?' William looks at Patrick, then at Grandma. With a pout he says: 'OK! I am willing to hear the rest of the story.' 'I too wonder where we are going with all this,' adds Sofia, looking intently at her brother.

William hears Cedric tell him, as he gets closer and puts his hand on his left shoulder: 'I'm no more reassured than you are. I am waiting to hear what follows and then I'll see. Imagine though, what if it is possible for us to travel wherever we want with these yellow dragons? Can you imagine? I think we would be so happy.'

'What are you saying Cedric, did you come across information William and I did not get,' questions Sofia, turning to stare at Cedric? 'I'm only assuming, that's all,' he responds, looking round for his grandparents, Ming and Patrick thinking: *'Come and help me please, because I have no answer to give them. I am in my imaginary that's all.'*

Grandma takes a long, deep breath, closes her eyes and then slowly reopens them, and then she moves towards the children and holding out her arms to them, says: 'Cedric got it right. Yes, you can travel with your personal dragon! He will take you wherever you please. The more you ride him, the more he will teach you and the more you will understand and live by a code of honour and the code ethics which commits him to you. The more you mix with them, the more joy and happiness you will have when riding them. They are magnificent animals, majestic, faithful, joyful, disciplined and great warriors,' says Grandma, so enthusiastically that William's attitude begins to change. 'You know, William, I have a dragonfly too that I carry discreetly and not one of our friends knows it, not even you, my children.' 'Really grandma! You carry it all the time,' questions Sofia, surprised at this little secret?

But of course, the Dragonfly is my principal power animal. It follows me everywhere I go. It is a very special jewel for me."

The children are astounded. They can't believe what is revealed to them. A tornado of questions remains active in their mind. Their eyes and mouths are wide open. Then, in turmoil, questions give birth to anecdotes, to bursts of laughter and new surprises. Several minutes elapse before Louise interrupts: "Come on, let's go sit at the table and we will continue to talk about it. Ming and Patrick will be with us for supper and afterwards they must return to Ottawa. During dinner, you may ask them for further explanations on the magical dragons because, you know, they too have a special relationship with these animals."

The meal unfolds in fun and relaxation. William is far more reassured. He is already making scenarios in order to hide the pin on himself; everyone at the table burst out laughing. All tricks are allowed. Cedric and Sofia add to the scenarios with many wacky plans to hide their bronze pins.

Ming gets up: "Not that we are bored, however, Patrick and I must leave you for now. We have to drive for four and half hours to get home. We have given you enough information about the yellow dragons for the moment. Enjoy them, you lucky guys." "*I will call and you can tell me all about your feats with your respective dragon, adds Patrick, who would have so wanted to live this adventure with Cedric, William and Sofia.*

Ming and Patrick get up, embrace Louise, Thomas and the children. They gather their belongings and when crossing the door Patrick says with a laugh: "Hasta la vista baby!" as in Arnold's film. They all burst out laughing.

"*Patrick knows how to lighten the mood. He is always happy and finds the appropriate words,"* thinks grandma.

The children accompany them to their car, a red Mazda. They hug Ming and Patrick one last time. They watch the car drive away and then come back into the house shouting to their grandparents: "May we try our dragonfly pins?"

They rush to grandpa. They are so excited since Patrick reassured them that they did not notice they had jostled grandma in passing. "Wo!" Barks grandpa. "You almost pushed your grandmother on the floor." "Sorry grandma! I can't wait to live the experience," apologizes Cedric. "And you, William, will you join your sister and your brother for this riding," asks grandpa sarcastically? "The pin doesn't embarrass you anymore? Are you ready to let your little 'peacock pride' make way for a most extraordinary adventure," asks grandpa?

"Leave him alone, Thomas," says Louise, knowing this teasing side of her companion! "I think it's rather his impulsiveness that takes over him when he experiences an unexpected fear or an unanswered question."

"Yes, you're right, I want to live this challenge with Cedric and Sofia as soon as possible. " Turning to his brother and sister, William heads towards the back-porch patio door saying: "When do we start?"

Cedric and Sofia are already there waiting for the approval signal for the departure. "You just have to follow the instructions I gave you earlier and your dragon will appear. It's simple, it's magic, remember," adds grandma, smiling.

At that moment, a flash of white light illuminates the entire back yard. An enormous animal appears in the middle of the neighbouring field. A yellow dragon of immeasurable greatness unfolds its magnificent wings.

"William, my little crafty devil, you preceded your sister and your brother. You still had doubts about the possibility of this gift of the gods." Grandpa points his finger at him: "It's only by experiencing yourself that you believe. I would like to warn you against this course of action. One day it will be necessary that your faith be greater than what you have shown for that dragon."

William looks at his grandpa questioningly. He does not fully grasp the meaning of these words. Grandpa realizes this and goes towards him.

"You'll have to deal with other situations that will demand that you have unwavering faith, the one they say, that moves mountains. For now, go enjoy these moments with your dragon, he's waiting for you."

"Wow! Wow! Wow! Wait for us, we too are sending for our dragon," say Sofia and Cedric, running to the field nearby. "Dragonfly! Dragonfly! Dragonfly!" repeat Sofia and Cedric, tapping gently on their respective pin.

No sooner said than done, two other dragons come to stand next to the first one. Enthusiasm prevails. The children are overwhelmed with euphoria. They are floating in a magical world.

Nevertheless, Sofia notices after a while that one of them is smaller than the other two. *"Ah! Strange, she thinks, why the difference in size? Is it related to the fact that we are two boys and a girl in our sibling group? Are there genders amongst the dragons? Surely, otherwise there would be no baby dragons. Come on, what the heck am I thinking here, they are magical."*

"You're right," answers grandpa to her questioning. "You have a male dragon and the boys have a female dragon. The symbiosis will be made far more easily by living with the opposite sex. Let your dragons introduce themselves to you. You'll hear them talk to you through your telepathic ability. This is how they will contact you. Now do you understand why we insisted that you practise your telepathy skills regularly. We knew that these beings of light would contact you only through telepathy."

"Thank you, Grandma! Thank you, grandpa! Let's go," shouts Will, rushing to the dragons.

"No, no, it's true, I do not know mine, continues William, while stopping and looking at Sofia and Cedric, astonished. He adds, I know, I must wait for my dragon to present itself to me. I can't wait to meet him."

Grandpa instantaneously remembers the description of the dragons, these mythical animals. He now realizes the importance of the gift that Master Xin presented him during his trip to China: an ancient book about dragons, their characteristics, their reason for being and their roles next to humans. Most particularly, with emotion, he can again see the page endorsed by Master Xin illustrating the yellow dragons, "Huang Long".[3]

What he sees corresponds with what he has read. They are absolutely huge: 15 metres from head to tail, the wings outstretch over almost 30 metres, looking at the size, they must weigh about 4000 kilos... They are beings altogether magnificent and radiant. The heads are adorned with impressive horns and their feet comprise five powerful claws. Their gazes, although benevolent and intense, command respect and inspire confidence despite their gigantic stature. These are messenger dragons from the coastal regions of Asia. Grandpa Thomas is amazed. He now knows that the children are blessed and protected by the Gods. "I tell you again that only humans with special gifts can see the dragons and feel their energy."

The children are amazed and in awe. Three yellow dragons are here before them, and the dragons are looking at them... Really, these yellow dragons are alive. They are breathing. They are moving on their two hind legs. Their nostrils are inflating with air and their tails are oscillating leisurely on the grass.

William, still reserved, hears a grave and imposing but reassuring voice vibrating in his brain that says: "Hello William, my name is DYRA and I am at your service."

---

[3]Huanlong, Yellow Dragon or Horse Dragon. This is the divine messenger who emerged from the River Luo to communicate to man, through Fuxi, the eight trigrams of the divination system known as the Yi-King. Wikipedia

The dragon on the left looks at him intensely, with respect, kindness and solicitude. DYRA bends down and, invites William to climb on his back. William does not move. He, so familiar with the dinosaurs of all his reading books, his imaginary adventures, is amazed ... he hears the dragon speaking to him ... he won't sleep tonight. "Come on William, what are you waiting for?" DYRA is speaking directly into his brain. He looks at his brother Cedric and questions him with his gaze. "How do we do that, ride a dragon? It's not like riding my bike."

DYRA hears William question himself and replies by advancing her right paw: "Put your foot on my right joint, then climb on my wing close to my body, pass your other leg in front of my other wing as if you were mounting a horse. It's not more complicated than that, mounting a dragon is just like mounting a horse." "I can't mount you the way I mount my black speckled gray mare. There's no saddle," says William, incredulous! "You do not need it, it's magic, and my neck adjusts to your energy. Your trust holds you in place and I do the rest. Take your place, William, we have some taming to do. Come on, get on! Trust yourself."

Thrilled and in a gymnastic move, he jumps onto the mount, sticks his plexus to the dragon's neck and feels the animal's full power, its strength and its confidence. He is reassured. Sofia is as in a dream. She too can hear the vibrations coming from her dragon: "Hello Sofia, my name is LYKA and I am at your service."

LYKA is slightly smaller in size and positioned between the other two dragons. The dragon looks at her intensely, with deference, kindness and solicitude.

Sofia scans her dragon with attention. She notices that the dragon has four claws on his left hind leg, while the other two have five. She keeps her observation to herself. Her dragon noticed it. He also keeps his reading for later, when Sofia will dare to ask him for explanations.

Beyond what she sees, Sofia feels the complicity between this fantastic animal and herself. Swiftly, at the invitation of her dragon, she finds herself comfortably and confidently sitting on that robust and protective creatures.

Meanwhile, Cedric has eyes only for the beauty, the harmony, the majesty and the strength that his dragon radiates. He also hears vibrating in his brain: “Hello Cedric, my name is MARA and I am at your service regardless of the day or night. You call me and I’m here.”

Already enthusiastic and understanding the procedure, Cedric rapidly finds himself sitting astride around the neck of this magical being thus becoming his faithful companion for life. He hears the dragon’s heart beating and perceives his own heart beating in unison with the mythical animal. He will never forget the sound of the dragon’s voice nor the feel of its heartbeat.

The First Flight

Louise and Thomas are very emotional. They are privileged to witness such an important magical and symbolic moment. They know that these yellow dragons are celestial messenger dragons. They are guardians of the divine residence and protectors of gods. They symbolize an elevation to a higher state. They are carriers of nine attributes: exceptional longevity, peaceful warriors, kindness, generosity, perseverance, willfulness, joyful creativeness, intelligence and magical. They are aware that the more these children will share their vibratory thoughts with these magical beings, the more they will integrate the same attributes.

Cedric, William and Sofia proudly mount their dragons. Their faces are radiant despite their tension perceptible in their grip.

With one flip of their majestic wings, the three dragons fly off together into the sky.

"Fantastic," exclaims William, clinging to DYRA's neck, his hair windswept, eyes twinkling with wonder, *"I must be dreaming,"* he thinks. *"No, you're not dreaming,"* telepathically transmits his brother Cedric. *"It's marvellous. I'm also living a magic moment."*

"I am flying like a bird," shouts, Sofia. "Rather like a dragon," quips LYKA. "Oh yes! Very funny, little dragon," replies Sofia, fondly hugging the neck of her messenger.

Only the wind whistles at the children's ears. They fly in formation like fighter jets. They feel they are in symbiosis with their dragons. LYKA, DYRA and MARA now test their confidence. Progressively, they twirl around, go up, dive vertically, straighten up with a sudden flip of the wings and soar at length. They dive vertically again and then pull back up drawing arabesques in the sky. Always sensitive to the quality of the children's embrace, they acknowledge the discomfort and the fear of the children, whilst developing with them the beginning of a magic complicity.

Eyes closed, teeth clenched, hands clinging to the neckline of soft and firm scales, Cedric, William and Sofia communicate their wish to return. "*Can we go back? We've had enough for a first time.*" The children, aching, tired, stunned and completely committed to their respective dragon, know that in the future they must develop stamina and a mutual trust. They sense the importance of developing their complicity with these magical beings. They are not merely entertainment mounts. The contact with each of their dragons allowed Cedric, William and Sofia to live an emotion of filiation, loyalty and companionship that they had last experienced with their departed parents.

"Whew! My arms are stiff as an iron bar," sighs William, extremely blown away by the experience. "And me, it's my legs," exclaims Cedric, excited by the short flight. "My heart is floating," adds Sofia, moved, close to tears. "I have not experienced this feeling since mom and dad used to play with us."

In silence, the flock of yellow dragons comes back to the house where Louise and Thomas are waiting. They are holding hands, filled with admiration and gratitude before this spectacular show, truly a magic moment. The grandparents never had information on the trips or adventures that the dragons will experience with their grandchildren. It is a secret, a hidden part of the information. These magical animals keep that information to themselves. The dragons received from their own Mage the mission to reinforce the respective gifts of the children. The dragons are at the service of their great Celestial Masters. Before being detached to serve the children, these great masters advised the celestial dragons: "Nothing is beyond their capability, they shall know how to overcome the obstacles, of course, with a little help from you, say the celestial guides smiling, looking the yellow dragons in the eye."

The children squeeze their chargers' necks and thank them. They're so happy that they are bursting with joy. They get off their mounts and respectively give it a hug. "*Bye for now, transmit LYKA, DYRA and MARA in unison. Be good, we will meet again soon to pursue your training. In the meantime, we are returning to our dimension.*"

The dragons vanish.

--- OOO ---

The first flight has been followed by many more. Since then, the children and the dragons frequently cross the skies and spaces of the Eastern Townships. The dragons intentionally and regularly move further away from the region and fly over unknown areas. The risks undertaken are consistent with the instructions received. The children must learn to live in a complete change of scenery. They must get used to living different topography and especially not to panic when they lose their landmark. They will need that confidence.

--- OOO ---

"Let's eat, says Grandma," recovering from her emotions. "Wash your hands," adds grandpa! The children look at their grandfather and ask in unison, "What for?" "You've just come back from a ride with your dragons," says grandpa surprised. "Why grandpa," says William, "my dragon, she is clean!" "It is a luminous animal," adds Cedric. "Magical gleam, now, that's clean, clean, clean," says Sofia, laughing.

"Thank you, children, I'm at a loss here, but go wash your hands anyway!" "OK we will," they say, laughing.

On returning from the bathroom, the children settle down at the table where the food cooked by grandma is ready to be served. The small family ask for a blessing. The children have put this ritual into practice since their childhood. Nothing is new for them.

The children experience a moment of nostalgia; they would so much have loved to share their dragon experience with their parents…

The children eat heartily while relating their respective adventure. They instinctively and continuously caress their magic pin.

The discussions, sometimes hilarious, sometimes in a low voice and secretive, continue throughout the evening. During this fantastic evening, grandma asks the children to get comfortable on the sofas in the living room.

"Oh! It must be serious," says William, with a touch of mischief in his tone. "Of course, it's serious," answers grandpa, settling down next to William, and squeezing his knees with affection. "Stop, grandpa, you're tickling me. I end up rolling down on the floor when you do that." "It makes me laugh so much to see you rolling down on the floor like bacon in a frying pan." "Well, here we go again," intervenes Louise, while staring William and Thomas down with her piercing blue eyes! "Can we begin; she asks?"

"Grandma don't bother with them, you know, they are always the same those two when they sit side by side," says Cedric, swaying on the couch. Sofia is looking at her grandmother: "Well! What is all this serious business? Can we move guys? What is it Grandma?"

--- OOO ---

The Prophecy

Thomas, Cedric, William and Sofia are sitting comfortably on the living room couches. Louise looks at them attentively: "Well, I consider what I have to share with you of utmost importance. You have heard your parents talking with us of a prophecy on a few occasions. However, we deliberately kept the secret from you. We did not want to speak to you about it until you had completed several specific training. We did not want you to be distracted by information that could be difficult for you to understand. Now that you are familiar and comfortable with your respective dragons, we believe that you are now able to receive more information about your forthcoming mission.

Grandma notices that their eyes are wide open and their mouth ajar. Yet she continues: 'We have another object to give you. You remember the other small bag, the velvet one in grandpa's false book?' The children nod their heads acquiescing. 'Well, it is the time to give each of you three the second objects. You may find me very solemn right now and I am. However, it is also an important moment, which, in time, will serve you well, yes; these gifts will be helpful to each of you individually and collectively.'

Grandma takes another pause. She turns to Thomas, comfortably seated on his couch and pensive. 'I am still your grandma, of course; however, grandpa and I also have a mission to accomplish. We made a commitment to your parents. I made a covenant with my guide Pheas and grandpa made one with his guides. I believe that before we speak to you of the prophecy, grandpa must tell you a story. Grandpa, are you ready, asks Grandma?' 'Yes, here I am.'

Thomas settles on the cushion besides his wife and faces the children in order to fully capture their attention.

'You may interrupt me any time. I will begin with a time dating back over 9600 years before our era. It is the Atlantis period.' 'Ah!' interrupts Cedric, 'I remember the film of Atlantis that I watched with you, Grandma, one night when you were babysitting me. William and Sofia were already asleep. The people from Atlantis were using crystals to power their spaceship. I remember those details.'

'Indeed,' answers grandma, 'you were so interested in the movie that I had to watch it a dozen times before you agreed to go to bed.' 'Grandma, I found it awesome to see their way of moving through space with merely a large piece of crystal.' 'Ah! Could we watch that film tomorrow,' asks William?

'Of course, it is in the movie library, you can watch it whenever you want,' answers grandpa. But now it is time for you to be attentive to what I must tell you. You understand?" The three kids nod while looking at their grandfather. "I will go on with my story. This great people of the Atlantis period declined they lost the vision of their society. They also lost the enjoyment of their special gifts. The gods decided to close the gates of their heaven temporarily because the people had become greedy and no longer believed in their gods. They lacked faith."

"Has it ever been possible to open the doors again," asks William? "Yes, according to what we know, an attempt was made in ancient Egypt around the year 3500 before our era. It was a very flourishing period in Egypt which contributed to the growth of humanity. By this, I mean that everyone wanted to remain in the glory of the Gods. They wanted to live a privileged life again. However, beings imbued with themselves, people who wanted to have more power for their own benefit, prevented the meeting of man with his destiny. They prevented the fulfillment of the prophecy."

"Oh, no! There we go again," exclaims Sofia. "Indeed, Sofia, humans have not understood the message since antiquity. I realize that it's the same today; not much has changed in 5000 years, if my calculations are correct. It's sad to say but it's true, except that the Gods have simply extended the deadline. They are offering a new chance for us humans. A new opportunity has been programmed. Encrypted hieroglyphic texts, dating back over 3000 years before our era were partially decoded by initiated Mycenaean around 1200 years, again before our era."

"Hiero! Hiero what?" Asks William, "I don't understand. What do you mean by that word?" "When you open your computer, you see a toolbar with small signs at the top to help you find what you need to work with. These signs give an instruction to the computer's brain. Is that not so?" "Well ... yes," answers William surprised at the question. "So, it's the same. The ancients discovered that in drawing and etching images in stone, they could, in this way, transmit their thoughts to different groups of people such as the different origins of their slaves. That is how they wrote their message. What you call icons, they called it hieroglyphs. OK, do you understand, Will?" "Yes, now I understand better than before."

"So, I may continue? Your nodding confirms that I may. However, the secret was closely guarded until now. It was hidden in a great library of the antiquity: that of Alexandria in Egypt. You're not lost when I speak to you about Egypt, are you?"

"No, says Cedric, recently we had to do group research at school on the subject. We went to the large library of Montreal by bus. The entire class participated. You remember, grandpa, you wanted to accompany us, but the teachers declined and thanked you for your generosity. Three women made the trip to accompany us: the science teacher, the French teacher and the history teacher."

"That's right, thank you for reminding me. So, I will continue the story. Beings of exceptional goodness, foresight and wisdom finally decoded the text of a prophecy that restored the hope. It appears it is now the time for the event to occur. You three, are part of the new hope for humanity." "You are the triplets of the year 2000," says Grandma. "That's why you must train hard to develop and master as much as possible the potential of your special gifts. This may seem unlikely. I grant you that. We ourselves were also flabbergasted when our guides transmitted us the news."

Thomas and Louise look at their grandchildren with admiration and affection. This moment of silence allows them to absorb the information.

Grandpa resumes: "As you know, you bear a sign on your neck, a mark at the level of the cervical vertebrae. This sign is invisible, for the moment, to the normal eye. This sign identifies you as those persons selected to fulfill this prophecy. Only the initiates and exceptional beings can detect that mark you bear."

"Ah! That's why our dragons emitted a comment amongst themselves saying that we were the triplets of the year 2000," says Sofia. "Now I understand what they meant. We looked at one another at that moment, hearing their message, but without understanding anything about it."

"They perceived the sign which gives them the authority, the responsibility to perfect your learning," says Grandma. "It is necessary that they do not make a mistake in the selection of the triplets, because to create a diversion, the Gods allowed the profusion of triplets currently in the world. This is to mislead and prevent groups with bad intentions to easily track you and divert the fulfillment of the prophecy to their personal advantage."

"You, grandma and grandpa, did you perceive the signs on our neck," questions William strongly? "Yes dear," answers Grandma. "We notified your parents of this immediately upon your arrival on Earth. That's why your mother asked you to accompany us to the countryside in order to prepare you for this great adventure. She asked you to make a promise to her. She knew that you are the triplets of the prophecy."

The children are speechless. They are in a meditative state. They review in a flash the events they have gone through in the last three years. They understand a little more the attitudes and demands from Ming and Patrick towards them. They also remember all the suspicious stares from their friends at school ever since they are in the region. *"Particularly the look from our science teacher,"* thinks Sofia. *"She never ceases to look us up and down every time we enter the room."*

"Are you with us children, you have been in a meditative state since we've announced you who you are and what mission is in line for you," questions grandpa through telepathy?

"I urge you to come back amongst us. I have yet to reveal to you the prophecy in question. It was forwarded to us on your arrival on this Earth, at your birth. I have always carefully guarded it in one of my false books. I'll get it to read it to you. Remain seated, do not follow me. It is necessary that the secret remains closely guarded.

Grandpa retrieves the book from the library. As he does so, he makes a special note of Sofia's thought on her science teacher. Later he must look into this matter. The children pull themselves together. They look at their grandmother with wonder. They look around for grandpa. He has not yet returned from the library of mysteries. He comes in with a parchment paper, yellowed by time, wrapped in transparent cloth to protect it as much as possible. Grandpa is wearing white gloves to hold it preciously. He heads to his cushion, sits down and declares aloud: WHEN GAIA, WITH HER LONGEST FINGER, SHALL PIERCE THE RING OF FIRE, THREE OF HER CHILDREN, MESSENGERS OF THE GODS, BORN OF ONE SAME CONCEPTION, SHALL RESTORE THE ERA OF LIGHT AND PEACE, DELIVERING LIMITLESS POWER TO THE NEW HUMAN.

A sepulchral silence is palpable in the living room. Nobody moves, nobody speaks and nobody dares look at each other.

The children are speechless. They understood nothing of the statement. Cedric, William and Sofia lift their shoulders in a sign of questioning. Grandpa observes them. They are seated in front of him. The grandparents maintain the silence. They are waiting for one of the children to shake it off and speak.

Suddenly, the triplets burst into laughter. They look at each other and make signs with their eyes as if to say: "have you understood anything? You? No, you? No. Neither have I."

Grandpa brings them back to reality. He tells them: "You do not need to decode what has been decoded hundreds of years ago, you should remember that this prophecy is real, that you are part of it and that the secret must be closely guarded, protected. You will understand it progressively as you get older. Your dragons will guide and will help you fulfill this prophecy."

"This is one heck of an enigma; I confess I can't make head or tail of it," says Cedric, dumbfounded. The other two just sit there without moving.

Suddenly, Sofia remembers the other small purple velvet bag. She looks at grandma sitting on a straight chair with a cushion on her back. She says as she approaches her: "Do you intend to give us the contents of the small bag, grandma? I'm anxious to see the item in question."

"*The prophecy went in very easily,*" thinks grandma In German. *"It was to be expected. Everything is so mysterious that, for children of their age, it goes beyond their understanding. All the better, it will allow the Cosmic energy to complete its preparatory work.*"

"Yes! Yes!" says grandma, coming back from her reflections that the children have not decoded. She picks up the little purple velvet bag, opens it delicately and brings out three crystals mounted on a silver cord. They are in the shape of a cylindrical spike with eight resplendent sides. She holds them at the tip of her right hand and lets them rock gently.

"Whew!" exclaims Cedric, "These are for us? We each have one! That's fantastic! I have a crystal like the people of the Atlantis had to get about. What is it for Grandma? I am intrigued by this object."

"Each of you has received a bronze pin that you need to carry to contact your respective dragons. Here you are with another item as precious as the first. From now on, this crystal must also accompany you in your travels with your dragons. With time, your whole-body system will be able to adapt, transform and adjust your A.D.N. Every time you travel with LYKA, DYRA and MARA, it will be essential that you wear it. It is like a key that will protect you and enable you to return to us. "Because we risk going further than usual," asks William, worried and little reassured by Grandma's message. "Will our dragons be carrying us much further than what we have been experiencing to date?"

"It's possible," answers grandpa. "Who knows what you can expect in the coming weeks?"

--- OOO ---

The Sun is rising over the trees on the horizon grandpa meditates by the tree dedicated to his daughter Marion and his son-in-law, Mark. This magnificent hawthorn in full bloom is his favourite tree.

This morning, the children woke up before dawn. They are busy drawing their respective dragon under the careful observation of Mimi the cat. Each child, in his world, relives the numerous flights with his dragon. Mimi is perched on the window sill; she perceives the happiness and wonderment of the children.

Grandma is still asleep.

Grandpa invites the children to help him prepare breakfast and surprise grandma together. "Look grandpa, look at my beautiful dragon, whisper the children with joy!" "Truly! I am impressed by your talent. Your drawings attest to your sense of observation. Congratulations children. Where are you going to post these beautiful drawings?" "Well, where do you think, grandpa? On the bulletin board in my bedroom," says Sofia, so enthusiastically. "Me too," add the two boys regularly preceded by their sister.

The group takes the stairs and goes into the kitchen.

While the group prepares the meal discreetly, Mimi the cat, accomplice, moves stealthily to grandma's room, jumps on the bed and presses her nose against grandma's left ear. Grandma wakes up to the cat's purring and smiles while also stretching, happy.

On entering the dining room, grandma looks at the children and notices their bare neck. With questioning eyes, she sends them the following message: "*Did you forget something this morning when you got up, after getting washed and dressed?*" Sofia, who hears grandma's telepathic message, replies, while touching her head: "I forgot to brush my hair!" William, who also heard the telepathic message, while passing his hand over his mouth, answers: "Oops, I forgot to brush my teeth." Cedric, also receiving the same telepathic message searches around and suddenly touches his neck and says out loud and clear: "Haaaaaa! My crystal!"

Immediately, the three children rush to their respective bedroom that grandpa and grandma made available to them since the death of their parents. Everyone picks up their respective pendant on the bedside table, passes it around their necks, run back, climb the stairs leading to the living room, at the top of which grandma stands waiting. "Ah! There it is... I strongly encourage you to never forget it again... It will be very useful to you when the time comes... However, I congratulate you, your telepathic system works perfectly, did you realize it?"

"That's right," answers Sofia, again surprised with her telepathic performance. William and Cedric too, are also surprised with the results in so little time.

At the table, the children are happy to show their drawings to grandma. "Splendid! What a wonderful gift! LYKA has green eyes and the others' eyes are black." "Yes, it's true, I had noticed," says Sofia. "What is this mark behind the right ear, Sofia?" "Grandma, I was going to question you on the subject in case you would know, you, who is in the secrets of the Magi?" "Ours don't have any, wonder the boys. Besides they are both female! No! No! It’s not what you think!!! They bear the Yin energy; this is what they told us.”

The boys giggle.

--- OOO ---

The Shadow's Hideout

The hallway is dark, blackened by time. A shadow moves on tiptoes. From time to time, this shadow lengthens and shrinks at the whim of the flames from the torches spaced along the walls. The shadow carries a huge black raven with dark green eyes on his left shoulder. "Crow! Crow! Crow! caws Kacouet." "Here you are my faithful companion. You never ask for anything except a little food from time to time. I like that."

The shadow's breath is deep, slow and lengthy. He strokes the bird with his right calloussed hand while moving along the lengthy corridor. He heads for his dungeon at the left end of his castle. The top floor of this dungeon provides for a 360 degrees' observation of the surroundings. It ensures early notification of any menace from land to the East or from the Ireland Sea to the North and West.

The shadow, Daarksoor, continues speaking to his faithful companion Kacouet. He just returned from a long stay abroad. His professional work is demanding and allows him less and less opportunity to live in his favourite castle. He's been back for just a few hours in this Castle of Legatyn, in Wales in southwestern England, in the land of the menhirs, the standing stones, bordering the Irish Sea.

This shadow bears an intimidating stare with eyes presenting reptilian pupils. He does not stand incompetence or resistance to his instructions. He draws his influence from a line of powerful characters in an organization that date as far back as the Atlantis era. The oral tradition and authority transmitted to him by his master and mentor goes way back in time. The legacy recorded in writing over the last millennium illustrates vestiges believed to be of Turanian origin.

Daarksoor has been living in this English castle for five decades. He decided to make this his official hideout under the direction of Brahima his master and mentor. Brahima heads the Curretaras organization. He purchased the Legatyn Estate in 1934 with the view to install there his organization's World Head-Quarters.

The external architecture has been completely modified and restructured. However, the interior of the castle has been laid out to accommodate the numerous collections of weapons, artifacts, books and very ancient archives. Recently several spaces have been modified to account for the more efficient information technologies. Several meeting rooms and research labs allow scientists to meet and remain at the forefront of their expertise. One wing, more secretive, adjoins the dungeon and protects the access to the underground. This section of the castle remains very mysterious and its access limited to few people. Highly secure mechanisms control its access and all displacements. Particularly, the inside of his dungeon is now equipped with several very private meeting rooms which are protected against electronic detections and espionage.

Currently, accredited persons are being escorted into a large rectangular room adjoining the library filled with occult books. Today's meeting is special. For the occasion, he brings together his principal collaborators involved in an investigation concerning the realization of an ancient prophecy of several millennia.

For over thirty years, Daarksoor has been seeking to clarify an enigma concerning triplets identified through a prophecy that dates to antiquity. Many slate tablets and scrawls in his possession remind him of this prophecy in one way or another. These works would be the envy of many archaeologists. No one other than him and his mentor knows of their existence or has access to them. He consults them during each of his trips to England. One Egyptian slate tablet captures his attention. He caresses it with his calloussed hands and sniffs it to absorb the ancestral odours to capture the Machiavellian secrets of its dark content.

The prophecy mentions three children from the same conception, therefore, triplets that should enable an inter-dimensional advent and are likely to provide an extraordinary power to the new human. As far as he can go back in time, from generation to generation, his predecessors have been working to find out who will be the keeper of the Gate, where and when the advent should take place.

For twenty years now, multiple signs indicate that the Earth is in mutation. Beyond the global warming, events emphasize effervescence unknown until now. The statistics of numerous countries and on all the continents show a substantial increase in multiple births, ranging, in some locations, to over three percent of the total births. Recent research indicates that, most likely, a group of triplets of the year 2000 would be the bearer of the keeper of the Gate to the new human. Every known partial document points to a key bearer.

"This meeting," Daarksoor believes, *"must put in place all the elements that will allow me to find these triplets and thereby assure that I am present at the Gate opening. I must be its only beneficiary. I need reliable collaborators that are going to track all the known triplets and determine which ones are potentially bearers of the key. Thereafter I will focus on a reduced list. For the moment, I know that triplets of boys are not important for me. There has to be at least one girl. It's a must. Currently the partial statistics show more than 5000 triplets. The task is enormous, since we must identify them, assess them discreetly and develop an efficient and flawless surveillance plan. No one must know that our organization is behind this effort. I will tolerate no compromise, no mediocrity and no negligence. I want concrete and quick results.*

--- OOO ---

Brahima

Despite his assiduous research and readings, Daarksoor hesitates. He wants to obtain the elements that can convince him unequivocally of the actions to take. He himself can make no mistake, his master and mentor Brahima, would never forgive him. It is the "raison d'être" of the organization. To find the Gate keeper, to acquire power for his lineage, which power sought for so many generations, that is the source of his inspiration.

"*This is the third time this month that I try to communicate with Brahima. It is as if he refuses to talk to me. I know he does not like to be bothered with requests. It is rather he who asks, I should say who demands. Nonetheless, I'm sure he is aware of our situation, particularly my personal situation right now. I am not his 'dauphin' for nothing. He did not prepare me during all these years for nothing.*"

"*Brahima, all the work that we have accomplished, all the teachings that you have given me, I use them and put them into practice. However, now, I need to talk to you. I need to coordinate with you. I do not want to jeopardize your plans. Please, Brahima, talk to me.*"

Brahima possesses the ability to be in several locations simultaneously. However, his real residence is situated in the cavern of the great dark sorcerer in the volcanic hills of the Reunion Islands. That is where Cremona, his adoptive mother and Voodoo priestess, presented him to the undisputed master, this magician, this dark sorcerer at the head of the global and ancestral organization: the Curretaras.

Throughout his childhood, Daarksoor was trained to control matters, to put it at his service. He recalls, amongst others, the beginning of his training with his mother. He still hears Cremona whispering in his ear words revealing to him partial truth and elements of his reality.

"You possess tremendous capabilities, rarely encountered in a human. With time, I have transformed your body so that it adapts to any terrain. You do not remember your arrival in my home. You had an enormous deformation of the spine, at the level of the lower back. I brought you in my home as an adopted son. I have been ordered by Brahima, our leader, to continually work with you, with all my power, to transform your body so that it would be more suitable to move freely. I was assisted in this task by my daughter Andreanas, your adopted and elder sister. She also has power over matter."

Daarksoor remembers the long sessions of intensive training with Cremona and his sister Andreanas. When Brahima headed the exercises, he pushed the efforts to extreme pain. Over time, Daarksoor earned the respect and affection of Brahima. Then, one day, Brahima handed over to Daarksoor instructions to ensure the dominance of the Curretaras organization on all continents. Since then, Daarksoor was assigned to the Curretaras headquarters located in Legatyn, England.

Daarksoor now runs, from the Legatyn Castle, the overall operations. He is responsible for the development and maintenance of the authority of the organization in all the social and economic fields. Brahima keeps the political and religious aspect for himself. Daarksoor is to communicate with Brahima solely in cases of extreme urgency or at the request of the latter.

In short, only a situation that threatens the realization of the final plan would allow Daarksoor to get in touch with Brahima, the supreme leader of the Curretaras brotherhood. They are hundreds of members planning for the millennia, the culmination of this final plan, which is to dominate earthlings by trickery, diplomacy and with weapons, if needed.

--- OOO ---

The Shadow and his bird enter a dark room. The original seven windows have been replaced with lead panels decorated with magic symbols. This room is protected against any energy or electronic intrusion.

"Kacouet, go to your perch," orders Daarksoor, sweeping his left shoulder with a sudden wave of his right hand. Daarksoor revolves around his Celtic cauldron, murmuring incantations. He seeks to contact Brahima, the only being who can check his brain, his thoughts. Daarksoor fears him to the highest degree. "*I'm in a total haze and I hate living surrounded by mist. Darkness and humidity suit me fine, but not the mist. I must find a way to contact him. But then this is not an everyday life issue. The life of all the organization depends on it.*"

Bang! Bang! Bang! Someone knocks on the door to the den. Only his personal secretary is authorized to approach this door. "Are they all present Henry," asks Daarksoor through the intercom? "Yes sir, they are in the big purple room, as you ordered." "All right, I'll be there in a few minutes."

"Master Brahima, maybe you don't answer because you are asking me to come to your Island. Anyway, I want to see Cremona and chat with her of my roots and my ancestors. I need to refresh my memory on my personal lineage of the sorcerer," thinks Daarksoor as he retrieves Kacouet, his faithful black raven. The bird positions itself on his left shoulder. "*It is becoming an obsession with me. I have some questions to ask my mother Cremona. I need more clarification. I will speak with her on my next trip to my homeland.*"

--- OOO ---

Daarksoor enters the large velvet room with confidence. The fourteen Curretaras regional dignitaries rise suddenly to greet him. The silence speaks volumes. Everyone knows Daarksoor's mood swings and customary intransigence. Not one of them defies this being with his stare. Daarksoor normally wears dark spectacles in public; however, when he wants to impress his authority he does not wear any. His yellow eyes with reptilian pupils and his haughty look are intimidating. His raspy voice, especially when he raises the tone, sends a shiver down the spine.

The Curretaras dignitaries are assigned a specific place around the table disposed as an enormous horseshoe. This table made of hardwood has its opening towards the sole entrance to the room. Each place is identified with the acronyms and symbols relative to the dignitary's region.

The fourteen windows have been modified and protected against any intrusions. They are adorned with old-fashioned purple velvet drapes. No light from outside can penetrate this room. Dark colours accentuate the glaucous and gloomy appearance. The participants remain always impressed and cautious. No one dares provoke master Daarksoor. *"Hum, Hum! That's good. They are uncomfortable but attentive. They are on their guard and know that I will not tolerate failure. A little bit of fear is useful to ensure performance."*

Daarksoor possesses the power to detect the energy that emanates from all these people present at this table. He has this power to detect the moods of others. Emotions of other humans fascinate him. He takes great pleasure in keeping silent and listening without their knowledge. He perceives their state of mind and all their weaknesses. He capitalizes on their slightest tendency to be deficient, and through a stratagem of his, puts them to his service by keeping them stuck in their devastating penchant.

Daarksoor with a deliberate stride moves to his chair in front of a majestic table situated in the opening of the horseshoe table. His chair, a throne of ebony wood, inherited from Brahima, and his table also of ebony wood, present beautiful carvings and ornaments highlighting the prestige and power of his position. Once seated, with a quick stare, he acknowledges the presence of each of his collaborators individually. Then with a nod he signals them to be seated.

The session begins without any preamble and is carried out with precision and brevity. Daarksoor, in his usual raspy voice, tells them: "You have before you a folder specifying your individual task… I ask all of you to inquire into the existence of triplets within your region and whose birth falls between 1998 and 2002 and especially those of the year 2000… You have access to all the technology from our network that each of you know of in your own part of the world… The most important thing is to trace triplets having at least a girl in their trio. Those with three boys may be identified but are of little interest… It is essential that you be discreet… You do not have to intervene. You must detect, identify and inform me. You have the details of the relevant information I am looking for in the guidelines in your file… Be like the shadow that is not seen but which is ever present as it follows its subject."

Daarksoor carefully looks at every one of the persons present. His piercing gaze, his clenched jaw and the rectus of his mouth stress the importance of the mission. "I want answers as soon as possible. Bring me names and especially precise locations. I want to know, amongst other things, which triplets possess special gifts. In this regard, it will not be up to you to act, but you are to notify me only."

Daarksoor, again, looks at each member who is present, and with a sufficient and haughty gesture, orders: "Go! I no longer want to see you for the moment. You know how to contact me."

A Magic Flight

The children are euphoric. They cling to the necks of their winged steeds, these magnificent Dragons. Hair in the wind, eyes bright with joy and curiosity, they telepathically share their impressions amongst themselves and with their mounts, these beings of love and magic. “I am so happy,” exclaims Sofia, her eyes sparkling with happiness. “You can say that again,” adds William, while letting out a conqueror’s shout. Cedric smiles at both his brother William and his sister Sofia, while also whispering “thank you” in his dragon’s ear.

The Dragons, accomplices, are testing the talents of their riders through multiple aerobatics. Suddenly, with a mutual flip of their wings, they fly towards the clouds and then penetrate them as a mental silence settles. The children, tense, respect their mount and keep silent.

--- OOO ---

The clouds become thinner.

Majestically, in close formation, the dragons fly in altitude over a beautiful area where checkerboard civilizations and cultures intertwine the greenery of the forest, sometimes dense and sometimes marked with the scars left by trails that are utilized.

The children note, impressed, the topology of the land with its hills, sometimes abrupt and rocky. The coastline of a rocky massif, caressed by a blue sea, frothy in places, presents an appearance of true lace with thousands of arabesques.

There is no landmark to reassure the children as to the place where they are. Questions and uneasiness are creating tension amongst the riders. "Where are we?" question the triplets together, surprised by this unfamiliar environment. "This is not the Sherbrooke area," mentions Cedric, having flown before over the Estrie region in a two-seater aircraft with Bob, a good friend of his uncle Patrick.

"*We are in another temporal dimension. We are flying over Ireland in the sixth century A.D.,*" replies LYKA, in response to Sofia's mental questioning. "How come? Why?" she asks, her voice betrays her worry. "What? What is going on? Where are you taking us," asks William, suddenly worried and gasping. "MARA, what's going on?" adds Cedric, trying to reassure himself.

"*We have a mandate to fulfill,*" *says LYKA.* "*We too have superiors. Their request is very simple for us; however, it is a little bit more complicated for you three. For some time now, you have been potentiating your telepathy and developing your physical and mental capacities through your exercises in known terrain. To date, this is conclusive. You use it with much discernment. However, you must experience it elsewhere, in another parallel dimension, and therefore, through new challenges, increase your telepathic abilities. In addition, you need to retrace your Celtic origins. That is why we will drop you off in these lands of the sixth century of our era, specifically in Ireland.*"

Stupefied, astounded, powerless, the triplets wait for what comes next. They can't get off their mounts. They are more than a thousand metres in the sky. They think: "*We are really jammed between heaven and earth.*"

LYKA continues : "*Our mandate is to drop you off in a specific location. You will meet a group of people who have a druid at their head. That druid is important for you; he must teach you and transmit to you a tool essential to your mission. While you are living your adventure, we will not be far away. We will never lose sight of you. No one will be able to see us, not even you, until the moment it's time for you to return home."*

"What will grandpa and grandma make of this? For sure, they are going to be worried. Will they know of our adventure?" "This does not make any sense," says William to his brother and sister. "I don't like it! I'm really scared," Sofia screams at the top of her lungs!

--- OOO ---

Ireland, People of the Earth and of Wars

Calmly, LYKA tries to reassure the children. He transmits secretly to MARA and DYRA: "*The children are terrified. Let's take the time to explain to them the whys and wherefores of things. The need for them to incorporate the teachings and to be put to the test, it can only be done through living situations that will allow them to experience their apprenticeship in action.*"

LYKA explains to the children: "*As you can see, this is not a game. The situations that will arise will be real for you and in line with your abilities and gifts. The challenges are there to prepare you, when the time comes, to experience something bigger, greater and more impressive. You must learn to live with the consequence of your decisions and your actions. You must learn to rely solely on you and the beings you will meet. Us, we have no right to intervene directly. But, remember, we will always be present by thought. One of our tasks is to ensure the continuous translation of the Celtic language. You will understand everything that will be said without your ever realizing our intervention. You have within you all the resources necessary to succeed your test.*"

MARA and DYRA, trying to reassure and motivate them in the face of the impending action, transmit to the group: "*take this as an extraordinary adventure*."

In turns, Sofia, William and Cedric refutes, questions, protests, expresses his concern: "It is not serious, all this," protests William vigorously. His cheeks are crimson. "We have to travel through areas that have no reference for us," objects

Cedric, raising his voice. "No! But do you see us landing in that era, not even costumed for their environment? We are going to be eliminated right away," Sofia stresses, really unhappy with the turn of events.

The three dragons were expecting strong reactions from the three children. After a few flaps of their wings over the Celtic forest, LYKA resumes: "*Ready or not, now is the time to test you. We will drop you off in surroundings that are unfamiliar for you. You will meet characters who will help you and others who will be menacing and dangerous. Remember, you have what you need to succeed. Moreover, this evening when the moon rises in the sky, you will encounter a druid called Taliesanic. You will recognize him thanks to two blue tattoos he has on his cheeks, a circle with a spiral inside on each cheek, and he will be wearing a white band with a drawing on his forehead, another circle with a cross inside it. In his belt, he will be wearing a small gold billhook. He is looking for three children, two boys and a girl. Three children who bear a birthmark at the base of their neck. Remember, this mark is solely perceptible by initiates. This druid has already seen you in a dream. Besides, never forget that we are here to protect you.*"

"So, everything is hunky-dory, as grandpa says so well," whispers William, sarcastically. "*He is tense. His breathing is becoming more and more irregular,*" says DYRA to the other two dragons. LYKA interrupts, *"I feel it as much as you do. However time is running out, I need to continue my explanations.*"

Such as a general giving his instructions, with assurance and authority, LYKA explains to the children that they are in Celtic Ireland at the beginning of the sixth century, a time when families, known as clans are revolting against one another in fratricidal struggles for power. "*Right now, in the region where we will be landing, an imposing group of warriors from the North are looting, capturing and ransoming to impose their laws all along the North-East coast of Ireland.*

"Just that! Then it looks promising!" interrupts William, still with sarcasm. He's ready to jump off his mount. He is becoming increasingly worried...

LYKA pursues his explanations with a sigh of hesitation. The children receive this information that resonates in their numbed brains. The situation seems implausible and catastrophic to them.

LYKA and his companions feel the children's anguish. They know it will be difficult for children of twelve years of age. They cannot intervene directly. Nevertheless, they are there to protect them if necessary. As per their commitment, they have the mandate and instruction to never abandon the triplets at the risk of their own lives.

LYKA continues. That information is necessary and valuable. At a minimum, their riders need to know in which ancestral context they will be living their test. "You sound like my history teacher. However, that is not what reassures me. It is not a history lesson that we need," says Sofia briskly. LYKA pauses then answers: "*What else to say, except, receive what I have to tell you for the moment. It is important that at least one of you three remembers this information; it will be useful to you in a timely manner.*"

LYKA pursues his explanations: "*Ireland is divided into five main kingdoms, each with a great number of small kingdoms. The whole country has about 150 kingdoms with a few thousand people in each. Local wars are frequent and this for all kinds of reasons. Power struggles are the most common. It is in this Ireland of princes and warriors that you are arriving.*"

The children are tense, nervous. They worry about their ability to react against these great warriors, especially William, whose breathing is becoming ever shorter. He is already anguished and feels the upcoming of an asthma attack. It has been a long time since he has felt so breathless. He is no longer listening. He did not bring his medical pump to breathe in case of a crisis. He is falling prey to near panic. DYRA, his dragon, perceives all of William's anguish and panic in her own body, and transmits to him: "*William! William! Listen to me! Come on, hug my neck hard... Yes, that's right, even harder, you can do it... Come on! Keep squeezing; try to make me say, 'drop."*

After a moment, she feels her companion's leg muscles relaxing. In a reassuring, soft, calm voice, DYRA adds: "*Well, are you feeling better now?*" "Yes, thank you," answers William in a barely audible voice. He is breathing more freely. He recalls, when his mother Marion reassured him, it sounded like that.

"*You'll see, everything will get better. Try to listen to the instructions LYKA is giving you. Are you OK now?*" "Yes," answers William, more relaxed and more receptive. DYRA pursues : *"You know William, the lungs, it is your territory. That is where you draw the emotional energy that enables you to shout, to speak as needed. Your lungs oxygenate your blood that feeds each of your cells. When you become tense, the little channels of your respiratory system shrink. The consequence of this is that you can't breathe and sometimes to the point where you can lose consciousness."*

DYRA pursues: "To help you when you don't have a pump with you or when you feel you are losing it, breathe very deeply and as slowly as possible. By doing so, you can use a trick that works well. Do you want to know what it is?" "Yes," answers William. "Here is a technique that works: *"Clench your fists as hard as you can and concentrate on your fists until you get the impression that it hurts. Yes, like that. See, your knuckles are turning white and your fingertips are inflated with blood. Super, it's like in your judo courses, in your rolls, you hit the floor and in changing your focus, you direct the energy by keeping in mind what you are doing. Do you understand?*" "Yes," answers William, with his eyes half-closed! He can see himself in his judo courses. "Hum! Yes! I remember. Thank you, I find it reassuring. Yes. The judo techniques, I will remember," he says, clenching his fists. "But you, how did you know that I train in judo?" DYRA smiles: "*Humhumhum! I know everything about you and your brotherhood."*

LYKA, MARA and their riders remain silent and give their support to William by thought. After a few minutes of respectful silence, the questions come from all directions. Will they be armed? Will they have allies? When will they see grandpa and grandma again?

The dragons hear their concerns. MARA transmits them: "*What have you learned on weapons and the art of war with your uncle Patrick and your grandpa? Amongst other things, have you learned nothing on the making and use of projectiles?*" "Yeah!" Sofia reflects out loud and shaking her head. "I am very skillful with a bow and arrows and I know how to make them," exclaims Sofia. It's as though her fear was disappearing. "Me, I am the champion of my school at javelin throwing," says Cedric, proud of himself and more confident. "There are so many stones here and nobody can beat me with a slingshot," adds William, now a lot more relaxed. Already, he can see how he will fabricate and use his slingshot.

MARA transmits: "These skills that you mention are nonetheless a start, is it not? Additionally, in your magic bag, you have what you need to live your experience." "A magic bag?" question the children in unison?

LYKA continues without paying attention to their questions: "*Now, Christianity brought by Saint Patrick is taking more and more space.*" "The Saint Patrick that the Irish celebrate with a big parade on March 17th of each year?" asks Sofia. "*Yes, says LYKA. Society at the time of Saint Patrick is essentially rural. Most people live on small farms. As Ireland is an island, the sea plays an important role in the whole evolution of the Irish people. Do you remember where Ireland is located on the map that your grandpa has in his office?*" "Yes, it is the big island to the West of England," says Sofia. "*Indeed, on one side there is England and Scotland and on the other side it is the Atlantic Ocean. Further North, there is an island slightly larger than Ireland that we now call Iceland.*" "Yes, it is located between Greenland and Norway. There are volcanoes on it," proudly responds Cedric.

"*It's true, you're right. This island, like Norway, is inhabited by seamen of the North, who were called "North Men" and later, they will be called "Vikings."*" "Yeah, the Vikings are explorer warriors, very good sailors. They are brave and can be very cruel. They do not know fear." "*Well done, William. You are right. During your adventure, you will have the occasion to get very close to some of them. You need to remember that when you arrive on the island, the men from the north are becoming increasingly present on the coast of Ireland. They are seeking to get rich through pillaging, or again, through trade and commerce with the village people they meet. The difficulty at present is one of language and customs.*"

The triplets, still in the saddle on their charger, look at one another and their eyes speak volumes. Yet, they remain attentive to the information they receive. The dragons are progressively descending and the children can discern the environment more precisely. "You will notice in the area the presence of many farms, often erected on a hill and surrounded by a circular wall and a fence." "There! Near the lake, that is not a farm, it is like a small fortress!" "You are right William; the homes of local chiefs or great warriors are more imposing in general and often serve as defensive positions in case of attacks. You will find them in strategic positions to control the coast, or in an important environment for survival, as for the croplands or the mineral sites, *or again, in a place to control an important access route like the crossing point of a river or a passage in the rocky hills. Most often, you'll also find several farms near these small forts, like the ones you see near the fort indicated by William.*" "No, but wait! Why all the history lessons?" interjects William.

Cedric knows his brother William well and insists that he remains calm and listen. They will need all the knowledge possible on the people and the land unknown to them. "LYKA would you please continue," demands Cedric.

"T*he clans focus mainly on family relations. The family is so important that loyalty to the clan cannot be questioned and that alone causes many disputes. The normal family group is composed of all those who descend from a great-grandfather. Every clan has a more important family which is called the royal family. It is the clan of the leader. Know that each member of the king's family is eligible to succeed to the throne.*"

"Is it important to remember that? Is it why they fight all the time?" "*Yes William, continues LYKA. Free men of the great extended family participate in voting for the election of the king when the throne becomes vacant. The system offers the advantage of ensuring that a fool or a cripple never becomes king. However, it has the disadvantage of causing terrible conflicts between two or more equally qualified heirs resulting in the battles that you allude to William.*"

"That scenario is not pleasant," sighs Sofia. "*Do you want to learn more?*" questions LYKA. "Yes! Yes, say the children, not having the choice to be elsewhere. They would like to break free of this gigantic titular, but it's impossible for the time being... Cedric remembers: 'As grandpa says, "knowledge increases confidence and confidence reduces fear." Grandpa always has a quip or a joke to say for us to better understand and remember.'

LYKA laughs inwardly, sensing this titular qualifier against him and continues: 'Land ownership also belongs within the family group and can create disputes within the family and the clan, especially between the most influential and ambitious members of the family. In fact, wars between blood brothers often occur. Families and clans are small companies with their rules and their influences. The more you are skilled at determining who has influence and who can be influenced, the more you'll be able to deal with situations because you will find out more quickly who can help you or who can do you harm.'

'That doesn't give me the urge to end up there!' sighs, Sofia. 'I told you about a druid that you will meet...' 'Taliesanic!' the three children say together. LYKA continues : "Indeed, Taliesanic. You have the memory of an elephant!!! .... (The other two dragons laugh mightily). Let's pass! ... No comments," replies LYKA.

"Remember this, it is very important: in the Celtic society, druids are men that are considered as sages and who are very influential. They form a special group amongst free men. They act as judges and doctors. They are soothsayers capable of predicting the future and they are generally great healers." "I have read that, in history, there were some who were very powerful and some very bad!" "Yes, it's true, Cedric they are human and many of them might be greedy and seek power. For these people, if they are not treated with honour and respect, or if the honours are not up to their expectations, they are to be feared. They are known not only for their language clarity, but also for their magical powers."

"Equally, women can be druids and have the same kind of power. In several clans, many women know how to fight with courage and great skill," intervenes Cedric. 'Good! Finally, some good news,' replies Sofia, encouraged by Cedric's comment, yet not reassured. 'In short, continues LYKA, what we have described is the social context in which we are dropping you off. As for the rest, you must listen, observe, make decisions and act to the best of your capabilities. The more you are informed, the more you will be able to take effective action.'

William, anxious, objects: 'I understand what you're saying, but we can't be projected into ancient times like that! We don't speak the language and we aren't dressed like them. We don't even know what they look like, how they live, or what they eat. It makes no sense!' insists William forcefully.

'Do not worry, William, rest assured, all three of you. You are in another dimension. Once you are in place, you will have a special look on matters which is in keeping with the learning you need to experience. Everyone you meet, they will see you as Celtic children. The situations will call on your knowledge and your skills. This adventure is part of your apprenticeship and is contributing to your preparation. Remember! You have a mission to accomplish someday. For now, you have what it takes to go through this test. Remember! Listen to your intuition, it knows. It will guide you. It is that little voice that tells you what to do, how to do it. It never makes a mistake.'

'*Now. It's time!*' The three dragons now fly increasingly lower over the Celtic region. The male dragon pauses: '*You have an appointment. You must not miss it!*' Sofia, Cedric and William retort successively, 'an appointment! What appointment? The one with Taliesanic. What will our test be?' 'LYKA, what lies ahead?' asks Sofia with an anguished look.

The tension is palpable in the children.

LYKA explains: *There is chaos in the region. A lot of people are threatened. Your mission...*" "As in the movie 'Mission Impossible'. Listen well, in one minute the reel will auto-destruct," replies William sarcastically. "William, listen, it is important!" says Cedric.

"*Yes, it is important, resumes LYKA. This first mission completes the first stage of your preparation. It will be like your initiation and you must be successful for yourself first, and ultimately, in a few years, for the realization of the prophecy. You will meet, amongst others, two characters who have to convey you a teaching and a secret that will serve you during the major event associated with the prophecy, the sage Taliesanic and the druidess Quelf...*" "Say that again, I did not get the name of the druid," asks Cedric. "*The sage Taliesanic and the druidess Quelf. You will be meeting these people. We are in contact with them and they are expecting you. That is part of their individual mission in this life. They must convey teachings to you. Once you have received the information that you need, they will protect you and guide you. Taliesanic will inform you as to where and when to find us.*"

"How will we know that it is the time to go and that you will be there?" Questions Sofia worried. "*You will know and feel it when Taliesanic tells you. At that moment, we will contact you telepathically. You remember that to contact us, it is essential that each of you always wear your crystal and your dragonfly pin. They are what keeps you in contact with us and will enable us to become visible for your return home.*"

"Wow! This adventure is really becoming more and more serious," whispers William softly. He looks overwhelmed by the events. "I believe you're right, William," says Cedric, looking at him very seriously. "*Now children, it's up to you. We trust you. You have all the resources necessary to succeed.*" "As grandpa says: "When the going gets tough, the tough get going," Cedric murmurs to himself. Phew! ...

"So, when you find it more difficult, call upon your will power which feeds your determination, your courage and your creativity. With that you will always find a solution. Do not forget, you are three, your efficiency and your result will stem from how well your trio operates," concludes LYKA.

The children remain silent. They stare at each other with questioning eyes. Uneasiness is becoming increasingly palpable as the mounts approach the unknown land.

LYKA remains attentive to the feelings of the children and mentions: "*Do not be surprised, you will understand what the people you meet are saying and they will also understand you. Your language will be that of the era. You are beneath a magical dome of protection. The dome protects you and provides a simultaneous translation. This translation will happen without you ever noticing it.*"

The children give each other an encouraging look. That's all they can do for now.

The dragons plunge in unison towards an open space to the east of a large lake located to the North of the island. "What is the name of this lake?" ask Cedric, anxious about the landing. "*Lough Neagh,*" answers MARA. She adds: "*have confidence in each other and do not forget what you have learned.*"

The landing is done smoothly and discreetly in a clearing surrounded by magnificent centennial oak trees. The greenery is dense. Birdsongs resonate. The children grip the neck of their respective dragons, perceive their trust, greet them, descend from their mounts and then, silently, move away towards the nearby forest. "Now it begins!" think Cedric, William and Sofia in unison.

Their legs are heavy. They look at one another. They hug each other in a brotherly embrace to give each other the courage and the strength required in the circumstances.

They become suddenly aware of their outfit. They realize the power of magic. They are dressed in accordance with a time they do not know.

Sofia notices her feet covered with leather galoshes tied with flexible leather. She is wearing a dark gray tunic, a long dress, tightened at the waist with a brown leather belt to which is fastened a wallet. This leather wallet rests on her pubis and serves as her magic bag. A knife is attached to her right hip. On her shoulders, she wears a cloak, a sort of thick woollen cape closed with a discreet bronze brooch bearing the image of a dragon. Magically, her long red hair is braided in the old style, the old-fashioned Gaelic way.

Cedric and William are both also shod in soft leather galoshes. They are wearing breeches (baggy trousers tightened at the ankles) dyed a sombre and discreet green. A cloak with a thick wool hood in the colours of the forest covers their shoulders. It is tied at the neck with a fibula to the coat of arms of the dragon, the same one as Sofia. Their breeches made of thick wool cover their legs. The half-tunic of linen clothes covers their torso and is made of the same fabric as Sofia's tunic. Their waist is belted with a large leather band on which is attached a magic bag at the front and a knife on their right hip.

Concerns

Louise and Thomas are currently busy taking care of their garden. “Tell me, Thomas,” asks Louise, while scanning the sky, “at about what time should the children return from their escapade with their dragons?” “I really don’t know,” he replies, shrugging his shoulders, attentive to his gardening near the grove of Bleeding-Hearts.

Both enjoy working outside amongst the plants. The garden brightens their environment with its colours and its odour. Any visitor may taste the harmony and appreciate the peace of the place.

Thomas continues: “They’ve been gone for a little more than forty-five minutes. They should not be long now. You know, these dragons are magnificent and I find it magical the relationship the children have with them.” “Besides,” continues Thomas, “they don’t need to give us a flight plan. They know what they should do. The children are in good hands, oops, good paws, he thinks, smiling. I don’t understand why you’re worried, Louise.”

“Very funny,” she responds telepathically and slightly worried. “I am not accustomed to seeing the children leave like this, unsupervised and even less without knowing the destination and the expected time of return. I prefer the planning to the improvisation, the foresight of the surgeon to the reaction of the emergency physician that you are, Thomas.” “Still, Louise, they are not babies! They can get out of any situation. They are courageous, creative, determined and they know a lot of stuff that we’ve shown to them.”

Motioning with her arms in exasperation, Louise heads for the house, not reassured. She tries to fill her waiting time. "*It's so hard to let them go, fly on their own ... stand on their own two feet...*"

Thinking back on what she just thought she bursts out laughing.

Thomas, who was close behind, heard her murmuring and he also bursts into laughter. "Come on! Let's trust that little acrobatic flying troop," he says, while gently clenching Louise's shoulders. "You are probably right, nevertheless, they are still kids," replies Louise. "Yes, I agree. They also have a great mission for which they must prepare and their classes are far from over. These dragons are here to contribute to their preparation. They are masters with a mission to accompany and protect the children"

Taking her companion by the hand, Louise suggests: "What if we make muffins together? The children will be happy to have a snack on returning from their adventure." "Hum! Muffins smell good," adds Thomas, his eyes sparkling and his mouth already filled with saliva. "What a delight! A good idea!"

The Magic Cauldron

Meanwhile, at the Legatyn Castle, Daarksoor heads for a small rectangular room located under the dungeon. It is in this room that he keeps his Celtic cauldron, an ancient and magical pot which transmits to him all the images of every dimension, from all eras according to his demand.

This magic cauldron, passed on from generation to generation for centuries, is his special means to maintain contact with and observe what is happening in the world. He has only to deposit a powder in the potion prepared for this purpose and to question the cauldron about a person or an event. He then automatically obtains a visual response. Never has the cauldron failed him in anything. Its loyalty is historic. Every image is real and true when it appears on the surface of the potion within the cauldron.

On entering the room, Kacouet, his black Raven, comes to rest on his left shoulder. The bird has been part of his environment for the past twenty years. It was given to him by a gypsy from the Carpathian Mountains as part of a ritual on the mastery over fire. The bird accompanies him everywhere in his virtual displacements. It shrieks with joy on perceiving its master. Daarksoor always brings it prey obtained through magic on the way to his den.

The cauldron, it is believed, dates to the pre-Arthurian period, at a time when the Druids made sacred use of it. In fact, this cauldron was used as a war cauldron for the Gallic leaders. It is a sacred object for the druids. They would prepare different potions in it: to heal, to celebrate, to prepare for war and even to punish.

When King Arthur conquered the King of Ireland, a similar cauldron filled with Irish money was the ransom to pay.

Daarksoor's cauldron is called the Sacrificial Cauldron. Brahima's family had acquired it long ago from a renegade Druid at their service. This renegade had obtained it after a conqueror had drowned in the cauldron a fallen Celtic king while he burned his castle.

Since then, Brahima's lineage exploit the magic of the cauldron for their own profit. Many a magician has contributed to the transmission of the cauldron's magic and power over the years. When Daarksoor, Brahima's adopted son took over the Legatyn Castle, the cauldron's magic was transferred to him to help and advise him over his tasks.

The cauldron has the allure of a huge soup tureen of about one metre in diameter. It is conspicuous, in the middle of this large rectangular room. All the walls of the room are garnished with illustrations and acronyms propitious to magic. The walls are made of gray stone, drawn from the same quarry in the Castle's environment. With the help of his subordinates, he redid this room upon his arrival in the area. This castle had in fact undergone tremendous damage over the centuries. However, many underground rooms have remained preserved and constitute a lure for the projects that Daarksoor nurtures.

Daarksoor slowly approaches his black cauldron with frescoes and Celtic symbols ornately carved in silver. With Kacouet on his shoulder, he looks over the magic cauldron and deposits in it a purplish powder drawn from the small black leather bag he carries with him, and he commands in a muffled and low voice: "What can you tell me about triplets in this current world?"

The smooth surface of the contents shows a swirl of clouds orbiting around the planet Earth for several minutes. Suddenly a continuous stream of teenagers, in groups of three, follow each other at very fast pace. These children come from all continents. They are dressed in varied and colourful costumes. The succession of colours and faces becomes staggering. “Cauldron, be more precise, what is your message?” interrupts Daarksoor.

The cauldron resumes its swirling. Images of triplets follow one another at a faster and faster speed to the point that the faces become blurred. Daarksoor interrupts again with impatience: “I do not understand you. I want to know what is happening. I think that, at present, events are under development. Yes, events that will have an impact on the future of our planet. What can you tell me?”

The cauldron again takes up his coloured swirl. The images are becoming less defined. “Ah! I see! You cannot help me. You need a more precise question. So, tell me, are the triplets that we must seek all boys?”

The surface of the cauldron turns opaque and then totally black. “OK, so we need to focus only on triplets having at least one girl. Anyway, it is the instruction that I gave to my research team in the field.”

The surface of the Cauldron turns opaque and then pinkish. “Perfect. I have to wait for the results from my research.” The surface of the Cauldron turns opaque then pinkish again. “Noted. We will continue this conversation later.”

Daarksoor remains pensive while pacing the room.

The Magic Bag

Cedric, William and Sofia, are sitting under a great oak. They assess their situation, confer and agree on a code of communication between them. It is now time to use their telepathic technique. They have been at it now for three years. They agree to protect each other and to keep aware of their individual movements. They do not want to be isolated.

They review the basic survival techniques learned with Patrick and Ming. They remember the importance to stay together. For now, Cedric assumes leadership. They must get organized. They agree on an action plan. “First, let us see what we have, to cope with the situation,” says Cedric.

Instinctively, the three children put their hands on their knives. At first glance, the rudimentary tool looks like a piece of wood, interlaced with leather straps. The handle somehow reflects the continuity of the sheath. The rustic iron blade reminds the children of the solid and rough cutlasses they made themselves at grandpa’s.

“This looks like the knives we used to make with Uncle Patrick,” exclaims William. “That’s right,” observes Cedric, “however in this period, there is no train to pass on a steel nail that has been placed on the rails like grandpa did in his youth. “Yeah!” Says William, eager to use his knife. “I think the way they made the sheaths and the handles is very ingenious. It is as if they had split the stick of wood lengthwise to place the blade in it. The handle portion is well wrapped in leather straps and I find it comfortable for the hand and the sheath seems solid, well tied up and secure.”

Suddenly, William takes the knife by the blade and throws it against a nearby tree. "Wow! Were you aiming for that tree or did you hit it by accident?" asks Sofia mockingly. "I just wanted to know if I could be as precise as with Patrick's knives," answers, William.

William had a habit of observing Patrick practising with his weapons, particularly, knife-throwing in the manner of the Bushis. Patrick initiated William in the rudiment of throwing knives, how to balance, hold, sight and throw the blade.

They all dump their magic bags in front of them to take the inventory of their contents. There is a good portion of dried fruit (walnuts, hazelnuts, acorns) that abound in the region. These dried fruits are usually collected by the women and children.

They remember LYKA's history lesson.

The Celts primarily consume pork and mutton. They also eat beef and the results of the hunt, such as wild boar meat. The Celts avoid eating all meat from animals living in burrows, such as hares or foxes. To them, the underground, is the place of the departed and that place must remain sacred. "To drink we have the water from the springs and the streams. Pollution does not exist in this era," says Cedric. "There is also honey," adds William. "We only need to observe and find honeycombs as the bears do. Do you remember our survival expedition with grandpa and Patrick?" "Yeah," answers Sofia, "70% of wild bees build their honeycomb in the ground covered with some vegetation, on banks or on sunny hillocks, facing the sun. The other 30% can be found on dead wood, hollow trees, in rock crevices or again, in certain talus, such as brambles or berries."

"How can you remember all that, sis," asks William? "You either have it or you don't..." answers Sofia, as William throws her a handful of earth.

"I'm sure we will be able to find milk and cheese amongst the farmers," says Sofia.

"We shall see, but first, let's look at what we have in our bags," answers, Cedric. "Me, I have in addition to the dried fruit, two flint stones to make fire, a long piece of leather straps, a piece of rope braided with rustic fibres probably from flax." "Me too, I have the dried fruit and two flint stones! But I also have a long piece of leather straps, a knitted wool hat and a ball of linen thread, two small bones as thin as needles and a lovely pin. I also have a leather bracelet, different from the ones you are wearing on your wrists," adds Sofia.

"Me, I have the same amount of dried fruit as you two have, but, I have only one big flint... Look, I can also make sparks when I use my knife on it. This looks like a ball of tendons, such as those used to make grandpa's bear paw snowshoes. Remember, he had bought them from the Aboriginal people near Quebec City. It's strong..." notes William, pulling it with all his might. "I also have some string, such as Sofia. I also have three flat stones with markings on them, I don't know what their purpose is," says William.

"Show me," says Sofia, holding out her hand. "These are runes! Look at the drawings. I do not know why you have them. Nonetheless, if you have them, it's for a reason. We'll know it soon enough. Be careful not to lose them."

"So what should we do," Cedric asks Sofia?

"I'm hungry," says William.

Cedric looks at his brother, his sister. He contemplates their assets, looks at the sky and the surroundings while pondering out loud. "I don't know what time it is; however, the sun is going down more and more. I think we should try to have some idea of where we are and orient ourselves. As well, I think we should find something to defend ourselves against animals or someone. I know that the Celts and the Gaul hunted boar. There are likely to be some here. Their tusks are dangerous.

"Cedric, you remember the rules of survival that grandpa and Patrick taught us? This time, they are not here to coach us. We must rely on our own capacities and work together. We also need to be ready to meet with Taliesanic and Quelf. Do you have any idea by where they might be," asks William? "We should have a plan but before, the most important thing is to have an idea of where we are. With that in mind we will be in a position to determine where we should go if we are in danger; have a shelter if necessary; especially have access to safe drinking water; and, know where we can make a fire. However, before making any fire, we must ensure that it is safe for us to do so." "Yeah, especially since warriors are walking around in the area" interrupts Sofia, not really reassured by her environment.

"To eat, we have the dried fruit," says Cedric. "As we do not know how long our mission will be, we need to explore to find out what else we can eat. Meanwhile, we should not squander." "So, let's not waste time," suggests Sofia. "We will do so, Sofia, however, we cannot act too blindly," says Cedric with authority. "Wow bro! Don't be so bossy!" asserts William as he walks away. "For starters, I need to know if I'm capable of protecting and defending myself. For me it's the most important. We can be caught by surprise either by an animal, or worse, by a warrior."

William seeks to prepare himself. Beneath the oaks, he finds a sturdy club. It gives him the confidence of a warrior. He also gathers round stones that he can throw with precision. "These will be useful to me until I make myself a slingshot."

"Good idea! You're right, William, I too will find myself a club. One never knows what he will encounter," says Cedric. Rather than a club, Cedric finds a very straight and dry shrub. Once the branches are removed, he notices the solidity and hardness of the wood. He quickly removes the bark and sharpens one end, transforming it into a small and efficient improvised spear. "This reassures me for now, but ideally, I would like to have two more. When we make a small fire, I will take the time to harden the tip."

"Look at what I found," says Sofia. She is proudly standing near a group of yews. This tree was prized by the archers of antiquity and the Middle Ages. Grandpa mentioned that it is this tree that allowed the making of the famous English longbow. The

English longbow made the decisive difference at the Battle of Crecy in the fourteenth century. Its wood is strong but also elastic. It was used to make bows, arrows and spears that were smeared with toxic sap from the yew (toxin).

She quickly identifies a piece of yew appropriate to her size to make herself a bow. She also finds twelve shorter and straight stems to complete her set of arrows. Suddenly, she runs towards the clearing and retrieves three crow feathers. She spotted when they arrived in the clearing. "Well, now I have what I need to make my weapon. All I need now is the cord. That is slightly more complicated to make."

"We are in late afternoon and I don't know how long our test will last we must find a shelter to protect ourselves and rest," mentions Cedric. "In the trees," answers Sofia. "In a burrow," suggests William, "the Celts seem to fear these places." "For now, I will climb this huge oak to get a sense of the surroundings to orient us. Meanwhile, examine the surroundings to see if there are animal or human tracks. Afterwards, we will decide."

--- OOO ---

The Locals

Cedric climbs the giant oak tree with ease while thanking it for welcoming them. "Gracias, Great Oak and thank you for protecting us. Please allow me to climb up to your top to examine the surroundings."

The late afternoon sun is usually located in the south-west. Looking in that direction, Cedric perceives a very large lake. The lake is calm and there aren't any boats on it. On the other side of the lake in the distance there are a series of green and rocky hills in some places. He is putting to memory every thing he sees.

"From my location to the lake, there must be one kilometre. I don't see any housing or movement. There, South of the lake, there seems to be a settlement. I see several wisps of smoke. The brownish patches are most likely straw roofs. To the North, it is widely forested, possibly a huge clearing at approximately two or three kilometres. To the East, I can only see forest and big hills. The furrows I can see from the treetops are either roads or rivers. To be confirmed..."

"Further South, the hills continue until the horizon. Oh! There, big black smoke, it's at least ten kilometres away. Would that be the North Men that LYKA was talking about? We will need to be on our guard."

"Which direction must we take to find the druid Teliesanic and how to recognize him? I really forgot the description of the druid that LYKA gave us before he left us. I must check this with Sofia and William."

Cedric takes the time to make another overview from the top of his perch and memorizes the directions. He estimates that they still have between four to five hours of daylight. He remembers grandpa's teaching: "to calculate the time remaining before the sun disappears, you extend your arms and with the number of fingers or hands between the horizon and the sun, you will have a good idea of the day time remaining." For Cedric, with his arm extended, one finger is equivalent to fifteen minutes and a hand, to one hour. Thumbs are not accounted for.

"We have at most five hours of clarity left! Five hands between the position of the sun and the horizon, I would say that it is about four o'clock in the afternoon. No time to lose. We have to get organized before dark."

He quickly comes down from the tree, branch by branch. Once at the foot of the tree, he hastens to draw his observations, some advice Patrick gave him. "*Drawing helps me to better anchor the topography in my memory. In addition, Sofia and William need to know, and even more, three to remember will facilitate orientation.*"

--- OOO ---

Sofia and William penetrate the forest, dense at times, but more often, relatively scattered. The terrain is undulating and the view frequently obstructed by numerous groves. They both agree to move around as they learned to do in their survival course. They remain visible to one another as much as they can while covering the maximum ground possible. From time to time, they make signs to each other to show that all is well or that there's nothing to report.

Sofia has an excellent memory. She records the distance covered and notices a peculiar rock; a tree struck by lightning or felled by high winds; a small swampy pond; or an embankment of stones gathered by humans. "*That looks like stones that have once been used to build a shelter or a small house,*" believes Sofia, signalling her brother to join her. "It has been a long time since someone came this way," says William. "Look at the size of the roots on most of the stones. They must have built the fire there; it looks like a huge fireplace that has fallen apart." "Yes, the stones are covered with soot," confirms Sofia.

"When I walked around the pond, I observed tracks that looked like those of deer hooves near the discharge, and a little further a pool of mud with a lot of pig tracks. It looks like the paddock on Lise and Michel's farm. It could be a gathering place for a family of wild boars. The stream flows down regularly. I did not follow it because I wanted to maintain visual contact with you. We should follow it a little way. I have the impression that there is a small valley, and that at the end, there is a rivulet. It would make sense, given the rough terrain."

"It's an idea. We have been walking for about half an hour. Did you count your steps," asks Sofia? "No, I completely forgot," replies, William. "Darn it, William, it is very important if we don't want to get lost. We need to go back where we came from. Did you at least observe the terrain?" "OK! OK, sister, don't get upset! I'm going to do it."

"I have the impression," resumes Sofia, "that we are about seven hundred metres from where Cedric is. Considering the detours; I calculated 1400 steps. I have seven knots on my rope, one at every two hundred paces. I also took note of certain landmarks and broke the tips of some branches to make it easier to find our way back. I think we should follow the stream a bit. We should go and see what goes on in the valley. How about it?" "We are starting to get far away from Cedric! And then, what do we do if we see Warriors?" asks William, worried. "We run away, hide or we fight... Your choice!" Don't be scared, teases Sofia.

--- OOO ---

Sofia quickly turns towards her brother, a finger on her lips and, squatting to the ground, she orders her brother to do the same. Uneasy, William crouches down beside his sister. Sofia, while looking at him, places her right hand in a contour up to her right ear so as to accentuate the auricle.

They have been following the stream for nearly an hour. They are silent and attentive to the landscape intersected with animal tracks. They saw two sites where some hunters had skinned animals. These sites are near the stream which is gaining more in magnitude because of the slopes on either side. This sector appears to be more frequented.

"What? What have you heard? Whispers William, his eyes round like billiard balls. Sofia points with her left hand in the direction of the curve of the stream at approximately one hundred metres ahead. Sofia hides behind the bushes. She accentuates her listening by putting both hands around her auricles. William follows suit.

Telepathically, Sofia, her left index on her lips, invites her brother to pay attention to a strange noise and transmits: "*I hear children who appear panicky and who are coming up the stream. Don't make a sound. Can you hear?" "Not yet!"* answers William, trying to concentrate.

Suddenly, three little girls and a boy aged between six and thirteen appear on the opposite bank of the stream. The boy, a redhead of vigorous appearance, is holding the hand of the youngest, a girl just as reddish as him. The two other girls are also holding hands. The tallest girl, with blond-brown hair, appears to be the same age as the boy. The third girl, a brunette, appears to be the most frightened. They are drenched, muddy and terrified. They are quickly progressing to where Sofia and William are hiding, while continually looking back.

The two girls slip and fall on the rocks while crossing the stream. The younger of the two stifles a cry by placing her hand over her mouth. Her torn skirt shows her bleeding knee. She is crying, begging her elder sister to help her. Having gotten up, she is walking with great difficulty, to the despair of the boy, who keeps looking around in anticipation of potential danger. His fear is tangible and is beginning to give way to impatience.

Sofia, less than twenty metres away, hears their moans of distress. She stands up and from her position, she waves them with her left hand to come towards her. "Over here, she calls out to them." The children are surprised. They stare at her, mouth open, bewildered are paralyzed. "Over here. Do not be afraid. We will help you; we are with you," calls out Sofia. Then, with a bound, runs to the rescue of the children.

The boy, emerging from his stupefaction, quickly wields a knife in his right hand, ready to defend and protect his small group. "Do not approach or I'll kill you! Yells the boy, his eyes filled with challenges while the three girls gather behind him as if to protect each other."

Sofia stops in her tracks. She puts her hands in front of her, open to show she means no harm. "My brother and I, we will help you, says Sofia calmly, looking the boy in the eyes and equally determined. What happened to you?" "I'm not afraid of you. I can defend myself. If you want to see what I am capable of, then come closer," the boy states with unwavering determination.

"*William, do you realize that we understand them and they also understand us?*" LYKA was right about the simultaneous translation. She then adds aloud: "William, come beside me and show them your bare hands. I think they really feel threatened by us." "Who are you? What is your clan? I do not know you, do not come closer or I'll kill you both!" shouts the boy, still watchful.

"We are three, two brothers and a sister. We are lost in a region that we do not know. My brother William is here with me, and the other, Cedric is a little further away in the big clearing. Come with us!" she says with much tactfulness in her voice. "My brothers and I will help you as best we can."

"*Sofia, what are you doing? We do not know them! You are placing us in danger! It is not what LYKA told us,*" transmits William feverishly. "*It is not what I feel. These children are not threatening. They are simply scared... They need us... I feel it's important that we help them... My intuition tells me that's what we must do!*" replies Sofia mentally.

"What clan are you from? I have never seen you! You could be our enemies. I will not let you do harm to my sisters." Sofia and William look at one another and do not know what to answer them. LYKA did not give them any clues on that subject… Sofia takes the initiative and responds with a verbal distraction. “Look at our hands. They are not armed. Listen to your little voice. It is telling you to trust us!” Sofia answers as quick as lightning.

The boy looks around him, to the left, to the right, then straight at Sofia. After a moment, he lowers his knife yet ready to strike if need be.

--- OOO ---

Allies

Cedric, worried, wonders where William and Sofia are. They left almost two hours ago and night approaches. Seated at the base of the Oak tree, he meditates: "*Great oak, you who is firmly connected, and through your roots, you know how to communicate with all the trees, I beg you, guide my thoughts to my brother and my sister.*"

Cedric transmits by telepathy: "Sofia, William, where are you? Come back to the clearing of the great oak. Darkness is coming in quickly and I prefer us to be together for the night. We need to prepare and go to meet the druid Taliesanic and the druid Guelf."

Cedric, attentive, perceives a message. "We will arrive shortly. Everything is well. William and I went a little further than expected, but it was worth it. We helped three girls and a boy. They are with us. They will help us in return." "How so, Sofia? What have you done?" transmits Cedric, tense. Sofia replies impatiently: "I did what had to be done! Now, we are not in danger! You should have confidence in me!" "Everything is well, Cedric! The children were really in danger, and now that they are with us, well, you can imagine, it's our turn!" adds William sarcastically. "Don't listen to him, he is exaggerating, says Sofia. You'll see. When you have met them, you will understand. These children will guide us to the druid, I can feel it. My intuition tells me so." "But I don't feel it!" intervenes William, always worried.

"It's your fear that keeps you from feeling!" transmits Sofia, looking her brother right in the eye. "Every human has intuition… Grandma taught me that one day, so use yours!"

"That's enough, what's done is done! Get back here, and then we'll decide what's best!" says Cedric. "I'm waiting for you!"

--- OOO ---

All along the trail, William discreetly listens to the silence of the children. He hears the thoughts and the panic of the girls. Most importantly, he pays attention to the aggressive thoughts of the boy who is walking in front of him, behind his sisters. Sofia is leading the group. She can easily identify the marks that she left. Every now and then she casts a glance rearward, adjusting her step to that of the group. The girls are following with more difficulty.

"*William, are you OK,*" asks Sofia? "*Yes, for the moment, however, I am reading aggressive thoughts in the boy's head. I am on my guard.*" "*I don't think we need to fear them. They are frightened by what they have seen, and of course, they don't trust anyone. I'd do the same if I were in their shoes. We are almost there. Another few minutes and we will listen to their story with Cedric.*" "*You always trust people too easily, sis. You will put us in danger one of these days!*" She answers him with a quip: "*You and Cedric, you are here and you will protect me, as grandma said...*" "*Grrrrrr!* howls William.

The boy and the elder sister, in silence, help the wounded girl, who is obviously experiencing more and more difficulty to keep the pace. "Are we arriving soon, asks the little girl? My feet hurt!" showing her wet and shredded galoshes. "We have arrived. That's my brother Cedric, near the old oak tree in the clearing… Cedric! Cedric calls Sofia. Come and help us!"

Nimbly, the boy places his right hand on his knife without, however, pulling it out of its sheath. William deliberately takes hold of his own knife to reassure himself. Both boys stare defiantly at one another, hands on their knife.

Cedric rushes to his brother and sister and greets the small group. The boy and the three girls remain distant. Cedric approaches and says gently: "My name is Cedric. You met Sofia and William. Welcome. We come from another region and we do

not know this area. Who are you?" He asks. Perhaps we can help one another.

He dares not say more for fear of betraying himself and putting them in a nice mess. The children look at Cedric, then at Sofia and William. In doing so, they come closer to each other, the girls behind the boy. The latter is acting as the one in charge. His right hand remains on the handle of his knife.

Cedric looks him straight in the eye and, in a reassuring voice, says: "Come. Sit on the ground in front of me on the other side of the trace I made." Cedric takes the lead and sits down. Sofia takes her place to the left of Cedric, and with an opening gesture, she invites the girls to do the same.

The boy hesitates. He casts a glance at William, who is observing him with his hand on his own knife. The boy removes his hand from his knife. Silently, William does the same.

The boy now looks at Cedric with caution and after a silent pause, he settles in front of him. He sits between his younger and eldest sister. The last girl settles down between the younger sister and Sofia.

Reassured, William settles down to the right of Cedric. The eldest of the girls keeps a distance between herself and William. William perceives the curiosity that appears in her mind. They look at each other and they both dodge their gaze, blushing slightly.

Cedric, looking the boy in the eyes suggests: "What if we take the time to introduce ourselves properly before we discuss?" Already, Cedric perceives that the small group does not feel safe.

Cedric asks Sofia and William to be attentive. "*Sofia, you were right, they are in distress and I don't believe they are dangerous to us. They are frightened and mentally tired. They want to find their own. Let's listen to their story!*"

Cedric smiles at the boy in front of him: "I know this is rather slim in way of explanation, however, here it goes: we have no idea where we are, therefore, while my brother and sister were making a reconnaissance of the area, I climbed to the top of this great oak tree to find signs of life in the region. The trace in front of you represents what I saw. I positioned the benchmarks according to the directions that I think they should go. Can you help me to complete the trace? However, before we begin, I would like to know your name."

Intrigued, the boy looks successively at Cedric, then at the drawing, then at Cedric again with a worried look. The girls remain silent, never taking their eyes off their brother. With pride the boy states: "We belong to the Bellinderry clan. My name is Aemonn, she is named Sinead" he says, pointing to the eldest, "Aisling is our youngest sister, and her, she is Ciara. "

"Do you have other siblings?" asks Sofia calmly. "Yes!" answer the three girls, with a unanimous voice. "We also have two older brothers!", continues Aemonn. "They remained with my father and grandfather to fight and allow us to run away. Father told us to flee to the druid's cave that he could protect us."

"And your mother?" "She died last winter."

Sofia observes that nothing is happening in the boy's tone in terms of emotions. She wonders: "*Is it possible that amongst these people living in an austere region, the children quickly learn to ignore their feelings? I have the impression that the survival of their clan is so important that the death of a loved one takes second place. This was not our case when Marion passed away... Hum! Something to think about...*" Sofia leans towards the boy and smiling: "Tell us what happened Aemonn, we too must meet the druid."

"Cedric, is the druid he is talking about our druid Taliesanic?" asks William. "I don't know... First, let's listen to their story," suggests Cedric, looking at his brother and his sister. Sofia and William look at one another and nod, "OK!"

Aemonn notices the little games on the part of all three. He remembers what his father taught him: "always keep 20% distrust towards new people you meet, so long as they have not proven their good intentions." With caution, Aemonn relates how a troop of giant warriors with axes and big swords attack the farms, slaughter the men, capture the women and do them much harm. They steal everything: cattle, food supplies and the family treasures before they set fire to the buildings. Aemonn concludes: "When they find liquor, they get wasted and then they become crueller. They even force their prisoners to battle amongst themselves. They are not afraid. They shout all the time and even fight amongst themselves."

"When I was up the oak tree, I saw a lot of smoke at a great distance in the following direction!" Cedric shows the direction and location on the drawing he had traced. Aemonn and Sinead look at each other and then lean over the drawing. Cedric adds: "Maybe you can give us more information on the region. If you can put that information on this drawing, it could be very useful to guide us and even protect us!"

"We don't know how to write!" replies the boy coldly. Sofia intervenes gently, trying to reassure him: "It doesn't matter; Try to recognize the waterways, the major roads or trails. Show us where the villages are and how long it takes to get from one place to another."

Together, Sinead and Aemonn indicate where to position the main locations in the region. "For starters, the great lake is well known because of the wars amongst the fishermen. It is called the Lough Neagh. Four clans constantly battle to control the fishing there. Aemonn goes on pointing to areas close to the great lake: there, is the Graigavon Clan, there, that of the Donaghmore, there, the Magherafelt and here, the Crumlin clan." Sinead intervenes: "The Crumlin are our cousins, their region is beyond the Portmore Lough, which is there." Cedric transmits to Sofia and William, careful to memorize the information. "Ah, it's a lake! I thought it was a large clearing!"

Aemonn points to a large discharge of the great Lake Lough Neagh. This discharge supplies a small river but with a strong flow. That river moves towards the sector where Cedric noticed the smoke. Aemonn also indicates two other discharges and streams that come from Portmore Lough and meet the first river.

Aemonn and Sinead identify the locations of the most frequented roads or trails along with the main villages in the area. The triplets can now determine important landmark points.

The children had fled from the Bellinderry Cove area. When Sofia and William intercepted them, they had been walking for almost ten hours. They had left their hamlet at daybreak.

Meira is the largest hamlet of the region. Its fortress controls the intersection of the three roads that cross the country. Sinead mentions having passed by Meira on a few occasions to travel to Craigavon with her father to exchange sheep wool. The journey time was from sunrise until the sun is at its highest in the sky, that is, between six and seven hours of walking. Meira is just a little less than half way, therefore about three hours walk.

From Meira to get to the Graigavon clan, it takes about four hours. "*I get the impression they do not understand the concept of hours*," transmits William. "*I believe you're right. We must be careful about what we say*," adds Cedric.

"Sofia, where were you when you intercepted Aemonn and his sisters," asks Cedric? "Around here." Sofia answers as she points to a bend in the small river that runs down to what Aemonn called AGHALEE. Cedric turns towards the boy and asks, "Aemonn, Sinead, where were you headed when you met Sofia?"

"Grandfather told us to go up the second river in the direction of Portmore Lough up to the three marshes. There, we will find the three sacred oaks, the Derves." "Three sacred oaks," William asks, surprised at this information that LYKA forgot to convey them. "Yes!" continues Aemonn. "They are easy to recognize because they are filled with requests and offerings that hang from the branches. From there, we walk towards the sunset until the healer druid finds us. Father says that he can see in the dark. He may even sense us better than does a bear."

"He knows the whole forest. He knows we are coming. Father said so," Ciara mentions, sure of herself. "Are there many druids in the region," asks Sofia? "Yes," says Sinead. "But father said that apprentice druids were living in his cave with him." "Taliesanic is the greatest druid, the greatest healer of the whole kingdom. He is very powerful," adds little Aisling.

--- OOO ---

The forest is beginning to grow dark.

Cedric, William, Sofia, Aemonn and Sinead linger around the layout they are trying to memorize. Cedric looks at the boy: "Aemonn, we will go with you to visit the druid. He is waiting for us too." *"Oops! That did not have any impact on him!"* "You know where he is?" asks Aemonn. "No! However, with the information we have, we'll find him together." Cedric continues: "How about if you and I, we take the lead, Sofia would follow with your sisters and William will bring up the rear?"

"Wow, brother! Why is it always me who must bring up the rear?" *"You have nothing to fear, Will, we are here to protect you,"* transmits Sofia, with a smile. "Grrrr!" retorts William. "Come Ciara. We must protect your feet better," says Sofia, hurrying to her side. Aemonn notices the gesture of solicitude on the part of Sofia and records this mark of tenderness in his heart. *"Hum! I'm surprised. She impresses me that girl..."* Sofia perceives Aemon's reflections and blushes while she wraps the young girl's feet. Sinead moves close to William and asks with a little mischievous look: "Can I be near you William?" Surprised by the request, William nods. He feels a pleasant tingling sensation at the back of his neck.

The Druid Taliesanic

An old man and a young woman are sitting near a huge rock some distance away in the forest. They are watching the sky. "The moon is round tonight. It is giving off a lot of light. However, it strikes me as quite sad," whispers the young woman with long red hair, braided down to her lower back. "Indeed, Quelf. It is bemoaning the massacres on the Coast. Ireland is due to give birth to its identity and it will not be easy." "What do you mean, Taliesanic? Did you have another vision?"

Silent, Taliesanic watches the fire devouring the logs. Sparks pop and fly away. The sparks remind him of the reality of the moment, allow him a glimpse of the realities of the future. He helplessly contemplates centuries of constant battle. Fighting amongst brothers, fighting with invaders, fighting in the name of Gods, battles forever commanded, initiated in the pursuit of power. Truly, the moon has good reason to be sad because, despite its light, this marvellous island, Eire, will know only very few good days during the next millennium. With a sad and aching heart, the old man with steel blue eyes and white beard meditates in silence: *"So many wars! So many massacres! Men are deaf to their hearts. They do not understand that by killing each other, it is to themselves they do harm. All living beings that populate this Earth are united by the air they breathe, the sun that warms them, the water that quenches their thirst and the Earth itself that carries them. This era of peace is long in coming..."*

The woman understands and respects the silence of this man. Taliesanic has been teaching her for numerous seasons the secrets of the plants that heal; the language of the birds who manifest the weather. Through the contemplation of nature she learned many teachings. She noticed the power of water which always finds its way and absorbs all the sorrows. She saw the wind that caresses or floors everything, carrying painful thoughts away. She observed the fire that transmutes darkness into light, cleanses and is an omen of a revival. She learned how easily the earth recycles indigestible residues and transforms them into nutritive elements. Doesn't the manure from the animals smoulder a new energetic growth? "*Gracias, Taliesanic, for your teachings, your guidance in the course of all these seasons.*"

Taliesanic tenderly observes this young woman that fate has entrusted to him. He knows. Yes, he knows what the Universe expects of this woman. She is ready. Quelf is ready for her integration into the Druids Brotherhood. She is qualified to provide care and to teach. Her wisdom and discernment qualify her beyond doubt. Moreover, she is determined. He knows.

He also knows that the children who are approaching carry with them the hope for peace so far removed... Hope for the discovery of a better world... He knows he must pass on to them his teaching for their world, for the evolution of humanity. "Quelf prepare the beverage and the victuals. They are coming."

--- OOO ---

The journey along the stream proceeds without incident and in silence. The group approaches the sacred oaks. The night spreads its shadow. Already the moon is rising in the horizon.

"We'll arrive soon. I feel myself drawn into this specific direction," whispers Cedric to his companion Aemonn. "I'm tired and my feet hurt," says Ciara. "The druid will take care of you," answers, Sofia. "He is a healer and knows all kinds of potions, you'll see." Ciara looks at Sofia with confidence and takes her left hand.

"*Cedric, notice how the yellow halo crowns the moon with sadness,*" transmits Sofia. "*Yes, grandpa would say, it's going to rain, that halo foreshadows wet temperatures.*" "*I kind of get the feeling that someone is watching us,"* adds Sofia. "*Where*?" asks William, anxious, looking around all the way to the dark groves? "*I don't know it's only a feeling. However, I don't sense any threat,"* completes Sofia.

Aemonn hardened to undergrowth shrubs identifies three superposed stones. "That is where we must go. It is with similar stones that father tracks our trails," he says. "OK, but, let's see if all are ready to continue," answers Cedric, who, for the moment, is assuming the leadership of the group.

Everyone progress along a discreet path, attentive to their thoughts, their worries and their hopes. Every now and then they see little columns of three stones which enable them to orient themselves. Then, slowly, a glow takes shape and warms the children's hearts.

"Welcome!" says the old man, with open arms and smiling. "Come, I believe you need to rest. We have been waiting for you. Quelf bring the hot soup for our guests."

Smiling and affable, the druid[4] Taliesanic welcomes each child. In turn, he faces each of them putting his left hand on the child's right shoulder and his right hand gently sliding from the forehead to the back of the neck. He needs to confirm his intuition and vision.

When touching the triplets, he comes into contact with the vibratory identification marks of Cedric, William and Sofia.

---

[4] In the Celtic tradition, the druid is essentially a priest. All druids of all ranks constitute the "sacerdotal class" of the Celtic society and are not a mere "college" of the Latin type. The sacerdotal class of druids is a constitutive element of the Celtic society of the Indo-European type of society with three classes: the sacerdotal class, the warrior class and the class of producers.

The druid received priestly initiation and he confers to the king the royal initiation. Consequently, the temporal and legitimate power proceeds from the spiritual power. This translates in the protocol of the court by the fact that the druid speaks before the king and that the king has no right to speak before his druids. It is the king who governs, certainly, but it is the druid who advises.

Taliesanic foresees the destiny of each child present before him. Each child, in her/his own way, will influence the evolution of humanity in her/his time. His eyes half-closed, focusing on his feelings, he acknowledges the vocation of these children, in the immediate and distant future. He lingers at length on the back of Sofia's neck, as if to collect an inestimable treasure. "*Universal Light, Gaia our Mother Earth, be blessed. I do appreciate this moment. I appreciate all your blessings in this world. I know now that everything is in motion towards this era of peace. Here I am. I am at your service as your humble servant. Guide my words, guide my actions.*"

The moment is solemn. The triplets hear Taliesanic's invocation. Without comprehending, everyone is aware that something important is happening here. Quelf, almost in a trance, accompanies and supports the sage. She realizes that, for her, the end foretells her departure. Serene, she relies on her Gods and her guides who have never abandoned her.

While the young people eat in silence, Quelf works on Ciara's feet. Once the wounds are washed, she pours a little oil on them. Her dexterous hands gently massage each foot. Quelf covers the little feet with some paste made from medicinal plants that she picked.

"Each of you in your own way has had a very hectic day. It's time for you to rest. We'll talk tomorrow. Quelf will show you to your beds. Sleep well," recommends Taliesanic.

A thousand questions arise. However, out of respect for their host, no one dares to ask a question. The children remain quiet.

Aemonn watches over and looks at his sisters fallen asleep. He recalls every moment of his day, from the violent beginning to the warm welcome of Taliesanic and Quelf. He does not sleep. The three strangers preoccupy him. "*Who are Cedric, Sofia and William? Where do they come from? When they look at each other, it is as if they are conversing together in silence. They are hiding something. They do not hold themselves like us and their hands have no story or injury such as ours.*"

While travelling in his thoughts, he hears Taliesanic's voice ordering him: "*Sleep now, Aemonn, it is time for you to rest. You will know and understand in due course. Sleep now.*"

--- OOO ---

The Opening

The light rain outside the cave pushes the young people to remain next to the comfort of the fire. At their own pace, everyone recovers their wits, their worries, their questions.

Aisling and Ciara huddle against each other as in another world, imbued with fear.

Sinead is standing next to William, comfortable and interested.

Sofia looks at Aemonn, intrigued.

Aemonn observes the triplets with renewed curiosity. *"What is Cedric thinking about? I have a feeling he is not with us."*

Sofia and Cedric are both attentive to Aemonn's thoughts and transmit their observations about him to one another.

The triplets comment on all the artifacts they see in the cave: drums, rattles and sticks decorated with feathers, drawings, stones and leather. Each of the sticks is placed at a specific place and in a precise position. Different plants are drying by the fire. Leather bags are lying on what appears to be an altar. Metal jars of various sizes give off fragrant smoke in various locations of the cave and especially near the entrance.

Taliesanic approaches the group with Quelf.

He invites everyone to come and sit beside him. Then, reassuringly, he inquires on how their night was. He knows very well that not one of them has slept. He and Quelf watched over them and captured their perturbed dreams. "I was waiting for you," affirms Taliesanic, looking at each child in turn, straight in the eyes: Aemonn, his sisters, William, Cedric and finally, Sofia.

Sofia, while feeling safe and comfortable, carefully look at this man who seems to exist only for them. "*I feel like I have known him for a long time*," thinks Cedric. "*Me too*," thinks Sofia. "*Yeah! But it is not an old man like him who will protect us from the warriors who walk around and massacre everyone*," transmits William, ever restless. "*I wonder why the dragons brought us here*."

"*You are here with me because together, we have events to experience. These events will prepare every one of you to live a very important mission.*"

"But he is reading in my thoughts?" Questions William distraught, looking at Cedric and Sofia.

Cedric and Sofia are no longer listening to Taliesanic. With a glance, they discreetly consult with William. Together, with a nod, they decide to close the access to their thinking as their grandma taught them.

The silence brings their attention back to the druid who, with the others, is looking at them. All eyes are focused on the triplets. They realize that their communication was not quite as discreet as they had thought. Each in their own way concludes that they must consult together and practise their telepathic method.

Taliesanic smiles and pursues. "You are gathered here with me and Quelf because we have something to teach you. In addition, you also have to convey amongst yourselves experiences that will serve you throughout your present life on this earth." "'*Present life on this Earth!' my eye! My world is not here. Here, it's a dream, no, it's a nightmare!"* ruminates William.

--- OOO ---

Taliesanic nods to Quelf. Quelf rises and signals Aemonn and his sisters to follow her into another part of the cave. Meanwhile,

Taliesanic invites the triplets to get up and follow him into a space where a heady scent prevails.

On entering the cave, the children note three bronze bowls generating a light bluish cloud. In the centre of the cave, there is a small fire. Four large stones covered with a sheepskin are arranged around the fire. The sheepskin serves as a form of cushions. In front of the largest stone lies a drum: a hollow log of wood covered at both ends with hide. The hides are decorated with drawings in black and white. One end of the drum, worn through beating, presents a stylized oak tree in the centre and different symbols around it. This decorated hide is placed to absorb the heat from the fire. The heat stretches the skin to provide for a better sound. A leather bag lies to the right of the stone. This bigger stone is Taliesanic's seat.

"What's that smell?" asks Sofia. "It is sage," replies Taliesanic. "This plant is sacred to us. It heals, nourishes and protects. In fact, come closer, before I begin, I will clean your body and prepare your spirit to receive what the Gods have prepared for you. Let's start with you, Cedric."

Before moving further into the cave, Taliesanic picks up a bowl containing wood embers reddened by a small flame, the sage, and invites Cedric to stand in front of him. Cedric slowly advances towards the druid. Taliesanic is holding the bowl in his left hand and in his right hand, a stick of sage plants tied up. The stick emits an odorous blue smoke. Respectfully, while humming unfamiliar words, the druid coats Cedric with sage smoke, from head to toe, from front to back, and finally, coming back before Cedric, he blows smoke towards his forehead, towards his heart and finally towards his abdomen. Cedric is then asked to take the seat to the right of the large stone, Taliesanic's seat.

William receives the ritual in turn and once his preparation completed, he takes the seat to the left of Taliesanic's stone.

Sofia, attentive and respectful, approaches. She perceives the intensity and respect of Taliesanic's gestures. The sage ritual completed, Sofia is invited to take the seat between her two brothers. She now sits facing Taliesanic, impressed.

Taliesanic settles down in front of the three children. His gestures are deliberate and solemn. His blue eyes, half-closed, reflect contemplation as he explains: "I invite you to be very present to your inner self, to breathe in deeply and to lock yourself into the sound and rhythm of the drum."

While singing in a strange language, the druid begins to gently tap the hide of the rustic drum. The rhythm is regular. Boom, boom, boom, boom, boom, boom, boom, boom,

In a very powerful voice, Taliesanic pronounces words in a language unknown to the children.

The structure of the cavern amplifies the sound created by the beating on the drum. The solar plexus of the children absorbs the rhythmic vibration. The magic intensifies.

The music sets a "to and fro" motion. The sound carries the children upon the waves of a sea of dreams. Their respiration is in harmony with the tempo imposed by Taliesanic. A festival of sound and light neutralize all thought. An intense vibration takes hold of their bodies. Suddenly everything stops, no sound, the three children are propelled into the silence of the cosmos. From afar a vivid red light, warm, reassuring heads to meet them, envelopes all three of them, and then penetrates their respective crystal. A single facet of the crystal remains highlighted in red.

A distant voice transmits them: "Sofia, Cedric, William, come back. It is now time."

Only the wood crackling in the fire breaks the silence. The children return from the journey with a feeling of extraordinary wellness. They perceive more than feel the warmth that their crystal is spreading on their chest. In a coordinated motion, each one respectfully touches his crystal aware of having received a magical and powerful gift.

They all feel connected with each other and with their environment. Rainbow sparks float around them, appease them. The children are amazed.

Tenderly, Taliesanic looks at them with admiration and gratitude. "*You are blessed. I thank the Cosmos for participating in your preparation. Numerous challenges await you both individually and collectively. Your interaction amongst yourselves and amongst different nations will ultimately lead you to the liberation of man. Humanity will again breathe the Light.*"

"*I hear you speaking in my head, Taliesanic, and I do not grasp what you are saying*" transmits Sofia in turn. "*Certainly, however, everything will fall into place in due course. For the moment note that the crystals you carry possess eight faces needing to be energized. What has happened a few moments ago, is very important. One face of your crystal was activated. It is related to your first energy centre, the one that connects you to Earth.*"

"Energy Centre! Our chakras?" Questions Cedric. Taliesanic continues: "Indeed, this energy centre represents the boundary between animal and human consciousness. It is related to the unconsciousness." "Unconsciousness, I have not fainted as far as I know," says William. "You are not aware of it, says Taliesanic laughing. It is magical." "OK I understand," replies William.

"This energy centre stores actions and experiences from your past lives. Also, according to what you have accomplished, it holds part of your future. This energy centre is the foundation for the development of your personality.

Taliesanic looks at each of the children in turn and satisfied of their attention continues: 'You have to choose. You have to choose all the time,' insists Taliesanic. 'Choose to be energetic and vigorous or be lazy. Choose to be generous and of service or egocentric and dominated by your physical desires. You are always confronted by choices. This energy you have been given is there to help you make the best choices.'

'The other faces of your sacred stone will be activated by otherwise persons you will meet during special events. When the time comes, the unity and complementarity you will have developed in your diversity will help you three, as a team, to accomplish what needs to be done for humanity. In the meantime, continue to learn and grow in gratitude.'

The triplets are astounded. They do not fully grasp what is being said. Sofia asks: 'Heck, what will happen to us? We have seven other faces to activate.'

Taliesanic ignores Sofia and tells them aloud: 'Some friends are arriving, do not worry.'

--- OOO ---

The Invasion

Six warriors appear in the trail coming towards the cave. At once, Aemonn and William lay their right hand on their knife.

With a posed gesture, Taliesanic signals the children with his hand to stay calm. 'There is no danger. They are warriors of the Bellinderry clan.'

There is no need for more. In two bounds, Aemonn has already burst out of the cave and raced down the slope and flown into the arms of Turlough, the weapons master of his clan. Despite his advanced age, this vigorous man inspires respect. He is accompanied by five young warriors. Aemonn recognizes them, he has trained with them on a regular basis.

Turlough greets Aemonn with a nod of the head, pushes down Aemonn beside him and, without stopping or speaking; he goes immediately to Taliesanic whom he salutes with infinite respect. With a look and a nod of the head, he greets Quelf, who hastily brings something to drink to this little group out of breath.

'Taliesanic, who are these three-young people? They are not from around here.' 'I'll explain later,' answers Taliesanic. 'For the moment, I believe that Aemonn grows impatient.'

'What happened, how's father, grandfather? What is the news? Speak!' Aemonn orders, tense. 'Alas, the news is not good,' answers Turlough, transferring his gaze from Aemonn to Taliesanic. 'It was very brutal. Despite the losses caused to the invader, the giants never stopped coming.' Turning to Aemonn 'your father hoped to see the reinforcements he had requested from your uncle. But the reinforcements never came.' 'The buggar!' interjects Aemonn, furious. 'Let him speak,' interrupts Taliesanic calmly, placing his hand on the left shoulder of the spirited young man. Then turning to the warrior, he invites Turlough to pursue.

Turlough quickly recounts the violence of the fighting. 'Aemonn, your grandfather died sword in hand. Your two brothers and numerous warriors disappeared in the battle. Shane, your father and our clan leader sensing that we could not defeat the enemy, ordered me to take five companions and come here as fast as we could in order to protect you, your sisters and the druid.'

'*Aemonn is the clan leader's son!*' think Cedric and Sofia at the same time.

'What else?' inquires Aemonn, tense. 'Despite my protests, your father insisted that I continue preparing you to take over from him,' says Turlough, putting one knee down on the ground before Aemonn in a sign of allegiance. He adds looking the young man straight in the eye: 'Moreover, your father requested that Taliesanic acts as your advisor with all his wisdom. You must act in a way so as to not go beyond the point of no return. The future of the clan is a priority,' concludes Turlough.

Turlough remains with his knee on the ground looking at the druid now standing besides Aemonn who affirms: 'Father is not dead! I know it. I feel it.'

'*Ha! He listens to his intuition also!*' Thinks, William.

'Your father insists that we go to your uncle, and with him, take back what must belong to you. He also told me that one day you'll be a great leader who will unite the clans. My mission is to push your physical limitations. Taliesanic and his successor's mission is to develop your wisdom. You will learn to properly direct the destiny of our people, of our clan, of your family.'

'*Aemonn is angry and frustrated,' thinks Sofia. 'He wants to rescue his father; he is mad at his uncle who did not show up to support the family clan. He wants to fight the invaders. He feels lonely and helpless.'*

Taliesanic invites Turlough to rise. The two of them get busy calming the young man's passion while the triplets and Aemonn's three sisters listen.

'*What are we doing here?' questions William mentally. We are not warriors, we're only teenagers.*" "*Teenagers admittedly, but with knowledge and skills that can make a difference. We did not come here for nothing. We have things to learn and to contribute. So, let's not get worked up now and let's be trusting,*" replies Cedric, reassuring. "*Trust whom, what?*" asks William exacerbated. "*I really like the druid,*" says Sofia, "*and besides, I find this old warrior very reassuring,*" she thinks, attentive to Aemonn's behaviour. "*We all know, sis, I saw you. You, you're rather interested in Aemonn.*"

The thought is barely formulated that William is already flat on his back. "Sofia, what's the matter with you?" grumbles William, both startled and annoyed.

Sofia, arms crossed, stares at her brother. In the stillness, her gaze says it all. All eyes are on her. "Well, what! He had no business saying that," says Sofia, infuriated. "Say what?" ask Aemonn and Turlough at the same time?

Only Taliesanic is smiling.

--- OOO ---

The Challenge

Sofia's spontaneous behaviour embarrasses the triplets. Sofia, still upset with William's indiscretion doesn't know what to say. Cedric, annoyed, looks at Taliesanic who is observing him with a smile. Aemonn and Turlough wait impatiently. The sisters, speechless, are looking at Sofia; only the female warriors of the Celtic clans dare shove the male.

Taliesanic maintains the suspense to the point of discomfort. Finally, he speaks: "Aemonn, these individuals are from another space and are here to assist us, that is you and your people. They are the future of your heritage," he says enigmatically. "I have been expecting their visit for a long time."

Addressing Aemonn directly, Taliesanic reminds him that the druidic tradition within the Celtic community is currently under pressure. That is why he is living away. Shane, Aemonn's father, had been his student for many years.

"For more than a century, with the coming of a new religion on the Irish Island, the druids lost much of their influence. They either integrated into the Christian religion or withdrew into monasteries. The political pressure was becoming too strong or dangerous. Several druids went with those who govern. Others like me withdrew from the social life in order to practice in that place our art of divination as well as that of healing. We study herbs and plants. Sometimes, as the need arises, we journey into different worlds. Some worlds are visible and others not. In the invisible worlds, we work with great magicians who assist us in advising the persons who need our services."

Everyone around him listen attentively.

"Cedric, Sofia and William are searching for their Celtic ancestors. They too have a great mission to accomplish in their world..." "Their world?" questions Aemonn. Taliesanic continues: "Their clan, if you prefer. My own guides asked me to welcome them with you and help prepare you to accomplish your mission, your duty." "*What does he mean?*" asks William, looking at Cedric. Looking at the triplets Taliesanic says: "These young people have developed a gift that we all possess but have neglected. They can read minds and communicate through thought." "*So, that's what was happening when I thought them odd,*" thinks Aemonn. "*Yes!*" says Sofia, looking at him.

"You have been reading my mind?" Asks Aemonn, surprised and outraged? "Yes!" says Taliesanic, "and I too can. We all have that ability. It takes listening, observation, discernment and above all, practice. You will learn, Aemonn. For now, they can really help you in your negotiations with your uncle." "I can't get over it," insists Aemonn, staring at Sofia. They both blush, feeling uncomfortable.

Quelf, silent until then, through a mental communication invites Sofia to join her at the back of the cavern, close to a drapery of black and white fabric on which a stylized oak has been drawn.

Sofia notes the medallion Quelf carries around her neck. It bears the same stylized oak tree. When questioned about the symbolism of the tree on her medallion and on the draperies, Quelf stresses the importance of the Derve in the Celtic tradition. "*Derve!,*" asks Sofia telepathically. "*Yes, what you and your brothers call oak*" transmits Quelf.

Quelf explains how the Celtic druids and shamans venerate this tree and consider it to be sacred. "Through its roots, it honours Danna[5], Mother Earth. Our elders call it Gaia. Through its branches, it honours the Father of All; through its leaves, it purifies the air and through its fruit, it ensures continuity and

---

[5] Celtic name for Gaia, Mother Earth.

nourishes man. The sacred oaks are found in different parts of the forests, in discrete places to avoid pressure from religious groups who seek to occult the ancestral practices. The druidic and shamanic practices will go through very dark days in the centuries to come."

--- OOO ---

Later that day, Quelf instructs Sofia and Aemonn's sisters on medicinal herbs and prepares a few pouches that may serve to provide care. Meanwhile, Turlough wishes to evaluate the combat efficiency of the teenagers. As a seasoned weapons master, he quickly appreciates Cedric's ability with the sword and javelin. Cedric defeats three of his men in succession. Aemonn has difficulty winning against Cedric who returns strike for strike. Turlough observes: "*That boy is very creative in his assault*".

Turlough is also very impressed with Sofia's archery skills. With precision and smoothness Sofia places six successive arrows within a fixed target the size of a man's hand at 30 paces. She also strikes five times out of six with the arrows a moving target: a small log at the end of a rope. She bested by far everyone present.

Turlough can't help laughing at the postures and movements displayed by William while throwing successive knives. He was even more impressed when he noted how quickly and precise this kid was with a slingshot. The rocks hit the moving log every time he fired his slingshot.

Aemonn, impressed, whispers to Turlough: "These teenagers would become great warriors in our clan. Cedric almost defeated me with the sword. You must teach me new techniques. As for Sofia, I think she can best almost all our archers. Belennos[6]! She

---

[6] Belennos Irish Solar God associated with Apollo.

can fire those arrows so fast and with precision! What a woman she is."

Aemonn has forgotten that the teenagers and Taliesanic can read minds. Sofia is blushing. Cedric and William consult one another and transmit: "*Our sister a woman! This guy is out of his mind!*"

Aemonn doesn't notice Sofia blushing nor the exchange between Cedric and William or Taliesanic smiling.

Aemonn, still thinking: "*This William is small but fast and slippery. He is very hard to get to the ground. I like him. He makes me laugh; more so, when he pulls his brother's hair to get out of his hold. Cedric almost gets mad. Perhaps I should go back with them to meet their clan and train with them.*"

Turlough considers the wrestling bouts of the teenagers with his soldiers and Aemonn conclusive. The bouts proved the determination, stamina and ingenuity of those new recruits.

Turlough is satisfied. He calls the little group of men and teenagers around the fire to prepare the next move.

Aemonn insists on finding a way to help his father and his clan. His firmness and his assurance already demonstrate his leadership. Turlough proudly supports this young man for who he foresees a great future. With Turlough's patience and Taliesanic's advice, Aemonn finally understands and support the course of action proposed by Turlough.

--- OOO ---

"It is time to go," says Turlough.

Before leaving, Taliesanic, Turlough, Aemonn, Cedric, William, Sofia and the warriors take their position in the marching column. They have discussed the behaviour they must have during the displacement should an incident arise. They also discussed what attitudes to maintain when meeting with the uncle known for his egotistical intrigues and deceit. Observation and mutual protection are essential for survival. To this end, Taliesanic and the triplets are to observe, read minds and discreetly inform Turlough on the intentions of their host especially if danger looms ahead.

Turlough and Aemonn take lead of the column of marchers. Taliesanic follows, flanked by William and Cedric. Sinead and her sisters are protected by two warriors in the middle of the column. Quelf and Sofia follow. The three most experienced guards provide security at the rear.

"Aemonn, we need to quicken the pace if we want to be at your uncle's in Glenaw before nightfall," insists Turlough. "One of the men will carry Aisling. I hope your aunt will accept to protect your sisters, If not, we will have to improvise." "Yea! This rain is not helping… The trail is slippery… As for my uncle and my aunt, we will see. One thing is certain, we need to find a way to help my father as quickly as possible. I hope we can intervene before everybody is massacred."

The small group continue to trudge into the abundant summer rain. No one escapes from the additional water dropping from the tree leaves. Everyone is soaked to the bones. Their hands are cold and wet. Holding on to their weapons is now a challenge.

Finally, the small group enters the hamlet of Glenaw. The triplets notice approximately fifty garrets surrounding an impressive construction. This construction is built as a stronghold to defend the clan's people. "What is this place?" Asks Sofia joining Taliesanic. "It looks bizarre, dark and is not very welcoming."

"Here is a little background to this place to help you understand the context," says Taliesanic. "In this part of the region there are many incursions from the Robogdii nation. The Crumlin clan has a mission to protect the Darini nation's Northern Territory. The Robogdii and the Darini nations have been warring for decades over the control of fishing rights on the Lough Neagh Lake." "Yes!" acknowledges Turlough. "To this end, the Crumlin clan accounts for over two thousand members. Of these, 150 are active warriors. In addition, the clan leader, if needed, can rapidly call to arms an additional 100 militia trained farmer warriors."

Taliesanic continues: "The clan leader, Finian Crumlin is the elder brother of Aemonn's deceased mother. Finian never accepted that his sister married Shane Bellinderry. He always considered Shane as his main rival for the leadership over the clans in the region. Since the death of his sister, relations between the Crumlin and the Bellinderry are not cordial, at best, they are polite." "Wow! We are really in another world," transmits Cedric. "*What is to become of us*?" Thinks, William.

Currently, few people are outside of their homes in the rain. Two guards at the fortress's gate observe the incoming group. Turlough orders to his warriors: "Be attentive, let us be on our guard and scrutinize the surroundings. We do not want to be surprised by an enemy. Your task is to fend off any threats and protect our chieftain's family, Taliesanic and his guests."

The troop quickly heads for the small fortress.

"Your uncle doesn't seem aware of the danger that represents the invader," remarks Turlough. "Yes! I noticed!" Answers Aemonn concerned.

Taliesanic observes and remains calm. He pays attention to his guests noticing how composed Cedric and Sofia are. Yet, he can see and feel how tense William is.

Aemonn does not know his uncle and cousins well. Whenever the families got together, their fathers would always argue. The women would withdraw to the gardens. His cousins would only try to prove their strength, often brutally. Colin is slightly older than Aemonn and he most of the time treats Aemonn as his scapegoat. He makes no bones about shoving Aemonn around with arrogance.

"This time, if Colin wants a fight, he will get one," thinks Aemonn. *"I will be able to put into practice all the close-combat training that Turlough and his companions gave me. I will not let myself be laughing at."* "Anger is a bad advisor," whispers

Taliesanic, capturing Aemonn's line of thought. "It's highly advantageous to remain secretive about one's strengths and let the opponent unveil himself first. The longer we remain calm and lucid the more information we'll obtain."

"Let's keep to our plan of action, Aemonn. Let Turlough make your demand to Finian for assistance and you, you pay heed to your uncle's response and especially to his attitude. Cedric, Sofia, William and I we will keep silent, observe and listen." Then turning towards Quelf: "Quelf, see if you can get information on Finian's intentions with the women of the clan."

The welcome, as expected, is cold. Quelf and the young girls are asked to follow the clan leader's wife companions.

Finian Crumlin, the uncle, initially ignores his nephew and Turlough. He only greets Taliesanic without looking at the group members that his guards are watching. Colin, intrigued, pays attention to the three teenagers younger than himself. "*Who are they? They are not of the Bellinderry clan. Why are they with the druid? They are spies. I will watch them*," thinks Colin.

Aemonn notices his uncle's affront towards him and Turlough. He clenches his fists and his jaw to control himself. He hears Taliesanic's voice in his mind: "*Gently, Aemonn, the plan, remember the plan, control your anger, you are the leader.*"

At the same moment, Taliesanic, standing beside Aemonn, places his left hand on the impetuous lad's right shoulder and says: "Thank you, Finian. I think your nephew needs your help."

Slowly, Finian tears his eyes away from the druid and turns, first to Turlough that he greets with a slight nod, before squinting and looking his nephew straight in the eye while thinking: "*What is Taliesanic doing with this Bellinderry cockerel?* Then with a slight smile: "To what do we owe your visit, nephew?"

Aemonn requests hospitality and protection. He invites Turlough to recount the events and then overtly asks his uncle to come to the aid of his clan and to support his father. During this time, Colin, his hand on his new sword, observes his cousin arrogantly. Cedric, Sofia and William listen to the unspoken and detect a lot of animosity. "*But we are in a real nest of wasps. These here folks really don't like each other*!" transmits William, jittery.

Mentally, Taliesanic reminds everyone to keep their cool and capture the intentions that are being unveiled as calmly as possible.

"I will send a scouting party to see if anyone pursued you," interrupts Finian. "Perhaps we will obtain news of your clan. During that time, we will eat and see what can be done, and then you will rest. Colin, go to the men's quarters and tell Lehmann to come here with his team of scouts. I must speak to them," concludes the leader of the Crumlin clan.

As Aemonn was going to protest, so as to push his uncle to take action, Taliesanic's thought modified his demand into a polite thank you. While the small group is being escorted to the dining room, Aemonn is fuming.

Throughout the entire meal, the conversations are held on two levels. Despite the civility of the exchanges, the members of the Bellinderry clan are not welcome.

"*These three silent teenagers intrigue me,*" thinks Finian. "*They seem to know more than they allow seeing: their way of looking, their gestures, their hands... Are they demons that Taliesanic is protecting? What are they doing with him... Damn druid, why did you come out of your cavern? You need not meddle in our affairs. It is imperative that the delegation of barbarians not arrive while they are here. I hope that Lehmann will have intercepted them... And that cockerel, he should have remained in his village and fought with his clan rather than be here. Yeah, another situation to deal with.*"

While the guests at dinner talk politely, the thoughts of the Crumlin leader roam. Taliesanic, Quelf and the triplets capture what is left unsaid and see their precariousness in this place. Telepathically, Taliesanic asks everyone to remain as discreet and imperturbable as possible. He invites Aemonn to ask his uncle for permission to retire. “Uncle Finian thank you for your hospitality. My sisters and I have had a very difficult day. With your permission, we would like to go get some rest. However, I would appreciate your calling me when your scouts are back.”

Finian acquiesces with a movement of his hand while he salutes Taliesanic with a courteous nod of the head.

As soon as the Bellinderry clan members get together privately in the garret at their disposal outside the fortress premises, everyone shares their observations. By agreement, they acknowledge that they are in danger and that it is urgent that they get away from the treachery that is forthcoming. Their safety is compromised. They must leave now.

The Pursuit

The downpour has ceased. Discreetly the group plans their next move. “I want to know what happened, insists Aemonn. We must go to Bellinderry Cove and see how we can help. That’s all there is to it.”

“Aemonn ! Calm down, control yourself,” says Turlough. “I know that you have knowledge of the surroundings. However, what tells you there is no danger? Do you understand?” “Hum! Hum!” Nods Aemonn. “We will go to our village," continues Turlough; “however we will do it my way. We must ensure maximum precautions and not approach our hamlet blindly. Hence I am dispatching two scouts to move ahead and warn us of any danger.”

Quietly, sheltered by the forest, the little troop walks away from Glenaw in the direction of Bellinderry Cove. They are all aware of the dangers that surround them and remain alert.

Meanwhile, in the fortress, Finian Crumlin discusses at length with his sons and the warriors who are totally devoted to him. Despite the insistence of his wife to respect the blood lineage, he gives the order to his weapons master to capture the visitors. “Take a strong and trustworthy escort and throw that cockerel Aemonn and the three strangers in the dungeon, and keep them under a strong guard.” He continues: “As for Taliesanic and Quelf, I don’t believe they will resist. However, we cannot release them, it would be too embarrassing. You will keep them under a strong guard until the return of Lehmann. When he has returned, tell him to take an escort of six men and deliver the druid and druidess to the monks of the bishopric. The bishop will know what to do with them. Besides, he’s been chasing all the Celtic druids and shamans of the region for a long time[7]."

"My three nieces can be sold to the Barbarians. In the meantime, keep them locked up. Kill all the warriors. We will show their bodies to the barbaric delegation. That should help convince them that we are their allies. Beware of Turlough, he is very tough. He has been the great champion of all the tournaments in Eire for several years. If possible, kill him from a distance. With him dead, the others should fall easily."

--- OOO ---

Quickly, the instructions are given and Finian's troops get organized. Colin, happy, accompanies the detachment in charge of throwing his cousin and the foreigners in the dungeon. "*I can taste the effect it will have on Aemonn. I am going to enjoy throwing him around again.*"

Colin, sword in hand, moves cautiously behind the weapons master. On the latter's signal, the guards move rapidly into the garret. Their yell resounds in the empty room. A quick search reveals no presence. "By Badb[8]! They are gone!" Screams Colin in anger. "Dad will have our heads!"

"Sound the alert!" Screams the weapons master.

"Alert! Alert!" Screams a guard while his companion blows the horn. The villagers are awake. The garrison soldiers dress up and rush to the call. One of the guards runs back to the fortress to inform Finian of the disappearance of the druid and the Bellinderry clan members.

Furious, Finian throws his wooden goblet which breaks into pieces on the hearthstone. Only his son Colin eventually calms

---

[7] In this Sixth Century Life, Christianity in Ireland is still fragile. The people too often turn to the archaic spirituality rituals.

[8] Badb, Irish goddess of wars, battles and slaughters.

him down. “Father, if I were in their place, I would try to reach the Bellinderry sector to find out what’s going on and possibly join the warriors to continue the struggle.”

“Lehann, our best tracker is not back yet,” says Finian speaking to his son. “Fetch the gamekeeper. He will guide you in the dark. He knows all the woods of the region. You will leave with him and the two platoons of ten men ready to go. Bring me back all those people, dead or alive. Is that understood, Colin?” “Yes, Father,” replies the young man, happy to fight with Aemonn! “*This time, it’s no longer a game.*”

Colin is getting impatient. The gamekeeper is taking too long to arrive. “At this rate, Aemonn and his group are taking a big lead. I hope the girls and the old man are slowing their pace,” thinks Colin. “You two,” says Colin pointing to two of his warriors, “go quickly around the village and try to figure out which trail they took.”

--- OOO ---

The rain is falling again. With it, detecting unusual sounds is more difficult and vision is much reduced. The undergrowth is dark.

Aemonn’s sisters have trouble following and Sinead requests a halt to allow the youngest to catch their breath.

Rapidly, a denser grove near a boulder provides a defensible space if needed. A safety perimeter is established by Turlough and his men. All of them are attentive to the slightest suspicious noise. During that time, Taliesanic talks with Aemonn and the triplets. He is preparing them for the throes of the battlefields. What will they find at the scene of the fighting? William asks: “Turlough, do you think we are being followed?” “Yes, I am afraid so. I think it is a question of time for them to get to us. I suspect Aemonn’s uncle will throw a fit and order a party of warriors to run after us.”

“Perhaps we could slow them down!” suggests Cedric. William nods his agreement and adds: “we can build traps wherever it's possible after our passage." Turlough finds it is a good idea, but it also has the disadvantage of confirming their direction and slowing them down. While Taliesanic and the girls are resting, Aemonn, Cedric, William and Turlough identify the inevitable passage they just crossed with difficulty. This is an ideal place to set a trap. The shrubs are taut, forcing the direction to take. Cedric points to the two mid-size trees coming out of the passage. "Hey! I think I have a plan." "We can sharpen the tips of rigid branches and cover them with mud. We attach them to a bigger branch that we pull back in such a manner that when the warrior comes out of the passage, he steps on a stick which sets the trap off. Then the tip penetrates the body violently and injures or kills the target depending on the point of impact. Generally, to neutralize a warrior, three regions of the body should be targeted: the legs, the pubic area and the upper chest.

Turlough is impressed by the simplicity of the setup and the probability of its efficiency. If people are pursuing them, it will be an element of surprise and incite all pursuers to greater caution. Consequently, this action will slow their pace. "Simple and probably very efficient," agrees Turlough. "Let's do it." Cedric, William, Turlough and three of his warriors work quickly and as quietly as possible. Taliesanic is protecting the girls. The rain is collaborating and camouflages the noise of the workers. Finally, the trap is in place.

"Where did you learn to set a trap," asks Aemonn. "We could use that kind of trap for the wild boars." "Yes, we can use it to hunt," explains Cedric. "That is why we learned it in the first place. Our grandfather and our uncle are great warriors in our world. They showed us how to survive in the forest and how to capture wild game for a meal."

Turlough observes these young strangers under Taliesanic's protection with admiration and respect. He thinks: "*So young yet so wise and well trained, Aemonn will benefit from their presence.*"

In the meantime, Sofia continues to question Quelf on how to communicate with plants. She explains: "Plants can communicate. Each has a way of telling you something. When you talk to the flowers you can sense that they are happy and responding. Sometimes it is the colour that appeals to you. Other times you feel it in your heart. All you need to do is pay attention in total respect. You will sense it. More so, plants can tell you how to use them to heal. Picking up a rampant plant[9] Quelf continues: take this plant; it is powerful against respiratory difficulty. When you chew the leaves, its juices will bring relief to your breathing difficulty. You can also use the pasta made with the leaves you chew to cure an infection or a wound that doesn't want to heal. You see, plants are alive and they can tell you how to use them."

Thus, Sofia is learning to use her gift of telepathy with plants. Quelf explains that this can also be done with animals. Sofia believes her. "My grandfather showed my brother Cedric how to communicate with a snake. Cedric had even patted the snake with his hand and the snake did not flee from him. The snake even left him a gift. The next day it had shed its entire skin and left it in sight for Cedric to find. It was at the same place he usually went to speak with it. As for my grandfather and my grandmother, they also talk to the trees and the plants."

"*Your grandparents, are they healers*?" asks Quelf telepathically, "I don't know," replies Sofia. "However, grandpa often calls grandma his White Witch." "Grandpa, grandma?" asks Quelf. "Yes, that's what we call our grandfather and our grandmother," says Sofia. "Ah!" says Quelf, smiling.

The group has been travelling for some time. The rain has ceased. Suddenly, in the distance, they hear a cry of distress followed by a scream of rage. Turlough nods approvingly and says: "We now know that we are being pursued and we are still far from Bellinderry Cove. They must have a good tracker. Let's find a good secure place to shelter the girls and set up an ambush." "The ford of the river near the three boulders seems to

---

[9] Glechoma hederacea, ramping plants.

me like a good appropriate place," suggests one of the young warriors who are accompanying them. "How far away is it Lian?" Asks Turlough. "Not very far, perhaps a dozen arrow shots away." "Then, go on ahead to make sure that we will not have any surprises and do a reconnaissance of the surroundings. We have no time to waste."

The Ambush

While the tracker is discussing with Colin, one warrior ventures into the grove to reconnoitre the restricted passageway before him. He bypasses the large boulder and when he displaces a shrub that is blocking the passageway, three popping sounds surprise him. "Touk! Touk! Touk!"

The time to realize that his shin is fractured, blood is pouring out of his two pierced thighs, whereas a stake crosses through the left side of his neck slipping close to the carotid artery. He isn't aware of the arrival of his companions alerted by his scream. He has lost consciousness.

Colin and the tracker realize that their adversaries can defend themselves. One warrior is detached from the group to take care of his companion while the others continue pursuing the fugitives, but with more caution.

--- OOO ---

Turlough is mindful that after having suffered the first injuries their pursuers will be even more determined to capture the fugitives. On reaching Lian he soon realizes that the place is difficult to access and may offer an opportunity for an ambush. He thinks: "*The position can possibly be bypassed. Nevertheless, the threat must be reduced and accordingly, the strength of our pursuers. It's important that we do not end up pinned between Colin's troops and the unknown threat that lies ahead of us.*"

Quickly, Turlough gives instructions. There is not enough time to set traps. However, the terrain offers some advantages to the defenders, particularly the high grounds. The attacker must climb a slope to attain their position. Additionally, the position offers protection for the defenders and little protection against projectiles for the attackers.

The serious injury suffered by a member of his group is an incentive for caution. Such prudence allowed foiling a second trap. In fact, this second trap, a huge log suspended by means of a thin strap strangely resembles the big boar traps he himself learned to make from his father as a teenager.

The tracker stops and asks for his leader, Colin, to join him. The tracker says uneasily: "Colin, I don't like crossing the ford here, look specially at the exit, it is an upward slope, the area is too quiet."

Colin agrees with the tracker. The place is well suited for an ambush. To save time they decide to treat the situation as if it was an ambush. Together they decide to divide their troop into two groups. "The tactic is to attack the fugitives on two fronts simultaneously," explains Colin. "We have the advantage; we have more warriors than them. One section will cross the river upstream to surprise them or at least make a significant enough diversion to weaken the defenders that could be waiting for us uphill."

Colin agrees with the section leader on a timing to enable them to cross the river, get into position and investigate the environment if possible. "It would be great if you could determine where and how the fugitives are set up. I will wait with my section for your signal before crossing the ford. This signal is the war cry that our clan uses. So, when you begin the attack let the Crumlin war cry terrorize them. When we hear the war cry, I will attack with the rest. Kill the warriors and capture the druid and the kids."

"If there is no ambush then send one of your men on the trail to notify us. So, we either attack on your war-cry signal or we move when you send us one of your men. While waiting for us to link up, you take position to protect our coming up the hill. We do not want to kill one another."

Colin reminds them of his father's order: "Do not harm the children. Mother would not forgive us nor my dad. God and all the men know that father is the clan leader. However, we all know that my father must contend with my mother's strong character."

--- OOO ---

Turlough observes the group on the other bank and wonders what is holding them back. They have been there for a long time. If the pursuit awaits daybreak, they will have lost the advantage of the night. Suddenly a clamour rises behind him at about two shots of arrows away, in the area where Taliesanic, Quelf and the girls await them with two guards.

Two cries of death make him understand that there is fighting at the rear. At the same time, those in front trigger their attack. Rapidly, the situation turns into a hand-to-hand combat and despite their courage, Aemonn, Cedric and William are finally disarmed.

Turlough and his last two men are surrounded by six warriors. These warriors remain alert and at a safe distance from Turlough. Six other warriors now join Colin who stands close to Aemonn. They have the three sisters with them. They are safe and sound.

Colin ties up Aemonn with arrogance and brutality. Two warriors tie respectively Cedric and William. William is gasping for air. Cedric immediately coaches William transmitting with calm: "*William be calm ... breathe slowly ... respect your rhythm ... breathe in ... breathe out... That's it... Keep going... Super don't lose your confidence ... don't let your confidence go away. Remember LYKA said we will be alright...*"

Turlough and his two injured men are disarmed and tied up.

Colin has lost six men and two others are injured. Taliesanic, Quelf and Sofia are missing. They ran away in the vicinity.

Cedric and William sense Sofia's presence nearby. She is repeatedly transmitting to them to stay calm. Taliesanic and

Quelf are protecting them. Cedric hears and understands Sofia's message. He has confidence in his sister. "*I hear you Sofia. I continue helping William who is regaining his breath. We will remain as calm as possible. Colin's warriors are big and brutal. We have killed several of them. Aemonn, Turlough and his warriors are being roughed up. Colin jostles Sinead roughly while Ciara and Aisling weep. Please do something quickly; I do not know how long they can stand it.*"

Colin's companions continue to shamelessly brutalize Turlough and his companions. Turlough flinches when he is hit yet he remains silent.

Aemonn defies Colin who ignores him. "Try me instead of my sister. Tackling a girl is only for weaklings and cowards. Untie me and see if you can best me."

Colin continues to ignore Aemonn. William rages at seeing Sinead thus treated. However, Sinead says nothing. She merely stares Colin in the eyes. William observes Sinead, defiant, showing her disdain for her cousin. This attitude arouses William's admiration and Colin's aggressiveness.

--- OOO ---

Taliesanic, Quelf and Sofia closely follow the events. They read the minds of everyone and anticipate their next move. "*Cedric, William, transmits Sofia, be ready, we are going to get you out of there.*"

Cedric and William heard the message and don't know what to expect. However, they trust their sister who never would have conveyed this message without reason.

"*Taliesanic, Quelf and Sofia heard our distress call,*" thinks William. "*I remember grandpa's teachings: 'As a soldier, when in a difficult situation, it pays to remain discreet, not to attract attention and above all, not provoke, even when one is pushed and shoved around with brutality. An opportunity always arises and it's important to remain attentive to fully seize it.' I think Turlough is doing exactly what grandpa was suggesting.*"

The opportunity is created when Taliesanic pronounces a temporary immobilization spell and Colin's group freezes in place the time needed to free the prisoners and disappear without their realizing what happened. Everything happens so fast. Aemonn and his sisters, Turlough and his men, together with Cedric and William have their bonds disappear by magic. Liberated, they run for the bushes towards Taliesanic who greets them.

--- OOO ---

Colin's men take quite a while to regain their thoughts. They have difficulty remembering what they are doing in the woods, in the rain. The tracker cannot detect a trace that might indicate the direction to take. It takes time for Colin and his group to get their wits together and remember they are after his cousin and his party. They remember the fighting and the losses. Colin asks astounded: "Where are the prisoners… What happened… They cannot have vanished… This is not possible… I am dreaming… Please wake me up somebody."

No one can answer. Pursuit is not possible. There is no indication of a direction to follow.

Taliesanic maintains his spell. Later, at daybreak, Colin, frustrated, tired is losing patience. He despatches four of his warriors: "I want you to circle around the emplacement to find possible tracks. It is not possible for a group of nine people to move about without leaving any tracks. Now go."

Taliesanic continues to maintain his spell. No sign can be detected. He keeps in contact with the tracker and Colin's thoughts. He inundates them with irrelevant information, sowing disarray.

Meanwhile, Aemonn and his party are still moving towards Bellinderry Cove. The party is moving within a more discreet footpath under the close protection of Turlough and his remaining two warriors. The warriors are injured but can provide some help to defend the party when and if needed. Sofia, Cedric, William and Sinead are also prepared to fight, if necessary.

Aemonn's companions are grateful to Taliesanic's undeniable magical authority.

Colin convinces his tracker to identify a probable and safe track that Aemonn's group might follow to reach Bellinderry Cove. Then he and his acolytes resume the search for the fugitives. This time their intentions are more warlike.

--- OOO ---

The Test of Courage

"I want to know what happened to my father, to my family, I will go alone if necessary!" insists Aemonn. Turlough, authoritative says: "We will in due course. For now we are walking blindly and we must get information to make a plan. Think Aemonn! This is not a hunting game! The dangers are real and we need to know what is happening in the village before we make a move. Your friends and Taliesanic will help us."

Taliesanic remains watchful and silent while the search for information is being organized. The two wounded warriors are to remain with the three sisters. Quelf and Taliesanic, both in a meditative attitude, guide Sofia through telepathic messages. Sofia communicates messages to and from Aemonn. Turlough, with Cedric and William, move around the hamlet in a different direction from Aemonn's. The interactive telepathic ability of the triplets enables the sharing of information between the two reconnaissance groups.

An action plan will be developed once they know more of the situation they face.

Cautiously, under the cover of foliage, Turlough and the boys rapidly progress up to the outskirts of the village. They note and transmit to their sister their observations on the destruction they see. They also transmit the invaders' activities as they observe them. "As my grandfather says, 'time spent on reconnaissance is never wasted'" whispers Cedric to Turlough. Turlough smiles: "Your grandfather must be a great warrior … good and relevant information reduces risk and mistakes."

Turlough signals to the boys to keep low and observe the site of the old mill near the river: "*Several warriors are discussing by the river. They appear to be resting near the mill, transmits Cedric. Turlough believes that the members of his clan have well defended themselves because there are many injured invaders; it's not a pretty site. Everybody seems tired. They are either confidant or negligent, because we can see only one sentry near the mill. However, they all have weapons at hand. They are impressive,*" continues Cedric.

Sofia acknowledges the information, informs Aemonn and in turn transmits: "*The women and children are in an enclosure with the goats. Six warriors are watching them. We cannot see the centre of the Hamlet; however, there seems to be a lot of activity there. Aemonn wants to get closer to see.*" William reacts and transmits, worried: "*Sofia, I don't like this. You're taking too many risks.*" "*Don't worry, Will, I'm with Aemonn. He's very skilled. He knows what he's doing. We are already in the village.*" "*Shit!*" mutters William.

While each group progresses, and obtains information, Taliesanic maintains his meditative attitude. Quelf reassures Aemonn's sisters and the two guards remain watchful, silent.

Quelf is also attentive to the transmissions amongst the triplets. "There he is," whispers Aemonn, pointing a finger to a group of weary men, sitting on the ground, their hands tied up in their back, staring at two fires where bodies are piled. He adds, worried, "I don't see my brothers."

Bodies of fallen warriors are burning in the two fires.

Warriors, both victors and vanquished, observe in silence, respectful, despite the smell of burning flesh that is spreading and racks the stomach.

Sofia perceives the anger rising in her companion. Only one idea occupies the mind of the young warrior, to free his father. She reads his thoughts and observes that Aemonn is about to commit a risky action. Telepathically, she seeks Taliesanic's assistance.

By thought, Taliesanic finally cools off Aemonn's temper.

Turlough, Cedric, William, Sofia and Aemonn continue to note all the information likely to help plan the next steps. The reconnaissance completed, they all return to Taliesanic's location.

--- OOO ---

Turlough, Cedric, William, Aemonn, Sofia and the two guards note everyone's observations and assess the situation.

Aemonn insists on going back to free his father and as many warriors as possible. His father has been moved into the building adjacent to the old forge. Only two guards are on watch. Most of the warriors are at the market place waiting to bargain amongst themselves the spoils they looted. The invader chieftain has yet to give the signal to begin sharing the spoils.

"We must act quickly if we want to free them. Tomorrow at dawn they may be gone. Now is the time to act," insists Aemonn.

"Let's wait a little longer, it will soon be night, it will be easier. Besides, we don't know where our pursuers are," recommends Turlough, with respect and the confidence that emerges from a life of fighting.

The triplets, in a common gesture, their hands outstretched, palms facing the ground, beckon everyone to be silent. "Taliesanic is transmitting us that a detachment of three scout warriors advances towards us," whispers Cedric. "They come from the hamlet and can't see us thanks to the protective dome that Taliesanic is maintaining," adds Sofia.

William, just like Aemonn, puts his hand on his knife. Quickly, Turlough takes the lead of the group. Together they get organized to surprise and capture the three warriors. Turlough, his two warriors and the three boys are in position and are waiting for the signal. Turlough will give the signal to surprise the enemy as best as possible. All of them are tense, watchful.

--- OOO ---

The surprise is total. Within moments, the three scouts are disarmed, tied up and gagged. One of them lies unconscious.

The prisoners remain taciturn. They stare at their captors unafraid. Turlough hesitates: "Having prisoners changes the plan. The prisoners must be guarded. The resources are limited and killing the prisoners is not an acceptable option." Taliesanic intervenes: "*Keep to the plan. Do not be concerned with the prisoners. We do not need guards. Now go.*"

Indeed, Quelf offers the prisoners herbal beverage to drink. The guards are now sound asleep and bonded.

--- OOO ---

The hamlet is relatively quiet. The women and children are still in the same pen. On the square, fires are glowing and illuminate the loot. The warriors are watching. The sharing has not been done yet. The guards would execute anyone who would dare approach it without authorization. For now, it belongs to the leader and he will determine who gets what share.

Aemonn finally removes a rotten plank and creeps quietly into the old forge. Scrubs close by are hiding his movements and actions. Meanwhile, Turlough and his two warriors are in position to protect, if need be, their leader Shane, Aemonn and the others at the time of their evasion. Cedric and William observe a group of invaders who are resting. They transmit all activity to Sofia. She is crouched in the shrubs outside the forge. She observes the two guards at the entrance. She is attentive to any noise that may signal trouble. The two guards appear to be asleep for the moment.

Rapidly and quietly, Aemonn soon frees his father and a few other prisoners. He passes his knife and that of Sofia around. The warriors free the person next to them so that soon, twenty warriors, members of the Bellinderry clan, escape in silence. Turlough and his men protect them and make sure there is no pursuit.

Sofia accompanies Aemonn. She admires the determination, the passion and the composure of this young warrior. Aemonn is happy to have found his father and sad at not finding his brothers. "Father, where are my brothers?" asks Aemonn, worried at the answer to come. "Aemonn, the body of your brothers are in the fire. They fought with courage, and like many others have sacrificed their life to allow several others to escape into the woods. You can be proud of them as I am."

Shane remains silent and melancholic for a moment. He then adds, placing his two strong hands on his son's shoulders and looking him in the eyes: "I am also very proud of you, your courage and your determination. Someday, you will be an excellent leader for our clan."

Aemonn weeps for his brothers. Vengeance rumbles within him.

--- OOO ---

Shane and his men fabricate weapons. These weapons will suffice until they retrieve their own in the spoils of the invaders. Aemonn and Taliesanic inform Shane, the Bellinderry clan leader, of the events and especially the reactions of his brother-in-law, Finian Crumlin and his son Colin. "We will deal with them in due time, for now, let's see what we can learn from those three," says Shane, pointing to the three prisoners who have awakened, surprised to see the troop around them.

Sofia and Quelf converse in private. Sofia is attentive to everything Quelf says to her. The two women are aware of living a magical moment that will mark their future. Sofia is getting attached to this woman. She cannot explain the special bond she feels for this woman. Quelf's gaze penetrates deep inside her. It's as if this woman could read within all her cells. And yet, she doesn't feel invaded. Quite the contrary, she perceives an immense respect. Sofia cannot define the joy, the happiness of being in the presence of this druidess. Quelf's energy nourishes her.

Taliesanic ignores Shane's question regarding these strange teenagers who speak their language. The explanations of his son and Turlough are not enough. He directly questions the man who was his mentor and guide during his youth. He has full confidence in Taliesanic, in his judgment.

Before answering, Taliesanic regroups Quelf, Sofia, Cedric, William, Shane and Aemonn. Turlough goes to organize a perimeter defence. "I have been waiting for the visit of these children for a long time," begins Taliesanic. "Many years ago, they were presented to me by the Gods in a dream. The Gods of our Celtic tradition were present: the mother Goddess Danu; the hero God Lugh, poet and magician warrior; 'the good god' Dagda, the prodigy; the god of death and king of magicians Balor; the god leader of the underworld Mider; the Celtic Goddess of battles Morrigan; and 'the son of the oceans and God of the sea and fertility Manannan MacLir."[10]

"The Gods showed me over a millennium of battles, of suffering for the children of Eire. They showed me how the children of our children would spill over the lands of exile and populate the earth, most often in suffering. They unveiled the cavalcade of the angels of light who will free man from his chains, from the darkness where his pride, his cupidity, his lack of love placed him. They told me how these three children, born of a single conception, would free the god Manannan MacLir, mounted on his lighted chariot drawn by white horses, travelling over the raging ocean and appease it in passing and leaving Lugh radiate his love and peace over the Earth."

"These children are messengers of the school of Gods, who are to ultimately accomplish their mission when the day comes. They are our guests and our guides," concludes Taliesanic in a solemn tone. Taliesanic looks affectionately at the triplets, fascinated by what they have just heard.

---

[10] Celtic Gods, Wikipedia

"*Whew!*" emits Sofia, impressed. "*School of Gods! Me, I want to go to grandpa and grandma's home,*" reflects William. "*It's not finished,*" responds Cedric telepathically. "*The dragons talked to us about a teaching that the druid must transmit us, we should not forget that. Anyway, we are protected.*" "*Indeed, you have other situations to live before your return,*" mentally transmits Taliesanic to the three Corribus children.

Cedric, William and Sofia observe the druid attentively.

Shane remains pensive. Aemonn looks intently at Sofia. She is unable to detect the young warrior's thought. Nevertheless, she feels a thrill at the back of her neck. She feels herself blushing. She looks away, uncomfortable.

--- OOO ---

Quelf tells the druid and Shane about the vision she had in a dream. This dream completes Taliesanic's vision. She now knows. She knows what she must accomplish. She knows her destiny.

Calm, serene, with the support of Taliesanic, her mentor, she convinces Shane, the clan leader, to go to the invaders so as to present her vision to their leader.

For her the stars do not lie.

The scouts, who are prisoners, will accompany the clan leader Shane, the druid Taliesanic, the druidess and healer Quelf, three bodyguards and the triplets. Aemonn protests vehemently. "Father, I want to be with you. It's my right!" says Aemonn, refusing all of his father's arguments. "Aemonn, that's enough!" cuts Shane with authority! "You are the continuity of our clan and wisdom dictates that you are not to be with me for this meeting."

Shane, unwavering, in front of his men, orders his son to stay out of the village until he is invited to enter therein. He adds: "The survival of the clan, the safety of the women and children who are prisoners depend on it." Then turning to his master of arms:

"Turlough, I order you to make sure that my son doesn't disobey me. I'll signal you with three long sounds of horns if your presence is needed. And if any misfortune should happen to me, you know what to do to help Aemonn."

"The protection of the clan is what matters most to me. Protect our clan against the invaders and against the Crumlin clan or any other clan. Is that clear?" Shane looks in turn at his son, Turlough and his warriors who with a nod of the head confirm they understand. Confident and proud, Shane sets off with his small group and the freed scouts.

The Agreement

At daybreak, the alert sounds with a lot of rackets. Orlaf, leader of the invaders, a giant with muscular arms, shakes his warriors still sleeping. His bare chest is adorned with numerous scars, evidence of his ardour in combat.

Twelve people stand in front of him. He scrutinizes the impassive faces of his disarmed scouts. He now focuses on the four armed warriors standing proudly, one of them strangely resembles the clan leader, his prisoner, a druid, a druidess and three children stand behind the warriors... "By Odin! What is this?" Bawls Orlaf.

A command, a runner, a hubbub, a sheepish-looking guard, confirms to him that his prisoner and the free and armed man before him are the same person. His initial astonishment quickly turns to rage. Orlaf grabs the sheepish guard by the neck, stares at him with burning eyes and with his knife marks the warrior's face.

Shane, his men, the druid, the druidess and the children remain dignified and impassive. The warriors quickly surround them.

Orlaf's scout leader, his right knee flexed in a sign of submission before his leader, explains that this clan leader wants to speak to him under the protection of the Gods.

His big axe in hand, Orlaf advances menacing. The two leaders eye one another scornfully. The silence is cruel.

The triplets capture the disconcerted and bellicose thoughts of the warriors present. They see Taliesanic, Shane and his guards, proud and confident, displaying no provocative action, simply attentive and imperturbable.

"By Odin! What is going on?" thinks Orlaf. *"This aphid of a leader was my prisoner. He managed to escape somehow. The guards will have some explaining to do ... and then this old man with his stick looking at me ... and this woman holding her pouch, she seems to me to be stronger than she looks ... and these three-young people with no weapons, who are they? They are not from here... This is not normal."*

Then aloud, he addresses Shane: "You are either an unconscious brave man or a lunatic to come back here, especially with an old man, a woman and children," starts Orlaf threatening.

"The man's name is Taliesanic, he is our druid," answers Shane calmly and confidently. "In our tradition, this druid is the wisest of the wise men; he is a messenger of our Gods and an advisor of kings. This woman is called Quelf. She is a priestess healer, according to our traditions. Both were aware of your coming and wish to speak to you. They have a message to deliver to you. It is in your best interest to listen to them."

Cedric, William and Sofia, under Taliesanic's protection, observe, listen, wait and remain as discreet as possible. They capture the emotions around them.

Orlaf takes a step back. The tension decreases a little.

The invader warriors are nervous. In their country, they fear sorcerers and priests who communicate with their Gods. No king ignores them. Often, one wonders if it's not they who direct the people. They are so feared, heard and listened to. The leaders consult with them before leaving on an expedition. And these two, here present, bear an assurance that they have never witnessed before.

Orlaf, hesitant, examines Taliesanic from head to toe then makes eye contact with him. Both remain impassive. One can feel Orlaf's tension vanishing. No one moves. The silence is astounding.

Orlaf backs up further maintaining eye contact with Taliesanic. Suddenly, with a quick movement of his hand, he orders his men to back off and slacken their guard. Orlaf turns to Shane "I invite you and your delegation to follow my escort."

Calmly, with a nod Shane accepts and heads for the Hamlet council hut. The hut is a large room where Shane normally holds his meetings and where he provides his justice.

Arrogant, Orlaf takes the seat that Shane would usually claim. Shane does not take up the affront. He merely invites Taliesanic to speak. Taliesanic, in a second state, unveils to Orlaf, personal information that very few people know: information from before their departure from the island of ice that this man couldn't possibly know.

"By Odin! May Thor take me! How could this man have gotten this information? By what witchcraft...? Do the Gods really speak to this man," Orlaf questions himself? Taliesanic continues to describe his vision of Orlaf's past ordeals. Then, he recounts the ordeals ahead that both peoples, his own and that of Orlaf, must live.

Orlaf asks: "How can I believe everything you are saying?" Taliesanic, turning to Quelf says: "Tell him."

In turn, Quelf recounts her vision. She describes the periods of war and of peace. She describes how, over the years, the blood of her people will mingle with that of the northern people, in the fighting and in the family, how entire colonies of peoples of the North will become established in Ireland to live their traditions, adapted to the ways and customs of the Eire. Quelf concludes: "In short, the ancestors are asking me to go with you and your men to your country that will become mine. I will leave with a group that our leader will choose, and you, you will choose a group who will stay with my people. In this way, we shall learn from each other. Many of your warriors will come to settle in this country, to fight herein, but also to develop trade. Your culture will join that of our country and ours, yours."

"Your people and my people will experience long periods of peace and prosperity. I will care for your warriors, I will teach the medicinal power of plants to your women. I will be an active member of your clan."

"She is going to live in the Northern Islands," reflects Sofia, surprised at what she is hearing. *"I don't know what we're doing here,"* admits William, his eyes open wide, fascinated by the gesture she is posing. *"She is going to live with the enemy of her people!" "We will speak with Taliesanic, for now, let's observe and listen,"* communicates Cedric, as flabbergasted as his brother and sister.

From questions to answer, the discussion continues a long time. An agreement takes form and is concluded.

--- OOO ---

Meanwhile, Aemonn waits in the company of Turlough. The latter has organized a perimeter of defence in case of attack. So as to prevent a surprise attack, he has also placed sentinels to protect the access to their waiting site. The general orders are to remain silent and wait for their clan leader Shane's orders.

"Ah! I'm tired of waiting," observes Aemonn. *"What can be happening in the village? What can they be discussing? Why did we not attack? After all, these men killed my brothers and several members of our clan. And then father who orders my exclusion. How can I learn to become leader when I'm kept at a distance? And Turlough who's always at my heels..."*

Aggressive thoughts torment the future leader, when one of the sentries warns Turlough of the arrival of a group of a dozen men from the Crumlin clan. They approach cautiously, weapons in hand.

Turlough was anticipating this eventuality. That is why he had chosen this discreet and easily defensible area to rest his people and await any developments. The location enables to respond to the threat of the Crumlin clan coming from the undergrowth, or invaders from the village. While the leader's son was sulking, entirely in his thoughts, he had discreetly prepared his group to this eventuality.

Careful not to create a situation where he would be caught up in a fight on two fronts, the invaders and the Crumlin, he opts for wisdom and decides to bluff and impress their pursuers. With Aemonn whom he quickly informs, he chooses ten men to stand before the enemy. The others will make noise by moving around to simulate that they are far more numerous.

Colin and his group have just come through a grove and wind up in a clearer space, when in front of him, emerge Aemonn, Turlough and several Bellinderry warriors. To his right and to his left he hears and perceives movement. "The Crumlin are not welcome on our territory, especially with weapons in hand," threatens Turlough firmly. "Go home, standing, of your own accord or lying down, feet first, when we are done with you. Which is your choice?"

"Where do their reinforcements come from?" thinks, Colin. "*Already, those that I see are as numerous as we are... How many are there in the bushes around us? Do they have spears and arrows? By Balor*[11]*, the risk is too great, the situation is too uncertain, we may die here.*

Colin straightens up and after a long moment of hesitation, replaces his sword in its sheath. His men do the same. His furious gaze never leaves his cousin Aemonn, who defies him, sword in hand.

Aemonn, Turlough and their men watch the Crumlin depart towards their territory. "I think we will live another period of battles with our dear neighbours," murmurs Turlough between his teeth. "Yeah, and this time, we will not be the fugitives" ... answers Aemonn, chest thrown out, proud of his response.

---

[11] Balor, Celtic God of death and king of magicians, Wikipedia

Three grave and prolonged horn blows reach them from the village.

--- OOO ---

The warriors of the north and those of the Bellinderry clan are gathered in the main square of the village. The tension remains high between the two camps. Everyone respects the orders of their leader. They keep their weapons down. Any quarrel or misbehaviour will see the culprits executed by their respective leader.

The two leaders reach an agreement. They are now discussing how to design their relationship in the future: which treatment to give to the respective warriors who will be living with the other camp; what tribute will be awarded to the people of the North; what role will be given to the druidess Quelf; what types commercial relations and reciprocal protection are to be put in place… In short, the history of power relations between two peoples is already initiated. A history of exchanges, wars, domination and turmoil has begun. It will end only in the eleventh century.

--- OOO ---

While the leaders deliberate, Taliesanic, Quelf, Sofia, William and Cedric withdraw into the forest. They are in the clearing of the great Sacred Derve, near the junction of the two rivers. There, they will spend the night. The next day, when the sun is at its zenith, Quelf will leave Bellinderry Cove with the warriors of the North.

--- OOO ---

The Celtic Initiation

The fire illuminates and warms Taliesanic and his small group. The moon, completely round, observes, a silent witness to a solemn moment. All of them are seated on the foliage, on the bare ground. Taliesanic is leaning against the old oak tree, his stick to his right and a sheep hide in front of him. On the hide, there are two golden billhooks, some herbs and a white quartz stone that shines in the moonlight, a falcon bird's wing and some sage powder.

Quelf is seated to the right of Taliesanic. She also has a sheep hide before her. On this hide, there are: a white swan feather, some medicinal herbs tied in small bundles, three sachets of powder and a blue chalcedony stone. Taliesanic invites Sofia to sit to his left, while Cedric takes his place to the right of Quelf, and William sits between Cedric and his sister. Everyone observe and listen carefully to Taliesanic.

The wise man, now in a trance, silently transmits: "The earth is like a fortress. Even the hosts of heaven cannot establish order, justice and peace on Earth because these entities are not made of physical matter. They don't have any power to act. It is the humans themselves who must offer them the possibility."

"On Earth, humans have another type of power, the power to choose. They can open to light or withdraw into darkness. If they want to resist to light, then the darkness will have the entire place. In order for the armies of Light to penetrate into this fortress, it is necessary that inside, someone open them at least one door. Do you understand?"

The triplets nod affirmatively. Taliesanic continues: “Never will the Earth be invested from the exterior by the heavenly hosts. It is necessary that from inside, beings open up breaches in the ramparts with love and light so that the heavenly hosts may enter.”

“For a very long … a long time … messengers from heaven have been announcing us the return of the Light. This light will be there only when enough beings have chosen and asked the hosts of heaven to come and bring peace, order and justice. You four, Quelf, Sofia, Cedric and William, you’re part of the plans of the Gods.” William asks, astonished: “Plans of the Gods?” “Yes, plans of the Gods,” answers Taliesanic, turning to William, “and this plan will be spread out over a thousand years. You and your brother will need to protect your sister. She will open one of the portals to allow the hosts of heaven to come and help us.”

“Protect me from what?” questions Sofia, worried. “There are generous and good people in the world. However, there are also greedy, malicious and cruel people. They live in the shadows, in darkness. When there's more darkness, greedier people take advantage. Those people will cause wars, great destruction and much suffering. Multiple massacres will take place in God’s name … but it will always be for the benefit of cruel and greedy men.”

The children look at Taliesanic in awe. “You are from a world in the future… You already know this. You know I speak the truth.”

Cedric visualizes his history class: crusades, inquisitions, invasions, genocide, world wars… William, anxious questions: “And, what should we do in all this?” “Don’t worry, you will be ready and strong in due course.” Taliesanic continues: “Your passing in this land of your ancestors is very important for you, for us, for Quelf and her descendents.

Numerous events will prepare you. You will experiment in different worlds, go through hardships and live moments of grace. Through them, you will discover your roots, strengthen your blood and purify your mind." Turning towards his sister Sofia, William asks: "What does he mean?"

Taliesanic looks at William and continues: "We are all artisans, builders, and in our own way, we are preparing the return of Light and Peace to this world of ours."

"You are with me because the messengers of heaven asked me to prepare you, to teach you how to protect yourself, to feel the energies around you. The more you are capable of feeling energies, the more you'll be able to hear and interpret the thoughts of others. You must also learn to protect yourselves from the intrusions of others into your thoughts."

Taliesanic, silent, remains in a meditative state. Quelf, attentive, perceives the triplet's emotions and transmits to them: "*Have confidence. You are surrounded by magic ... you have your dragons... You will be guided and supported by exceptional beings through every stage of evolution you have to complete in the years to come.*"

The tension drops amongst the children.

--- OOO ---

Taliesanic and Quelf exploit the rest of the day and the evening to complete the triplets training. Cedric, William and Sofia are attentive. They receive the teachings that are intended for them. Thus, from explanations to exercises, they reinforce their gift of telepathy and their capacity to feel energies. Quelf also teaches them to communicate with plants, to ask the right question and feel the answers.

The children are impressed. As they dance around the fire, they feel the energy from the air which feeds their chakra. Their movements executed in thin air give the impression of being in water. They feel the pressure, the displacement, the heat and the freshness caused by the movement. It's magic. They learn, motionless, to listen and feel the energies around them. They experience how to feel each other's energy, their actual or simulated emotions. In the dark of the forest that surrounds them, they guess their positions. The children are enthusiastic and eager for knowledge and skills. They hear in their head the voice of Taliesanic: "*Coucou ! Where am I*?"

No visual or energy contact. The children may well scan the surrounding area and even the tree branches, nothing. They don't perceive anything. They see nothing. Quelf, who accompanies them, smiles heartily. She knows her mentor. He likes to play tricks while also teaching. "*Come join me.*" Taliesanic allows the children to detect him.

The children orient themselves and perceive the druid's energy at less than fifty paces. He is sitting on a large oak branch and delightfully observes the children who rapidly move towards him. "What did you do to block us, to prevent us from reading you?" Sofia, questions Taliesanic both amazed and curious. "I'll teach you how," answers Taliesanic, all smiles.

--- OOO ---

Midnight, Taliesanic takes the children near the great Derve. The triplets observe. The moonlight is impressive. Fireflies are dancing in the glade and amongst the trees. "*They look like fairies… It is magic*," thinks Sofia.

Taliesanic speaks an unknown language, interspersed with raucous sounds and deliberate movements. His attention is focused on Quelf, kneeling before him. Several logs have been consumed. The children observe fascinated.

Suddenly, Taliesanic imposes his hands on Quelf's head. Then, all smiles, he helps her to stand before him. Quelf stands before Taliesanic. He gives her a very ceremonial hug. In a sacred gesture, with both hands, Taliesanic presents a golden billhook to Quelf while uttering a magic spell. Quelf is radiant.

The children maintain a respectful and appreciative silence.

--- OOO ---

While the boys are resting and the dawn drags on in the horizon, Quelf and Sofia discuss by the fire. “Sofia, there is a part of my vision that concerns you personally … my voices told me to keep a part of this vision for you alone. I am asking you to lock your telepathic channel on me.”

Sofia diverts her eyes from the fire and turns respectfully towards Quelf. Quelf looks at her with intense emotions. With a slow and respectful nod of the head, Sofia signals her attention. Solemnly, Quelf relates: “I have seen you liberate Manannan MacLir, son of the Oceans and his army of Angels of Light. I have seen you, with the help of your brothers, open the portal. Yes, I have seen you succeed, not without some difficulty though. You will experience sufferings in your heart and it’s these sufferings that will give you the courage you need to defeat the darkness. You were born of the stars and you are guided by the Gods.”

Dipping into her pouch, Quelf brings out an acorn, polished like a jewel: “You see this Derve that is sheltering us. It originated from a grain like this one. I am handing it to you and I call upon the Stars to make the Sacred Derve grow within you, with righteousness, courage and generosity. The day will come when you know how to accommodate and protect the beings that will come to you.”

Stunned, Sofia does not know what to say. She doesn’t grasp the full impact of Quelf’s words. In a flash, she reviews her three years of teachings with grandma, grandpa, Patrick and Ming. She remembers the prophecy concerning her brothers and herself. She knows in her heart that this is a moment of truth for her. Her destiny is taking form. The druidess confirms her intuition. However much remains unknown to Sofia.

Sofia accepts this gift with deference. She clutches the acorn in her left hand and brings it to her heart. Then affectionately she snuggles in Quelf’s arm, who welcomes her tenderly. A tear runs down Sofia’s cheek.

--- OOO ---

Taliesanic greets the rising sun, and then meditates.

The triplets share with Taliesanic and Quelf the dried fruit in their knapsacks. After this frugal meal, Taliesanic moves near the fire and spreads his supple sheep hide in front of him. He pulls a small leather sack out of the pouch he carries on his belt close to the golden billhook. This billhook never leaves him. With a quick movement, Taliesanic spreads stones on the hide, his improvised tray.

William is astonished. He notices that the flat stones from his magic pouch strangely resemble those before him on the hide belonging to Taliesanic.

The druid is now looking at him with affection. "The ancients call these stones runes. They carry the tradition of the people of the land of ice. They were given to me by a wise man. Some time ago, my messengers asked me to bury three of them at the foot of the Sacred Derve and that these stones would be returned to me when the time is right. Last night my messengers showed me all the runes gathered together."

Taliesanic observes William who timidly puts his hand in his pouch and takes out the three missing stones. The three of them are fascinated. How did those buried stones end up in William's pouch?

"It is magic!" exclaims Sofia. "It is also a teaching of the Gods!" declares Taliesanic. "It's a sign to make us believe that we are not dreaming!" says Cedric, impressed. "Phew! How is this possible?" asks William, disconcerted.

Taliesanic explains extensively to the children and Quelf the significance of these stones in the daily belief of the peoples of the North. One should note that the secret of the runes can only be unveiled to those who practise the art of divination. Only an initiate can use them wisely. Taliesanic concludes by placing all the runes in the pouch.

Taliesanic turns to Quelf and gives her the small leather pouch while uttering these words: "These stones are now ready to return to serve the people living in the land of ice. Quelf, these stones are now yours. They acknowledge your vibration and you will know how to hear and understand their messages. They bear their original wisdom enriched with our Celtic wisdom. Both wisdom will accompany you always."

The Dragonfly

The reconstruction of the Bellinderry village is ongoing since the departure of the warriors of the North. They left three days ago.

Orlaf chose well his ambassadors to integrate into Bellinderry community. His men work actively, with energy and strength. They are strong and do not fear the toil. Shayne, the Celtic leader, as Orlaf, the Northman leader, has pledged to treat their guests with respect and integrate them within their respective clan.

Quelf is "en route" for the land of ice. Sofia feels an enormous grief. She cannot control her tears. She sobs and finds this separation difficult to live. She thinks, suffocating with pain: "*Yet another loss, one more in my life. I am only twelve years old and already my heart is bruised like a woman of fifty!*" She asks Taliesanic, her heart full of bitterness and desolation: "Why is the universe picking on me?" The druid comes closer and softly, silently, like a loving grandfather, puts his firm yet supple arms around her.

Sofia wants to see her grandparents. They would know what to do and what to say on such occasion. They are so good for her and her brothers. Sofia can take no more. She snuggles in Taliesanic's arms. "The pain is so strong I think my heart will blow up in my chest. It hurts!" "Take your time to get through your pain. It is present like a red iron that burns you. It will fade away with time. For the moment remain in my arms and breathe slowly," says Taliesanic with compassion.

Taliesanic breathes in tempo with Sofia, in silence. Sofia appreciates the safety of his arms. She knows… She is not alone. Moments pass. She withdraws from his arms. The pain is simmering. Her eyes say thank you. Taliesanic holds her hands tenderly. He knows he can talk to her now, she will understand.

"My dear child, I understand your pain. It stems from within your heart. It can only be healed with time. All the losses and separations that life puts on your path will be roses of pain and sorrow. Those roses will build your heart with strength. It is in sacrifice that the Earth will bear new fruit of love and peace. You are chosen to make a difference. Through your mission, you will bring relief to the suffering of your fellow humans."

Sofia hears his words, but does not grasp the scope of Taliesanic's message. She misses Quelf's advice. She misses her druidess friend, counselor and teacher. Someplace within herself, Sofia feels that she is bonded by blood to Quelf. It is inexplicable, however, her intuition, that little voice, incites her to believe in that blood ties she has with Quelf. "Taliesanic, I don't understand. I feel I have a strong bond with Quelf. I feel like her blood is flowing within me. My intuition tells me so. And now she is gone… Please, Taliesanic help me understand." "This bond exists. One day it will become clear to you. For the time being, believe in your intuition, it is your greatest ally!"

Sofia breathes deeply. Her chest, so contracted since Quelf's departure, relaxes.

--- OOO ---

The three boys come in rushing towards Sofia and Taliesanic. Cedric, boisterous: "Morning Taliesanic! Morning Sis! Sofia! What's up? You look awful… What happened? Did you lose something? I have never seen you like this since mom died!"

Aemonn, Cedric and William are baffled by Sofia's state of mind. They know her as a strong person, one with a warrior attitude. They don't know what to do, what to say or what to think. Aemonn consults Cedric and William. "What's going on with Sofia?" whispers Aemonn, intrigued by the emotional state of the young woman. "I think you should go and talk to her!" says William. "After all, in her eyes, you are the warrior that fascinates her."

Aemonn blushes on hearing William's comment. "You think I can do something for her?" he asks, surprised at William's request. "Me, actually, I don't know a great deal about talking to women." "Woman! He already calls her 'woman,'" think Cedric and William simultaneously. *"Wow! thinks William, my sister a woman! She still has a long way to go."*

--- OOO ---

Sofia is looking for her dragonfly brooch. She can't find it on herself or in her pouch. She especially doesn't want to awaken suspicion in her two brothers. She doesn't remember at what moment she could have lost it. She doesn't want to live, under any pretext, in this Celtic environment. Even though her heart beats wildly for Aemonn, she doesn't accept to be stuck in time. It's very difficult for Sofia to feel stuck. It's like taking away all her freedom of action, her freedom to think and to act. *"Where could I have lost my brooch?"*

Taliesanic hears her question. He knows whom to contact so as to end Sofia's uneasiness. He says: "Go to the edge of the river, near the mill. Someone will render you your jewel that is lost or borrowed."

Sofia, clenching her fists thinks within herself: "*I would not have lost it! Who would do that to me? William can do that just to provoke me. If it's him...*"

She heads at a run to the river, furious. She is preparing her revenge against William. At the river, she sees no one. Sofia sits on the rock near the mill. As she watches the water flowing and she thinks how much her life is like this water. The movements of water remind her of her turmoil. She cries softly. She leans over to pick up a stone when she hears Aemonn coming behind her at a running pace: "Sofia... Sofia... Sofia ... are you OK?" He approaches with caution.

Sofia turns around swiftly and lets her wrath explode: "Where is my brooch? You're the thief? It's you that stole my brooch, my dragonfly? I thought it was William, who was again playing a trick on me… No, but who do you think you are?" She yells at him. She approaches Aemonn with both fists raised, ready to hit him. "Come on, answer me!" Shouts Sofia, gripping him by his tunic.

Stepping back two paces, surprised, Aemonn thinks: "*The women of our clan don't speak like that to men!*" "*Well, if the women of your clan don't say what they think, it's completely the opposite for my own people. You know my way of thinking; I do not like cheaters, nor thieves!*" transmits Sofia, indignantly. "*It's true, she can read in the thoughts! My, oh my!*" thinks the Celtic warrior.

"I need this brooch to return to my land!" continues Sofia, hitting him on the chest. "Do you understand?" Sofia is glaring at him. "Did you steal this brooch from me to keep me with you?" Sofia pulls him firmly, her two hands gripping his tunic.

Intimidated by Sofia's proximity and her intense stare, Aemonn admits with a slight affirmative nod of the head, mouth agape and eyes wide open. Sofia blushes… After a long silence, she bursts out laughing conscious of the situation, at the way she is gripping Aemonn.

With an uncomfortable smile, Aemonn takes Sofia's hands delicately and breaks free. He looks into her eyes with such affection that Sofia relaxes her muscles. Her anger subsides. "Yes, says Aemonn, with desolation! Yes! I want to keep you with me and make you my life companion. It is what my heart tells me!" Aemonn said the words with conviction and firmness.

Sofia looks him in the eyes, then softly: "Aemonn, I have strong feelings towards you. I look at you and I see and feel your vigour, your strength and your dignity. You will be a brave leader. You will be a great leader for your people. However, I can't stay with you and your people."

Aemonn says with intensity and sadness, "I love you, Sofia, princess from another world!" "I admire you, Aemonn, peaceful warrior and leader of the Bellinderry clan. It is an honour for me to have met you and mixed with your people."

The two timeless teenagers move closer to one another gently. Aemonn embraces her in his already muscular and protective arms. She snuggles, feeling cuddly and confident. A kiss seals their affection over time. The magic moment passed, Aemonn hands the brooch back to Sofia who recovers it with relief.

"Whew! Thank you," she says, with a radiant smile. "I know you must return to your people. I want to offer you a gift. Will you accept it?" "I would be honoured; however, I cannot bring anything with me," breathes Sofia. "I want to give you this little leather bracelet given to me by my mother before she departed. In its centre is the symbol of our clan, the triskelia. I know that you will wear it on your wrist with as much respect as I have in offering it to you."

"Aemonn, I can't accept it, because where I'm going, these objects cannot follow. However, I will note all the details of this bracelet, and when I'm back in my world; I will make a similar one with a triskelion in the centre. Therefore, it will be more than a memory, she says with emotion. This will be my gift of moments beyond time and space."

Sofia looks at Aemonn intensely. She fastens all the traits of this great Celtic fellow in her heart, her soul and her brain. He is scanned, as she knows, to do so well. "Before leaving Quelf handed me an acorn from your sacred tree. I cannot bring that acorn with me for the same reasons that I cannot accept your mother's bracelet. I was hoping that together, you and I could bury it in the ground, in an appropriate place where you could see it grow. Once it has grown and you are the leader of your clan, you can come to rest in its shade."

Aemonn looks at her, then suddenly, he gets up, takes her by the hand and they run to the river. "There, let's plant the acorn on that mound near the mill. I love to come here and look at the river and catch fishes."

Sofia engraves in her memory this space and its surroundings. Aemonn deposits the acorn in a hole they dug with their hands, in silence and in meditation.

They both return, accomplices, to the village centre.

--- OOO ---

Cedric and William are overwhelmed with joy when they see their sister returning with Aemonn. Cedric says, to his brother: "Aemonn succeeded, he knew what to say to our sister Sofia." "What a relief!" said William, as he had heard her thought about him, accusing him of stealing her dragonfly-shaped brooch. Taliesanic, seated near the clan leader's hut, is content to keep still. He observes and treasures in his wise man's heart this youthful and pure demonstration of love between Sofia and Aemonn. This is a refreshing balm after so much agitation, so many battles and intrigues.

--- OOO ---

Cedric and William observe the flurry of activity in the village.

Life is being reorganized. It is necessary to complete the reconstruction, regain trust, adjust to that which is real and be aware that the unknown is forever lying in wait. The past is no more, just as the arrow in the target gave its result which cannot be changed. Tomorrow does not exist. However all is possible. What only truly counts is the reality of the moment, with its possibilities, its resources and its constraints. The choices of the moment will shape the future.

Suddenly, William asks his brother: "What can we expect in our future?" The two brothers discuss their reality, the recent events, the teachings just received, the prophecy… They know that their preparation is just beginning. Sofia will have a special role, still unclear. They will have to take it up with grandpa and grandma.

“You know William; you know how Sofia can be unpredictable?” “Yeah! Sometimes it even becomes very complicated,” says William. “Especially when she doesn’t agree with us or we stand up to her cheesy ideas!”

“I think we both should watch out for her without her noticing and without committing any indiscretions. You know, I find she is quick at guessing and drawing conclusions,” says Cedric. “Yeah, and besides, her intuition is very strong!” adds William.

Cedric and William continue their reflections. They validate their understanding of the teachings Taliesanic gave them. They are also very proud of their contribution in the events. Taliesanic observes the two boys, smiling affectionately.

The Return Flight

The day is already well advanced when Cedric, William and Sofia hear LYKA: "*It's time to leave. Accompany Taliesanic; he will guide you to the clearing where we left you.*"

"*Children!*" transmits Taliesanic, "*come join me at Shane's hut. I will be there waiting for you.*"

The triplets arrive there together and find Taliesanic in private conversation with Shane. Turlough, Aemonn and his three sisters are also present. They acknowledge their arrival. The emotions are heavy. Turlough looks at these young persons with respect and admiration. Aemonn knows that Sofia is on her departure. He takes her hands and looking at her tenderly brings them to his lips without saying a word. Then says: "Can I speak to you in private?" He pulls her to a corner of the hut? "Certainly." Sofia follows him.

"I will keep your image in my heart as a warrior and chief," whispers Aemonn near Sofia's ear. "I will make myself a leather bracelet like the one you are wearing. That way I will always remember our encounter and my bond with you. You are to become a great warrior and a great leader with your clan. I will wear it I promise."

The two teenagers oblivious to those present, embrace each other

Cedric shakes hands with Turlough. Each has their right hand grasping the other's right wrist in a warrior's grasp.

"I'm sad to see you go," says Sinead moving towards William and embracing him with affection. William blushes and welcomes the affection in silence.

Taliesanic and Shane reckon and appreciate the friendship shown here between the youngsters

William checks his dragonfly, sees that of his brother and asks Sofia: "Sofia, I don't see your dragonfly, where is it?"

Sofia rummages in her pouch, takes it out and secures it to her tunic. "There!" she says with a smile.

After the emotional exchanges, the guests look at everyone, registering every Celtic detail they observe. Taking a respectful step back with Taliesanic, Cedric, William and Sofia thank Shane the clan leader, Turlough the weapons master, Aemonn the courageous son, Sinead, Aisling and Ciara. The three sisters are impressed with the triplets. They register their courage, their determination, their strength, their behaviour and their attitude. Everyone silently think about the recent events.

Taliesanic, happy, asks the triplets to follow him. The small group silently heads for the clearing of the Sacred Derve. Fog is spreading in the night that begins. "*Mission accomplished, I can leave whenever you want, Danna!*"

--- OOO ---

Despite the ambient fog, the clearing features a peaceful luminosity. "The airstrip is illuminated!" says William, with his own special brand of humour. "Airstrip?" questions Taliesanic, intrigued by this term.

The triplets burst into laughter at the same time. "In our time, we have big metal birds that displace humans over great distances, says Cedric. They need space to land on the ground and at night, these spaces need to be lighted for them to land." "Ah! I see," says Taliesanic, smiling, not convinced...

The children feel the presence of the dragons close by. They all hug Taliesanic affectionately. "It's time for your departure. I will sit near the Great Derve and rest. Be blessed and may the Gods protect you. Awen!"

By magic, Taliesanic falls asleep for eternity next to the Great Derve. The triplets, in a simultaneous gesture, tap their dragonfly brooch three times: "Dragonfly! Dragonfly! Dragonfly!" LYKA, MARA, DYRA appear at once.

Cedric, William and Sofia rejoice and keenly jump on their mount. They hug the neck of their respective dragon. They feel the affection of these winged companions. They are accomplices of their adventure. The dragons question in a playful tone: "Should we go back to your grandparents' home?" The children answer in chorus, moved: "Yes!" "Congratulations to each of you," says LYKA with pride. "You have passed your first test with flying colours."

--- OOO ---

The return trip is uneventful. They are happy to return to their environment. They recognize the Stokes Mountains and their grandparents' garden. They breathe with relief: "Finally!" The dragons notice that the children began their adventure anxious and perturbed. They come back confident, enthusiastic and ready for more adventures.

--- OOO ---

Louise saw them first and rushes towards the garden. She cries out: "Quickly Thomas! Here they are!"

Cedric, William and Sofia get the impression of having lived a dream. It's magic! In the space of two hours in real time with Louise and Thomas, they lived almost ten days in Celtic land.

--- OOO ---

Nostalgia: Country living

The days go by rapidly with all the work to be done around the farmhouse. The children take every opportunity to practise their telepathy with greater interest and determination. The experience with their dragons brought about the necessity to develop their capacity to communicate amongst themselves. They learned a lot, but, they must now become subconsciously competent. Meanwhile, Thomas and Louise know their mission. They endorse their responsibility. They remain vigilant. They use every occasion to challenge and upgrade their three grandchildren's gifts and potential.

In this regard, they make use of every challenge possible. For several weeks now, the children are encouraged to meet all the farm animals: pigs, chickens, horses, cats, birds, and when the occasion arises, foxes or deer that appear in their area.

This morning, Sofia is trying to capture the language of chickens. She hears cackling coming from the neighbouring farmhouse, in front of grandpa's property. She pays attention to this cackling that never ceases. She lends an ear: "What is causing the chickens to cluck that way? Is someone or some animal slaughtering them?"

Sofia decides to go to the neighbour's henhouse and check it out. When she arrives at the scene, nobody is there. The owners must be at work. Sofia heads for the barn. The doors are wide open. A hen slips through her legs in a panic. A rooster pursues her intensely. She seems crippled. One leg keeps slipping under the weight of her white feathers. "Oust! Oust! Be gone, you bad rooster, stop pursuing this unfortunate hen! Let her be! Leave her alone!" She chases away the brownish rooster.

Sofia approaches the hen gently, trying to take hold of her by the body. The hen tries to flee as best she can. "Ah! So, that's it, you have an injured leg. Poor little thing. Let me help you. You know, I can put you back in shape. I've done it before with our cat Mimi. She had been in a fight with a yellow cat and her paw was in very bad shape. My grandmother told me to be self-confident and to place my hands on the wound. You know little one, it worked. After spending a few minutes with her, Mimi licked her paw and set out again, purring. Let me try. I know how to place my hands. I don't know how it works, but it does."

The white hen lets Sofia come closer. Sofia bends down and takes her gently. Then, sitting down on the ground, she poses both her hands on the left leg bent under the feathering. For several minutes the hen remains motionless aside from her head that keeps turning from left to right. Suddenly, she flaps her wings signifying that she wants to leave. Sofia sets her down and the hen quickly moves away. She is already much better.

As she returns to the house, Sofia thinks: *"Really, chickens are not my pet subject. I don't grasp their cackling. Still, I'm able to guess their nest-egg-laying time. I like that a lot. I like good fresh eggs. Hum!"*

A flash crosses her mind, she suddenly remembers her dad Marc. She sees him at the stove, cooking succulent pancakes to be served with delicious maple syrup. How nostalgic. Tears blur her gaze for an instant; thoughts crowd her mind and wring her heart: *"It's almost four years since you left, dad. I miss you. It is incredible how time flies. When mom passed after you, I thought I would never get through that ordeal in my lifetime! I wanted to die on the spot, in the hospital, so much my heart wanted to burst. You and mom, I miss you both so much."*

Sofia remains pensive. She is sad. A tear runs down her left cheek. She hears her brothers calling: *"Sofia, where are you? What are you doing? We need you to solve an enigma."*

The boys search everywhere. Suddenly, they see their sister coming out of the neighbour's henhouse. Gesturing with her arms up in the air, she tells them, excited: "I guessed your question faster than what I experienced amongst the Celts! Wow! That's cool! I have finally achieved instantaneity. I'm cool!" she exclaims, on reaching her brothers.

"Don't go off your head sis!" retort the two boys. "We too have increased our telepathic ability and power. We are much stronger than when the three of us were amongst the Celts. It's unbelievable what that trip brought us. I'm beginning to believe what our dragons told us before they left us in that hostile forest," replies Cedric, suddenly thoughtful.

"We focused on the horses. They are extraordinary animals. They cooperate very easily. They have the friendliest of languages. Nonetheless, they are hesitant towards us humans. They say they see us much bigger than we actually are." Sofia interrupts: "In my opinion, it's grandpa who has the information. He can answer your question. He has so many books on the subject. I'm convinced he will be able to tell you." Sofia looks at Cedric with a smirk, her nose up in the air.

"Are you still reading our thoughts?" question the two boys. "Be careful of being indiscreet, sis. We are no longer on hostile terrain," says William, who always feels being spied upon by his sister.

"That's enough, it came to me automatically," replies Sofia firmly. "I can't help it! I'm faster than you two! It gave results when we were with Aemonn, his father, the druids Taliesanic and Quelf, especially when guessing what the enemies were thinking. We were all so helpful!" adds Sofia, with her cajoling eyes. "Yes, that's right!" answer Cedric and William, staring into the air, as if to say "girls are annoying! ... They always want to be right."

The three of them rush into the house to find grandpa and grandma. "Grandpa, grandma, where are you?" "Where are you, grandma Louise," shouts Cedric, as he and his brother cross the threshold of the back door.

They are not in the inter-room. The work clothes for the fields are on the hooks hence they should be close by. It's in this area that grandma keeps the preserves she makes: jams, green and red ketchup, small bitter and sweet gherkins along with the pickled beets that grandpa Thomas particularly likes. He enjoys them with Louise's traditional meat pies. "We are here, in the library of mysteries, as you usually call it."

Cedric rushes into the library: "William and I have a question for the two of you." Sofia jostles her brothers as she enters the room: *"I too want to know."* She doesn't want to be left out. "Be careful, my beautiful girl," says grandma gently, retaining her granddaughter by the arm. "Calm your 'pompom'! There is no need to jostle the others around."

Sofia apologizes to her brothers at grandpa Thomas's request. "What is your question?" Grandpa, looks Cedric and William in the eyes, in turn. "What did you want to know exactly? I know it concerns telepathy, however, if I want to give you the exact answer, I have to pay attention to all your words, your gestures, your voice intonations."

"Grandpa, the last time I checked the books in your library I spent a lot of time over a book that talked about the transmission of thoughts," says Cedric, more relaxed. "An old worn out book with index cards inserted inside it?" Grandpa is trying to visualize what Cedric is referring to? "Uh! I don't know if there are index cards in it, except that I retained the title and the author's name: Emile Hureau: De la Télépathie Étude sur la Transmission de la Pensée, 1920 (Telepathy Study on the Transmission of Thought 1920)."

"Yes! Yes! Yes! I know which one you mean. Wait, I will go to find it without too much trouble I believe!" His fingers move along all the books. One by one, he touches them with so much affection, as if they were made of rare silk. These books are his accomplices; they have helped forge his thoughts. The children are moved. They watch their grandfather go over the books like a general reviewing his soldiers lined up for an important inspection. "Here! I have it! I love this book! It's a treasure, a marvellous tool box! I used it regularly during my university sessions in communication. "What is it you want to know Cedric?" "I want to know how telepathy works. As you say, if we understand it then it is easier to remember."

Grandpa turns a few pages and says: "Ha! Here it is, are you ready to hear what it has to say on the subject?" The children nod as they settle down, legs crossed in the manner of the American Indians. They are attentive and want above all to understand the mechanics of this phenomenon of nonverbal communication, because even if they experienced it on Celtic land, they want to understand how it works.

Grandpa reads the following: "*The brain emits complex waves that constitute a thought that another brain in harmony with the first one can receive. Also, examples of telepathy occur most often between beings bound by sympathy, such as: between a mother and her child, between brothers and sisters, especially between twins.*" "Even more, if they are triplets like us," intervenes Sofia with assurance and conviction. "What we have experienced proves it, does it not?" "Of course," answers grandma.

Grandpa continues: "*The vibrations caused by your thought propagate in ether which is a subtle, expansive fluid that fills space. It is the environment, the medium that transports all vibrations: heat, light, and thought.*[12] Is it OK so far?"

The children look at one another and Cedric answers proudly: "We understood everything, even the word 'ether." "I know that you are learned children for your age. I am really impressed with your intellectual curiosity and interest in older books. Even though you are proficient with computers which are highly effective and useful in your searches, you also have the reflex to check out some old books. Yes, I'm impressed because you may not always have access to computers, then books become your information source!"

---

[12] Hureau page 5 (Author's translation)

Grandpa continues to read and explain the telepathic process. "In short what you need to remember is that each sound has a vibration mode. Likewise, so does the thought and when it is projected with intensity it can go a long way. In Australia and South Africa, the indigenous people are known to communicate this way over very long distances. Through training we can develop the ability to transmit images with great efficiency. Experiments have shown that a person at some distance has reproduced a picture described by another person that cannot be heard or seen." "I want to do that," says William. "In due course, you will all do it; it is planned as part of your training to come." Retorts grandpa.

"You know that it is said that many ideas and inspirations come to us suddenly . In fact, what occurs is that there are energy forms that are being captured in mid-air which we often refer to as the 'sea of knowledge'.[13]"

Grandpa asks his grandchildren which ocean he is talking about. Sofia, who is quicker than her brothers to give answers, says: "That's right; you spoke to us about it. I think we had a little attention drain at that time. We must have been in orbit, as you say so well when you call us back to order." "You make me laugh. It's really nice to have you with us," chuckles grandpa.

--- OOO ---

Thomas pauses for a moment, looks at Louise with affection and gratitude before adding: "With the loss of your parents, the Universe gave us an invaluable gift with the coming of you three into our home. I say this with all my heart. You are a true gift to us!" Thomas remains pensive.

The children and grandma Louise let him live his emotions. It's rather uncommon to hear their grandfather communicate his emotions, especially about the loss of his daughter Marion and his son-in-law... The children never saw him cry or get angry

---

[13] Hureau page 6 (Auther's translation)

with life, nor against the medical people, or for that matter, with God, the Creator of all things… Grandpa always gives the image of being a strong man, ready to face any challenge… He mechanically wipes his eyes with the back of his hand. He looks at these children with love. Silently, with his eyes, he thanks them for having allowed him a little time to get his breath.

The children respect his silence. Grandpa learned to master his emotions through his daily meditation. They know from experience; emotions cannot be concealed forever. The bubble must be punctured to release all the stress and emotions stored up in one's heart. Grandpa just did so and everyone is happy for him.

Louise, Cedric, William and Sofia look at each other and realize they thought the same thing at the same time. They smile at one another, eyes narrowed with pleasure and their right-hand thumbs obvious, as a sign of connivance. "*My-my! I'm really impressed! Their experience with the dragons is truly contributing to their telepathic abilities! They integrate the teachings very fast!*" Grandma, witness to their subtle joy, wraps them tenderly in her arms.

--- OOO ---

Grandpa resumes his statements on telepathy and then looking at them with the eyes of a professor alerted to students lost in a field, he asks: "Do you need further explanations on telepathy or the terms I used?"

"Listen grandpa," replies Cedric, "later, we will look up the meaning of the term 'pineal gland' or perhaps grandma will provide us the answer." "We are OK" add William and Sofia, eager to learn more about the mechanisms than on the terms of the text. "OK then," answers grandpa, "you can ask Louise about it or search for it on your PC." Grandpa resumes: "Once the telepathic organ, the pineal gland, is sufficiently developed, as in some ancient cultures, we receive the thought waves through this gland as we receive sound waves through the eardrum. Two conditions are necessary to practise telepathy: concentration and externalization of the thought of the issuer, who directs his thinking persistently towards the chosen goal; and a receiver with a sufficient degree of sensitivity. Success depends on the perseverance of the persons, their energy, their conviction and their mental effort capacity and infallible complicity."

"If I understand you correctly," says William, "because we're triplets, we are strongly advantaged! If you only knew to what extent it was useful to us during our last adventure with the dragons. He looks at his brother and sister with complicity and pride in his eyes." "You're absolutely right, William!" says grandpa. "You are blessed by the Gods, don't forget it. It is said in the ancient books that the gifts you now possess were present amongst the first humans. Everybody had them. We must rediscover them again. That is the reason your dragons have you live all these trips. It's for you to put your gift of telepathy into practice, regardless of the circumstances."

Grandpa believes they have had enough for today and proposes, in conclusion. "As you see, you have learned to effectively use telepathy. You are better able to protect yourselves against all dangers. Your dragons and the druid you met, have probably initiated you to several of their formulas of protection." "*They have a nostalgic look in their eyes, notes grandma. What are they thinking now? I can catch part of their thoughts; however, there seems to be an insurmountable wall presently.*"

The three of them smile at their Grandma, then rush into the kitchen where an excellent snack awaits them. The school year is advancing fast. They are two weeks away from the start.

Family history

"Grandma, you should take the time to tell us the story of your family. You told us that it's very important to know where we come from, to know our genealogy, especially for me," insists Sofia. "Yes, it's true, it is important and I promised! Today is a good time, especially since you go back to school in a few days. Come the three of you, let's go to the library of mysteries. We will be far more comfortable. Besides, I need to refer to my private book for some details."

Sofia, William and Cedric, excited, settle comfortably on the black leather couch. "This story is my story and that of my ancestors. This story also concerns you, Sofia. It concerns your mother Marion, it concerns me, my mother, my grandmother, and a whole line of extraordinary women who preceded us. These women, as we are, you Sofia and I, were called white witches." "White witches! What about us," asks William staring at his grandmother.

Grandma smiles at both Cedric and William. "You will learn what you truly are in due course, boys. For now, let me tell you more specifically the story of the family of a woman who came from the Northern Countries: The Vikings, the North Men." The children look at one another, surprised, frowning.

Louise heads towards one section of the library. She withdraws a big red book from the middle bookshelf. The gilding bears the mark of assiduous reading through the passage of time. Many hands have touched this book. Grandma handles it with great care and respect. As she opens it, one can see the sheets yellowed by age. It's the book of her ancestors. This book is very precious. On the leather cover is a coat of arms, that of her family, «the Mans.» The armorial bearings consist in a large oak tree with five important branches, a lot of leaves and five acorns that are hanging down. The roots are, too, five in number, largely rooted in the ground. The original armorial bearing was of solid bronze. She gently flips the pages and finally finds the section concerning the history of Islanda.

The room is filled with emotions. "It is a magnificent book! I love the 'coat of arms' on the top of the book," exclaims Sofia. Then, cutting the vibration so that Louise cannot guess her, she says to herself: *"Is this the same symbol as I saw at Quelf's?"* She hears Grandma: "Here it is! I will tell it as it is written and as I was told by my maternal grandmother. She was of Irish descent."

Grandma begins the epic story of her ancestors with much respect, pride and joy. "The king is dead. Kandar, great warrior and explorer has passed away. His serious injuries suffered during the last expedition on the coast of the North Sea got the best of him. His wife, priestess and mother, completes the ritual. Algard, called the Brute, was chosen to succeed him. He dreams of conquest and riches. He is cunning, sometimes perfidious and never gives up. He pulverizes any obstacle to his ambitions. He declares; "The debate is over, Islanda comes with us."

"Who is Islanda," asks Sofia, attentive and curious to know the importance of this character? "Wait!" says Grandma, "let me continue! Where was I again? Ah! Yes! Islanda.... "The debate is over, Islanda comes with us." This is how the new clan leader ends the lively discussion that takes place the day after the funeral ceremonies. Islanda, widow and priestess of the clan, awaits the verdict of the implacable new leader. Algard is now the leader of his people. He does not support contradiction and much less that coming from a woman, even if she is a priestess. He has long awaited the opportunity to conquer and get rich.

Algard has uncommon physical strength, and his pride is equalled only by his ardour to punish and hurt his enemies or whomever resists his desires. Kandar, the only one who could physically best him is no more and Islanda, who knows how to influence the clan, must be neutralized. She must be removed from the clan. She must disappear. It is Algard the Brute's turn to rule the clan, on the coast, on the seas. "We leave at dawn tomorrow morning." "Ah! No, they're not going to abandon her somewhere," exclaims Sofia, breathless, indignant at the lack of respect for her ancestor. "Calm down my dear, it's the story of our ancestor, as a female in the line of white witches. She is courageous; you'll see what she will do. This is a great lesson of faith, determination and willingness to fight for your beliefs. I consider her one of my mentors. I often read this passage. Frequently I question Islanda before deciding. Can I continue, Sofia?" "Yes grandma, I can't help it, my anger rises by itself." "I understand you Sofia but let me read on.

At nightfall, Islanda defers to the Vikings' law. She prays the gods to protect the people and her daughter Yolanda. Algard has placed Yolanda under the responsibility of Princess Awan, his mother. Yolanda needs to be prepared for her work as a healer of the body and soul, in the tradition imposed by Algard.

Algard now shares his thoughts and intentions with his close guard, those warriors most loyal to him: "We are Vikings! Our destiny is to conquer, to be the strongest and for that we must be feared. Islanda has been speaking of love and peace to our nation of warriors for far too long. We must not cease our fights. Conquer or die! That's my law. The peoples must respect us. Only strength deserves respect. Kandar was weakening under Islanda's influence. He wanted to cease our expeditions. No! We are Vikings and Odin is with us. To survive, it's up to us to be the strongest, the most feared, the richest."

"Islanda must disappear… She is poisoning the minds of our warriors with her messages of peace. We are meant to fight and conquer. If for that, we must slaughter and pillage, then so be it! It's our destiny! Islanda must disappear, and by Odin, we will find the right moment to do so."

The children listen attentively, their fists clenched.

Grandma continues: "The aurora borealis dance amongst the stars and provide a mystic light that shines over Islanda's face. This woman with extraordinary talents and abilities is on the lookout for a sign. The Northern lights metamorphose themselves in an emerald sky, drawing a magnificent tapestry with delicate patterns. Suddenly, a flashing star, Islanda, attentive, is transported into the universe of the Gods. She hears. She understands her mission. She accepts to be the messenger and to live the exile imposed upon her."

"The people fear Algard's brutal force. Islanda knows that her predictions, her advice, her omens are now banned. It's forbidden for her to speak to the people, to speak to her daughter Yolanda, a twelve-year-old teenager. Her heartbreak is palpable. She knows what awaits her. Through vibration, she transmits to her daughter Yolanda courage and determination. She knows that her daughter, coming from a long line of women of wisdom, will be the bearer of a succession of women with universal powers and with limitless mind capacities."

The triplets wipe their noses and misty eyes. Sofia sniffles: "Grandma, please, wait a bit before proceeding." The children are so disappointed and shocked to learn what this priestess must endure because of that Algard's selfish attitude. Cedric, William and Sofia breathe at length and looking back at grandma, nod their heads to signal her to continue the story. Grandma then takes the book she had placed on the table and continues reading.

"Dawn colours the horizon. The crews of the three Drakkars are on board and await the signal. In the lead Drakkar, without a word Islanda transmits with her gaze all her love to her daughter Yolanda, who observes the apparel under Awan's supervision. She is restrained by force, because she can't hold back her tears, her rage and her secret desire to join her mother. One day for sure, she will only need to find the moment, the person and the means to achieve her ends... She must reach the Grand Island coast, Eire, the island that her people conquered."

"The coastline slowly disappears. The Drakkars sail on an increasingly hectic sea. They are headed for the Greenland territories, the destination, unclear. For days now, the sailor warriors are relentlessly busy coping with the battling waves that splash noisily against their ships. Many are worried and fear the power of the priestess just as much as that of the waves. Islanda observes and her silence disturbs. For eight days, she says nothing. The tension is palpable. 'Land! Land! Land!' cries the lookout man."

"Algard, the leader and captain of this expedition, gives orders, brief and firm. Everyone is busy and acts with force and dexterity, insensitive to the bite of the icy water. They know the importance of their task as sailors. They are aware of their leader's intentions. Many fear the consequences of his decision. One does not get away with dismissing the messenger of the divine. Odin does not appreciate that one plays with the Gods."

"Finally, someone who will intervene!" casts William, content that this character, named ODIN, is on the side of the priestess. "She will have the support of the Gods, though not as you think, children. Wait for what follows." Grandma continues her story.

"Only the crashing waves break the silence. Their thundering sound, a warning, as they hit the shore. Do they welcome this great lady or are they threatening the warriors of the consequences of their action?"

"The crew, under Algard's stare remain apprehensive. No word, not even a glance is transmitted. A pouch, a few clothes, some provisions, a couple of spark stones and a cutlass are deposited. Algard the Brute and his warriors return to their ships."

"The Drakkars quickly disappear on the horizon. The priestess observes. She has been exiled, isolated, banished from her clan. Her heart hurts. She fears the unknown. She always had the support of all her family. She never had to look after her daily necessities. In accordance with her priestess status, she did not have to worry about her food, her defence against any invader…

Uncertainty inhabits her, invades her. Images of wild animals, of peoples, surely warriors, disturb her. "What am I going to do, alone in a strange country that is as wild as its vegetation?" Her people do not listen to the call from heaven; do not listen to the message that the infinite wisdom of the Gods dictated them. "The price for my failure, she thinks, is this new, unknown Land, where the wind and the waves compete to be heard, where the horizon presents a succession of glaciers that melt and vanish."

"Odin! Are you here, standing beside me? Will I have the courage to live in this new-found land? What must I expect in this unknown country?" Suddenly, she hears within herself an answer to her prayer. Looking at the sky, she recognizes Odin's sign. In a firm and loud voice: "God of love and peace may Your Will be accomplished." Then, Islanda reconnects with her inner strength, looks at her surroundings, and in peace, prays: "*New-found land, I salute you. What do you have for me? I am ready to meet my destiny. Thank you for welcoming me.*"

"Of all those warriors, not one knows that this exile prepares the fulfillment of a prophecy that will be realized a thousand years later. It is then June of the year 1000."

--- OOO ---

A sepulchral silence reigns in the room... The children look at one another. Together, their thoughts relate to their adventure in Ireland. Cedric mentions aloud: "Phew! Now, I understand the importance of the status given to Quelf! Yes, as a priestess warrior she has quite a lot of influence." William and Sofia approve with a nod, just as pensive, as if they were still out there, in that Celtic land!

"What are you saying Cedric?" Asks grandma, surprised. "If I hear you well, you met a Celtic priestess warrior? Where did you go with your dragons while grandpa and I were waiting patiently for you three? "Hummm! I was not aware of this small detail, she sighs... Ah! The Magi dragons have tricks in their 'magic pouch'!" Continues grandma while pinching the bridge of her nose with her left thumb and forefinger, her questioning reflex... Grandma awaits an answer to her questions.

"Oops! We didn't say everything," whispers, William... Cedric looks at grandma and says: "Uh! Yes! ... We crossed through hundreds and hundreds of space time with our dragon friends. They have the capacity to transport us through all dimensions in a flash. It was magical, grandma. It's amazing what they can do. They transmit us the information telepathically at the speed of lightning. Besides, it was extremely helpful because, we admit, it was quite dangerous at times. To understand the language of those Celtic peoples ... fortunately, the dragons were translating us their discourse simultaneously... You know, grandma, what's cool, is that nobody could see them! They have this possibility of transparency, where appropriate, when it is needed," completes Cedric feverishly.

William and Sofia support their brother's story. They believe he knows so well how to tell it. Grandpa moves closer on hearing his three grandchildren. He quite simply can't get over it! He thinks: "Did I hear them correctly? The Celts! They deliberately failed to tell us the tumultuous passages of their journey with their dragons." Looking at the children: "Hold on! I believe it's important that you fill us in. What happened with your dragons amongst the Celts?" Says, grandpa. "Hum! I would have liked to be there, too," thinks grandpa, with a hint of nostalgia in his soul... "I remember my adventures when I was their age. Adventures I created with my imagination. I was the leader and hero of an entire band of Native American warriors. We would cross mountains and valleys of various countries. I faced huge monsters that would come from other planets..." Thomas mumbles words that seem unintelligible to the children and grandma who stare at him.

"Where are you, grandpa, asks Sofia? What are you mumbling between your teeth? We don't understand your language." Grandpa pauses before saying: "Excuse me children, I was gone into my childhood memories. I would have liked to take part in your adventure too. I suggest you tell us all the important parts of your inter-dimensional journey. That's what this is, is it not, asks grandpa? I am curious to learn more about these peoples from the land of druids, the deadly fighting amongst the other conquering peoples, their magic power..."

The children look at each other with complicity. They agree to disclose to their grandparents their incredible adventure: the experience with their dragons and the friends they made during that adventure. Sofia, Cedric and William describe in turn what they lived, what they learned about themselves and the teachings from Taliesanic and Quelf. Thomas and Louise frequently request clarification or simply ask the children to slow down. The children get carried away with their enthusiasm. They recount their individual and collective adventures well into the evening.

Truly, Louise and Thomas are happy to see that their initiation has paid off. Cedric, William and Sofia are courageous, generous and show a lot of creativity. Their gift for telepathy seems well acquired. All the tests told by their grandchildren demonstrate that their learning is progressing well. The efforts are worth it. The program devised with Ming and Patrick must continue. Furthermore, let us not forget the contribution from the three dragons.

Before going to bed, Sofia takes her grandmother by the neck and whispers in her ear: “Grandma, the coat of arms that is on your book, I saw it on the medallion around Quelf’s neck.” Louise, cheerful, looks at her intensely and whispers: “It’s truly extraordinary; I’m pleased to see that nothing has been lost with time.”

Fondness

Cedric, William and Sofia avoid thinking about the incident that occurred at the beginning of the week in their new school. They need to practise Taliesanic's teaching on how to block information at the brain level. They are aware of their grandparents' gifts, their capacity to read minds. They certainly don't want to have to give explanations. They do not want to explain why and how they called their respective dragon. Hence, after the evening meal, the triplets rush to their respective bedroom, indicating to their grandparents that they have a lot of homework to hand in. The rest of the week goes on without any other incident.

Cedric, William and Sofia have invited their school friends, the Wangtans, to come and share a weekend of fun with them.

--- OOO ---

Saturday morning, the household wakes up slowly even if the farmyard rooster is hoarsely singing his morning Gregorian chant.

Thomas and Louise await the visit of Peter and Jocelyn Wangtan. They are to spend the weekend with them.

Sofia opens her eyes. The sun is already shining. She stretches in her bed, gets up, quickly washes her face puts on her track suit, then rushes up the stairway and meets her grandparents in the kitchen. "Good morning, my beautiful little princess," says Thomas smiling.

Grandpa prepares breakfast for the whole family on weekends. During the week, they all prepare their own breakfasts and lunches. It's easier this way and everyone is happy with this situation. "Mimi!" calls grandma, gesturing her to get down from her perch. "What are you doing on the kitchen counter?" She thinks: "*Cats! They are always perched as high as possible. It is an observation tower for them. Yet Mimi knows I don't like it when she does that. It is forbidden.*"

"Grandpa, do you remember that Peter and Jocelyn are going to spend the weekend with us? We asked you earlier this week." "Yes, Sofia, it's already on the agenda," replies grandpa, while preparing his popular oatmeal. Everyone enjoys grandpa's oatmeal. He makes it as smooth and velvety as a milk chocolate bar.

"Sofia, your friends will settle in the blue room down the hall near the cold storage room. I made the bed with sheets that smell like a breath of fresh air in late Summer. Hydrangeas smell good at this time of the season. The rose bushes are still blooming and their scents and colours are breathtaking. All my senses are excited."

"Wow, grandma, you're in high spirits this morning," exclaim Cedric and William as they enter, all smiles. "Your garden is a real paradise," adds Sofia. "Ah, my dear children, when I feel in a state such as this, I can't help but declaim, as you say so well, on everything that surrounds me. I feel being part of the whole creation in a single instant."

"Right now, I think you're very shamanic, grandma. In fact, you are that all the time," corrects Cedric, taking his grandmother in his loving arms. "You talk to plants, to birds, fawns come to you, foxes come in your plants to play with their young and chickadees come to nibble in your hands. If you're not a shaman, you're not far off." "Hum! I like this," answers grandma, hugging her grandson. As she hugs Cedric, she says: "You know, children, as we get older and our skin begins to show creases, we wonder if you, young people, will continue to give us tangible signs of affection…" "Ah, beautiful grandma," giggle William and Sofia, leaving the table to go and place a kiss on her rosy cheeks, always so kissable.

“So, my love, you’re feeling nostalgic this morning,” says grandpa breathing deeply. “You know Louise; I always find you as attractive as the first day I met you. Wrinkled skin, to me, it’s a sign of great wisdom and experience. I think you’re not through collecting ‘wrinkles’ because, from what I see, you’re here for many years to come.”

Roaring with laughter, grandpa hugs her tenderly and says: “You’re such a darling, my beautiful Louise!” The children laugh to hear him speak to their grandma like that.

“Thomas, I thank the Universe, because the more my skin creases, more your eyesight decreases,” exclaims grandma, laughing. “*That is what must be called loving presence,*” thinks Sofia. “*Yes, it is, my beautiful girl,*” transmit Thomas and Louise, smiling. “Wow! This is a great start to the long weekend!” say William and Cedric, savouring their Saturday oatmeal with appetite.

A Secret Unveiled

"Pierre, Jocelyn, welcome to you both in our home. We are happy to see you again. I heard that you had a lovely family trip to Mali… Here, leave your luggage near the entrance wardrobe," says grandma. Jocelyn says as he puts down his weekend bag: "Yes ma'am, we had a very nice holiday, though I must say, we found the temperature very hot and humid. It's always sunny in the land of my ancestors."

"Come and enjoy a hot beverage with us. It's Saturday and today is our day to relax and chat," says grandma, waving to Peter and Jocelyn's parents, who are driving away in their car. "My parents will pick us up around 4:00 P.M. on Sunday," mentions Jocelyn. Grandma ushers the two boys towards the dining room, calling: "Sofia, please bring two more cups to the table."

Sofia crosses into the kitchen and as she passes near Jocelyn, he addresses her with a half smile, hiding a slight juvenile shyness in her presence. She smiles back to him with eyes filled with laughter. Grandma notices Jocelyn's ploy towards Sofia. He is one year her senior. Pierre, on the other hand, is a year younger than the triplets. He hastens to give a hug to William, his recreation and weekend friend.

Together, they chat and enjoy the hot chocolate with marshmallows prepared by grandma and Sofia. Grandpa notices the impatience of the youths who wish to be amongst themselves. "Go, shoo, grandma and I have things to do. See you later for lunch. We'll call you. Have fun."

Pierre and Jocelyn are children who have been initiated to elemental energies. Their mother, an African shaman, transmitted them her knowledge and ability to communicate with gnomes, fairies, goblins, trolls, jinn and all those beings that inhabit the gardens of Mother Nature.

The triplets are already anticipating magical moments with their friends. "*It's fascinating to see Pierre and Jocelyn getting in touch with these magic beings*," thinks William. "Yeah! It's wonderful to have friends like them," responds Cedric telepathically.

Suddenly, Jocelyn leans towards the grove of orange daylilies close to the red barn that houses three horses! "Hello Epona!" Pierre then explains to the triplets: "Our mother has taught and shown us how to communicate with the Goddess Epona. Epona is also the Queen of Fairies. She watches and reigns over the kingdom of horses. The Romans and the Celts erected temples to her at a time when horses were part of everyday life. She is responsible for the welfare and health of horses. In addition, on every continent, peoples consider Epona as the protector of the environment and the spirits of nature." "Hello Epona!" The triplets greet the Goddess in unison and with respect. "Thank you for protecting our horses."

"*Ah, really! The Celts erected temples for her! ... So, that is what we observed there... Yes! That's right! We saw her*," thinks Sofia...

Cedric, William and Sofia recall the acquisition of their three horses. After the death of their mother Marion, grandpa and grandma offered their grandchildren these animals that are known for their great emotional availability and their ability to help heal and reconcile. Thomas often says: "Horses are not here to please us as dogs do. They are capable of penetrating the human heart and pour out one's pain and suffering gratuitously." These horses have developed an exceptional complicity with their riders. Cedric's horse is the completely black stallion with a white inverted triangle between the eyes. The gray mare with black spots belongs to William. Sofia mounts her mare with the dazzling white coat with pride and fondness.

The acquisition of these noble animals accelerated the children's healing process. Their attitude towards life has gained momentum. The care they brought to these animals channelled the orphans' emotions while also developing their sense of responsibility. Over time they became proud riders. Their "joie de vivre" is reflected by their infectious laughter. Their frolics in the house and in the surrounding countryside, their crazy races with Rocky the dog, their hide and seek games with Mimi the cat, their bicycle hikes to the village, the ardour they bring to their martial arts training sessions, all these activities testify to the healthy evolution of these children. They are preparing for their life mission.

--- OOO ---

Grandpa and grandma are busy at their weekly Saturday tasks while the children continue their activities in the surrounding country. "Honey!" asks Thomas, "what would you say if I spent an hour with the children to give them Greco-Roman wrestling training? The youths all seem in top form and I need the exercise." "It's a good idea; ask Sofia if she wants to participate."

OK, after the training, we'll go to the movies for the 4:00 P.M. representation.

It's OK with me. I'll prepare a snack for you all, adds grandma, pleased that the young ones are having fun together.

--- OOO ---

The five friends return from their morning play and wrestling training famished except for Sofia.

The table is set: spaghetti, meat sauce and white sauce on the menu, along with an appealing Caesar's salad. "Hum! It smells good," intone the boys. As for Sofia, she's not very hungry. Something else is bothering her. "*It's probably her menstruation period, thinks grandma. We are not hungry 48 hours before that and we feel 'lousy.' We don't want to be pushed around and certainly not be annoyed... Especially as she agreed to live the Greco-Roman wrestling experience*." Looking fondly at her granddaughter, Louise asks: “Do you want to rest awhile Sofia? You can come back when you’re hungry. Everyone should respect their bio rhythm in life, especially us women. You know, Sofia, we are more cyclical than men; we follow the cycle of the moon.” “Yes Grandma, I’ll go lie down for about half an hour, I feel awkward,” answers, Sofia.

Sofia feels the abdominal cramps invading her. She has trouble breathing; the pain is so intense… Louise follows her to her room and offers: “Would you like me to give you a light abdominal massage, just enough to help the passage of the blood clots that are stuck to your uterine wall?” “Yes grandma, your «massage» is miraculous!”

Gently, with tenderness and love, Louise delivers her massage. Sofia relaxes and falls asleep. Louise covers her with Sofia’s preferred “doodoo blanket.” The soft fabric of the blanket brings Sofia back in contact with her mother Marion. She gave it to her for her eighth birthday …, already four years ago, …

--- OOO ---

In the dining room, the men are splitting their sides laughing while enjoying their meal when Cedric interrupts suddenly very serious: “Well! I think now is a good time to give you answers to the questions you’ve been asking about our family.” “What do you mean,” question Pierre and Jocelyn, intrigued by their buddy’s formal tone?

“Listen boys, grandpa Thomas hastens to say, I think Cedric is referring to a secret he wants to share with you. We believe that you are capable of understanding and coping with it.” Cedric and William look at each other, surprised at their grandfather’s attitude. “Tell them your story since you came into our home.” Louise had just returned from Sofia’s room to join Thomas. They are now looking at Cedric, encouraging him to speak.

Cedric leans on both of his arms on the table as if for assurance. “You know that we are orphaned of father and mother.” Taking a pause, he looks at his brother, William, and reveals with emotion: “Sofia, William and I, we promised our mother Marion, before she died, to follow a rigorous training that prepares us for the future. For three years now, grandpa and grandma have been preparing us to live different experiences." William quickly adds: "Mom's brother, Patrick and his wife, Ming, are martial arts experts. They have been teaching us self-defence including the use of knives, archery and most importantly, when and how to utilize muscular strength to defend ourselves. It's tough but fun."

Cedric resumes: "Grandma has been teaching us how to communicate with plants. Grandpa has been teaching us to meditate and develop some skills we have. Above all, both of them are preparing us to meet special teachers who are to train us through rituals for a specific mission we have to prepare for. We made a promise to our Mom. So, every year until we are ready, we must live many experiences that we will discover as we grow older. This Summer we had our first initiation."

Pierre and Jocelyn are staring at Cedric. Their jet-black eyebrows are raised in surprise. "What is this story about initiation?" Jocelyn, the eldest of the siblings raises the question. Sofia, coming into the room, continues the explanation: "We had our first big test last June at the time of the Summer solstice, which is also our birth date." "We're glad you're back," says Jocelyn, pulling a chair beside him for her to join the group and continue the explanations.

"All that to say, continues Cedric, that as we grow up with you, you will notice that we will be increasingly different. We were told that we are part of a prophecy. There are many children like us in the world who are being initiated to support the global energy movement. They, too, are living the same thing as us but in other countries. Apparently, we are connected to a prophecy to happen during our lifetime." Cedric stops talking and looks straight at his friends.

Pierre and Jocelyn are intrigued and surprised. They perceived long ago that the Corribus were different from the other classmates. They look at each other and note that their perceptions were accurate. However, to realize that their friends have decided to share this secret with them, it's awesome. At this very moment, they feel they are participating in a grandiose event, an astonishing adventure. This is happening around them, and their friends are sharing their secret with them. "Wow! This is cool! We are very lucky to be your friends…" Both boys are enthusiastic. Their thoughts are soaring at full speed. They are already in movie scenarios.

The triplets consult one another with a glance and now know that they can pursue their story. They heard their thoughts, their reflections. They know that Peter and Jocelyn will keep the secret on the revelations they are about to deliver them.

The afternoon passes quickly. Curiosity and enthusiasm feed the exchanges. All the subjects are tackled: the ritual with Taliesanic, the adventure amongst the Celtic people of the sixth century, the experience and complicity with the dragons, the painful experiences of the physical and martial activities. In brief, Pierre and Jocelyn are at the paroxysm of excitement. They can't take any more. They want to live the experience on the dragons of their friends. "Would it be possible for us to meet your dragons," asks Pierre, timidly?

"First, interrupts grandpa Thomas, you need to know something. Only initiated or prepared individuals can see the celestial dragons. Perhaps these master magicians can make an exception. We must ask them. As they say, there are exceptions to every rule." Turning towards the triplets: "Do you have your pins, children?" Thomas looks at Louise with a knowing look. In a flash, William rushes to his bedroom followed by Cedric and Sofia, saying: "They are in our treasure chest."

The two Wongtan boys eagerly wait for the moment of truth and wonder. Cedric runs back from his bedroom, followed by William and Sofia. They stop, look at their grandparents, and quickly, they go outside while tapping their respective pin three times. And here, LYKA, MARA and DYRA appear, ready to assist the triplets. Telepathically, they each consult with their dragon simultaneously. LYKA responds to the children's request: "Yes, we have this privilege of disengaging the magnetic field that surrounds us to allow other humans to see us. However, we need to do so with discernment. For your friends, the Gods seem to agree, they have just communicated it to us."

"Youppie ! "exclaim the children, in unison. "Super! Gracias! Jocelyn and Pierre will be happy as birds flying in the sunlight," exclaims William. "I beg your pardon," says MARA. "Don't you mean 'as Dragons'?"

A great dragon laugh is heard. Jocelyn and Pierre are more and more able to make out the gigantic forms that are appearing in the garden, while Cedric, William and Sofia laugh their heads off. The cloud that surrounded the dragons has dissipated and now they are dazzled. It's utter surprise.

The shock is brutal. Jocelyn and Pierre fall flat on their back. They can't believe their eyes. They are before huge dragons emerging out of a Hollywood movie. Fear sets in. They are shaking all over.

Seeing this heartrending scene, grandma and grandpa rush to pick them up and give them assistance. "Don't be afraid! They are so kind and helpful. It's their size that is impressing. Their goodness of heart is as large as their stature and more. Allow yourself to be tamed. Trust your riders, Cedric, William and Sofia. They will be able to guide you. You will not be able to hear their language. They communicate through telepathy amongst themselves and with the children. Cedric, William and Sofia will translate their conversations."

At the sight of this scene, the triplets burst out laughing and roll about on the ground. They let their grandparents take care of their friends.

Once the presentations are done, the five friends head for their respective dragon. "Two females and one male. That's cool!" says Jocelyn, who had just received the information from Cedric.

Returning from their emotions with difficulty, Jocelyn and Pierre hesitantly accept to mount astride behind Cedric and William.

Pierre stands beside William. "I'm so happy to share these moments of flight with you Pierre. You'll see, it will be fantastic. I'll guide you. Get yourself behind me. Hold on tight. Take me by the waist at the level of my belt. Does that suit you?" "Well, I'm a little hesitant, but I want it so much. Ah! I'm getting on regardless of my fear of heights. At worst, I'll close my eyes and I'll live the thrill of the adventure from within." "Yeah! That's right! You've got it! Let's go!" shouts Will, hooking on to his mount with his teammate.

Cedric does the same with Jocelyn, who now feels ashamed facing Sofia. Cedric notices. He wanted to impress her by his courage and determination. He lets his sister resolve this little discomfort.

Sofia hears his cerebral verbiage. She waves her hand to him and shouts: "Let's go! Climb on! I am following you closely. You're good! Jocelyn, you managed to overcome your great fear facing this gigantic and beautiful being. Have confidence, we're safe with them! Open yourself to this magical moment. Capture all the beauty of the landscape and enjoy the ride." "Well, Sofia, I'll trust Cedric *and his dragon.*" He hesitates a moment and between his fleshy lips, adds: "I would like to ride with you, Sofia. Another time, perhaps." He looks at her intensely, inviting her to live a moment of complicity.

Sofia knows that there will be no second time. This is the only experience that he will live with the celestial dragons. She smiles at him anyway before they depart. She is still thinking of Aemonn too much to fall for Jocelyn's emotional blackmail.

The departure is very smooth. The dragons heard the triplets' simultaneous messages to the effect that their friends were frightened.

The flight is magnificent. Grandma and grandpa are again marvelled by so much grace and strength flowing from these mythical and magical animals.

Aerial aerobatics succeed one another, vaulting in one direction and then in the other. The dragons remain sensitive to the different emotions of their new riders. Everything goes smoothly. Jocelyn shouts in Cedric's ears to overcome the noise from the wind. "Your dragon is really nice." "It feels good to hear you shouting," answers Cedric loudly. "For a moment, I was wondering if you had lost the use of your tongue! Bravo! You are much more relaxed. Besides, MARA told me so a few minutes ago, she feels you are more at ease. Don't forget, she senses all your emotions. The three of us experienced the same stress as you on our first flight. It will pass." "Thank you for telling me that. I suspected a little that you had been through the same path but I didn't dare ask. Luckily, you're here. It really reassures me."

As for DYRA, she respects the pace of taming of this new rider. Pierre is starting to relax his legs. "Tell him that if he had continued to squeeze me like that, I would have had bruises on my glittering scales." DYRA laughs heavily. William joins in. "What did she say to you?" Pierre knows that William and his dragon communicate through telepathy.

"She told me that if you had not loosened your legs, she would have had bruises on her scales. That's why we both laughed. These dragons are capable of making jokes, you know." Pierre mutters through his teeth: "That's very funny! You, you're used to riding your dragon. You've been hanging out with your dragon for some time now. Me, it's only been a few moments." "Still, it was very funny, don't you think? No hard feelings, OK? Let's have fun. Let yourself be lulled by the motion of the wings." "It's true. I close my eyes and feel like I'm floating on air."

These are magical moments. The children don't want to come back. What a fantastic trip. The return is executed smoothly as it was for the departure. The landing is easy for these great celestial dragons. They deposit the children in a fluid and secure movement that impress the two African boys. They thought that they would be shoved and shaken as they had experienced during their last airplane flight to Africa. Jocelyn and Pierre share a thought: "These dragons could give great flying lessons to all the airline pilots!" *"They're right!"* reflect Cedric, William and Sofia as they smile at one another, happy.

Jocelyn and Pierre, reassured, ask Cedric and William to thank their dragons for this gift of riding and flying with them. It was incredible. Grandma and grandpa, present at the landing site hear the brother's request and inform them: "Tell them yourselves. They can hear you cerebrally as well as vocally." "Gracias from the bottom of our hearts. This will remain etched in our memories forever." "Go! You can get closer to them. Lean on them. They are so friendly. It feels good to touch them. It increases one's self-confidence. They will let you glide your hands over their shimmering scales. You'll see the feeling is great!"

Jocelyn and Pierre comply. "The feel of their scales is very soft and comforting," reflects Pierre. "It's a magical and mythical life that you are touching there," says grandma affectionately, as much for the two boys as for the dragons.

All this has been wonderful, but all good things must come to an end. "The dragons must leave," says Cedric, smiling at his friends. "They told us that they were happy and fortunate to have shared these moments with you."

"A word for you, Jocelyn, from my dragon," says Sofia... Sofia gets closer to Jocelyn's right ear and kindly whispers three words: "Vigilance! Vigilance! Vigilance!" Jocelyn turns to Sofia and asks her discreetly: "Why just me? Why am I the only one to receive a message from your dragon," he asks Sofia, astonished? "Well, I don't know," replies, Sofia. "I am merely transmitting his message of kindness, concern and foresight. He often speaks in riddles. Do you know what that means for you?" she asks. "Yes! Of course, I know," answers, Jocelyn. "Well, I'll see what I have to do about that!" Louise, who heard the conversation between the two, asks: "Is everything alright, children?" "Yes! Yes! It's just that LYKA had a little personal message for Jocelyn. That's all."

Louise heard LYKA's message. It's the same message that her guide, Pheas had left her one day. She thinks: "Hum! What does it portend?" *"Grandma, I hear you, what are you thinking, what do you mean by portend?* Asks Sofia telepathically. *"One day, I heard the same warning from my guide Pheas. I think we must increase our vigilance towards Jocelyn.*"

Grandpa, approaching their grandchildren's friends, makes them an express demand. "No allusion, not a single word to any one of your adventures with the dragons. You must promise us. It's essential for what is to come."

Jocelyn and Pierre look at one another and in a single heartfelt voice, promise: "Yes! We promise! Scouts promise! That is priceless!" says Jocelyn, looking deeply into grandpa's eyes.

Pierre comes close to grandma and dares take her by the waist. "It's comforting to feel you are confident, Pierre. You are always welcome here," adds grandma warmly, hugging him against her.

"Not a word to your parents," say Cedric, William and Sofia. "Even if you're dying to," adds Sofia. "OK, we promise."

--- OOO ---

Sunday afternoon at around 4:00 P.M., Jocelyn and Pierre's parents arrive as expected. The parents notice the sparks in the eyes of their two children. They set out again, happy.

Thoughtful, Jocelyn continues to be troubled by the three words Sofia mentioned into his right ear. "*What does that message really mean? Why me? Vigilance, vigilance, vigilance, those words keep running through my head.*"

--- OOO ---

The Clash of the Dragons

The training continues, just as intense on the ground as in the air. Sofia, Cedric and William understand the merits of the physical and mental demands imposed on them by their instructors. Not a day goes by without a lesson being retained. Sweat and joy are mingled with work and work brings success. As grandpa Thomas so aptly says: "The only place where success comes before work, is in the dictionary."

--- OOO ---

Sofia, Cedric and William enjoy and always look forward to riding their dragons. Time does not exist when they are riding them. Their practices have enabled them to develop the confidence necessary to ride their mounts with ease, complicity and efficiency.

Today, the flight plan aims to tweak their communications and reactions when facing danger. LYKA in the lead, the three dragons complete various acrobatics. The acrobatics are becoming increasingly surprising and challenging. The dragons twirl to the right, then to the left, and plunge gently to the ground, followed by vertiginous accelerations towards the clouds where they all play hide and seek.

Suddenly, the three dragons stiffen and remain hidden in a dark cloud. They perceive hostile energy in the surrounding area, a sure danger.[14]

A huge black dragon of more than fifteen metres long and impressive volume is approaching dangerously closer from cloud to cloud.

LYKA transmits to his companions: "The children are not ready to experience aerial combat with a dragon as powerful as Taurarok. We knew he was going to appear one day or another, but it's a bit too early and really not the time…" "I agree with you," adds MARA. "Let's quickly deposit the children and then come back and drive this monster away. He must not attack the children. If possible, he must not see where they live. Sofia must be protected at all costs."

The children, surprised, are horribly afraid. While MARA, DYRA and LYKA plunge at high speed towards grandpa and grandma's house, Cedric asks: "Taurarok! Who is that?" "Taurarok is a black dragon we have known for millennia. We have fought against him repeatedly. He is a cruel, brutal and destructive being. He is a worthy opponent."

The dragons perceive the inevitable fight. The three mounts nimbly reach the garden, deposit their riders and, in tactical formations go back to meet the threatening giant. They are here to protect the triplets and help them pursue their destiny, whatever the challenges. "Under no circumstances is Taurarok or any of his accomplices to approach the triplets," transmits LYKA.

---

[14] Dragons feel energies from tens of kilometres away just as does the polar bear, who, thanks to this keen sense of smell, detects the presence of a seal a dozen kilometres away, and the odour of a beached whale at more than 30 km radius. Wikipedia

--- OOO ---

Thomas and Louise are appalled. They suspected that one day, beings from the shadow world would show up and intervene in the lives of their grandchildren.

Louise perceives Cedric, William and Sofia's emotional state. She approaches them. She invites her three grandchildren to join her and their grandfather. Precipitously, Cedric, William and Sofia come close to their grandparents. Sofia, worried, asks Louise: "What will happen to our dragons?" "They are capable of fending off the enemy, even if he is gigantic," answers grandpa. "They are also well surrounded with energy, don't forget that children." "Yes, that's right," answers William. "I would so much like to be with mine to live a fighting experience, he says aloud with ardour and readiness."

"Come on, Will, you're not serious… Aye! They move, those beasts, when confronted. You're not thinking! C'mon! You'd risk leaving your hide there," adds Cedric, astonished. "I recognize you William. I'm not surprised … even at the risk of your life, you are ready to take up arms. You're really a fighter," says grandpa! "Let them confront him, three against one, and we will see. Your dragons are aware of their mission. Let's await the outcome," says grandma, inviting the children to come into the house. She continues: "Pay attention to your breathing and pull yourselves together. You can't do anything in this situation. Besides, the dragons know how to fight."

Much time goes by. The children are still waiting for the return of their dragons. They are nervous and impatient.

Suddenly, the triplets see MARA and DYRA approaching the house. They immediately go out on the lawn and Sofia starts running towards those enormous creatures and shouts out to them: "Where's LYKA?" She is anguished at the mere thought that something bad might happen to him. She rushes beside MARA and DYRA who don't move.

"What happened to him? You left him alone with that monster? Did you not defend him at the risk of your life?" She cries, upset and shocked at the mere thought of losing her aerial companion?

The boys reach her, surround her and try to calm her. Nothing to be done, Sofia is in a terrible state. She is torn by the possible loss of her magical companion, she weeps angrily. "It can't be true, not him, not another being who is dear to me." She sobs torrents.

Grandma approaches and calmly lays her right hand at the back of Sofia's head and her left hand on her solar plexus. A few moments suffice. Already, Sofia is breathing more calmly and looks at her grandma with tearful eyes, desperate. "Let it out, Sofia! I know it's painful. It's difficult to live a moment such as this. But we don't know what happened during the aerial combat. Perhaps we would have explanations if we listened to MARA and DYRA tell us what happened. What do you think, child?"

Louise looks at Sofia calmly and gently. "You know Sofia, during our menstrual period; we women are much more vulnerable to emotional shock. It takes years for us to understand and manage this overflow of energy." "I'm afraid grandma. I fear that something happened to him." "I understand what you are feeling. Maybe you're wrong. How about asking MARA for explanations." "Yes grandma. Let's hear MARA and DYRA tell us what happened," suggests Cedric.

As they prepare to recount what they know, a gust of wind jostles the two female dragons, the children, Louise and Thomas. It's LYKA who lands on one leg, imbalanced and a little bashed up.

Sofia exults with joy. She rushes to her dragon and jumps to squeeze its neck and says: "Oh, LYKA, you've returned! I was so afraid you would not come back. I don't want to lose you." "Hum!" breathes LYKA. "You're very good for me. It's your love that allowed me to fight that monster at the risk of my life. That's why I pulled away from my two companions and could surprise Taurarok, darting him on his left side, close to his cardiac centre. It was a surprise assault and he let me know he didn't like it. He retaliated by throwing darts of fire at me with his powerful breath. I lost my orientation and balance. I almost crashed into the forest of Mount Stokes. It's thanks to my survival pouch, located just under my two small ears that I quickly recovered and could resume the combat. MARA and DYRA attacked Taurarok who was pursuing me. That diversion allowed me to recover and counter-attack. I regained control in no time and asked MARA and DYRA to let me take care of him."

LYKA turns towards Thomas and Louise: "I've known for a long time that such an encounter was forthcoming. That black dragon has been looking for me for several hundred years according to the linear time of you earthlings. It's not the first time he attacks me. I give him no chance. You don't give any respite to a being like that one. His vigour and his agility are amazing and he can catch you by surprise." Then turning towards his dragon companions: "I can tell you that my two companions are magnificent warriors, with their wings outstretched in attack formation, they bore down at full speed, stumbling head first into that black monster. That stunned him so much that he fell in a dive and struggled to resume his flight. It was at that moment that I resumed combat with him. He defended himself very well. He saw that the fight was uneven and he chose to disappear. This time, he again yielded. However, we know that this fight is only postponed."

Looking directly at Sofia: "That is why MARA and DYRA arrived before me, my dear Sofia. I am touched by your concern for me. Be reassured, I have more than one trick in my bag." LYKA laughs with an impressive guttural sound.

MARA addresses LYKA : "I believe that now, we must consider this threat during our outings!" "And prepare ourselves accordingly, especially if the children are with us," adds DYRA. "Yes, we will adjust the training," concludes LYKA.

--- OOO ---

Taurarok

Thomas, Louise and the children regain control over their emotions. They are reassured. The children are all safe and sound. A combat training program is scheduled. Sofia remains pensive.

"LYKA, how is it that it's you that Taurarok sought to combat. Who is this Taurarok to you? Why does he want to fight you?" The three dragons look at one another. MARA speaks to LYKA : "I think you should tell them about our history with Taurarok."

"Ah! So, there's a history amongst you four," exclaims grandpa, "That's interesting, we're all ears" says grandma with concern. She insists: "We're listening. Our brain is adjusted to your vibrational frequencies. There is surely an explanation for that dragon to be tracking you."

Louise. Thomas, Cedric, William and Sofia settle down in front of the three dragons. Everyone feels LYKA's telepathic contact.

"Well, then! At the outset, know that Taurarok has not always been on the dark side. He once was a magnificent and great fighter, adored and respected by all the dragons. For this story, consider that we don't calculate time as you earthlings do. So, I speak to you of those moments that are immemorial and off the temporal clock. This story begins with a flight executed by Taurarok and his faithful companion, Drago. Are you following me, asks LYKA?" "More than ever!" Sofia's tone shows how anxious she is to know the truth about this aerial monster.

--- OOO ---

“It happened on the day of the Celestial competition organized by the Gods. This competition allows the Gods to evaluate and compare the prowess of different groups of dragons. Teams of dragons come from different dimensions and from all the regions known of the Gods. This activity also procures moments of rejoicing for dragons. As you know, dragons intervene a great deal with humans without them noticing. They work discreetly without being perceived or seen by the earthlings.”

“Formerly, humans could see them with their third eye. However, with evolution the third eye integrated the skull and the other two eyes appeared in its place. Since that time, humans became afraid of the gigantism of these magnificent beings. Currently, only initiates can see and contact dragons.”

“This competition is a veritable obstacle course. Each team comprises two dragons working together. The race calls for, amongst other things, intelligence, endurance, various flight skills and combat techniques. The competition is a real challenge especially when a trophy is to be awarded. There are many types of competition.”

“Now, just imagine hearing Drago talking to his teammate, Taurarok: ‘Go, fly higher, still higher, faster, hurry up, I want to win the race against the others.’ Those two have always won any competition ever since they began flying together. Their complicity is remarkable. Every year, all the other dragons tried everything possible to beat them.”

“Every type of challenge they entered was won by this hellish duo. They were always crowned with glory and recognition. However, with the honours and visibility they became imbued with themselves. It seems that all this glory made them inaccessible. They took delight in their joint success until one day, at another race organized by their Gods, a large yellow dragon named LYKA, here present, from the Asian territories, rose to the challenge and won the race accompanied by his partner, MARA, also here present, another yellow dragon, as burly as Taurarok.”

“Taurarok lived the defeat very badly. As for Draco, he took this defeat as another challenge to face. He is remembered for a famous remark he said that day: ‘Good, we no longer had fun doing these races. Nobody was up to us. None had the power and the strength to stand up to us. This is a team that will compel us to excel. I like that. Don’t you, Taurarok?’ It seems that at that moment, Taurarok rallied to his companion, saying, ‘You’re probably right. In fact, it’s true; I was bored in the end. For the next race, I will be prepared, you will see, they’ll get an eyeful. I will not let us be surpassed this way. We will again be the inter-dimensional world champions. Between us, they will see nothing but FIRE.’ At that moment, we heard a low rumbling coming from Taurarok and Draco. They were projecting blue flames of joy. That is one of our ways, we dragons, to demonstrate our pleasure and satisfaction.”

“As promised Taurarok and Draco trained secretly and eventually participated in the race organized in another inter-dimensional context. Hundreds of dragons of different colour, shape and size were competing. The race was to honour a goddess acknowledged by their Gods as being an important entity for the world of humans. This goddess had the mission to wrap the earth’s aura in a veil of protection against spiritual wickedness. All the available dragons from every inter-dimensional space were to be present. It was to be the most important race ever organized by their Gods.”

“We could see Taurarok and Draco were ready. They had prepared their scales, their horns and their claws for the occasion. Taurarok has always been the most beloved and admired dragon. He is truly magnificent especially when he spans his huge gleaming black wings to full size. His horns styling his triangle-shaped head give him an air of a combatant prince. His presence is worthy and noble. He is easily incensed because he gives a grandiose show. His pride is equalled only by his gigantic shape. As they say, he has a lot of panache. Draco remains in the shadow of his companion. He is an excellent wingman in races. His shape and size allow him feats that Taurarok can’t do due to his immense deployment. It is an asset for their duo.”

"The signal to begin the race must be given by one of the Gods. The crowd is excited. The competitors are focused. All the dragons, whatever their size, have settled in an immense area prepared for this purpose. Everyone can hear the loud breath emanating from their muzzle. Everyone's eyes are glued to the god that will give the signal of departure. A shockwave is triggered by the signaller. The competitors open their wings; take flight towards the location of the imposed obstacles. It is grandiose. It's a giant rainbow. It's a moving kaleidoscope. It's a colour extravaganza as far as the eye can see."

"The objective is to win the trophy, yes, however, with it comes a beautiful golden crown and associated privileges. Multiple obstacles must be overwhelmed. In this race, attitude counts as much, if not more than skills. The judges consider criteria such as ingenuity, resourcefulness, 'fair play' amongst competitors and compliance with the rules in force at the time of such obstacle course."

"Everything is going well. The dragons fly two by two, stimulating each other. There it happens: breathtaking unimaginable arabesques, nose dives, some courtesy gaps, winged confrontations and especially headbutts amongst rivals. This is all part of the competition and is accepted by the Gods. They know it's just a game."

"Only Taurarok does not see it as such. He has a hidden agenda. He must not lose the race. It is a matter of honour and pride. He must prove to everyone that he is still the undisputed master of all these races. Besides, he and Drago are favourites to win. Imagine this type of exchange where Taurarok asks Draco, his wingman: 'Take care of the dragon accompanying LYKA, while I take care of him.' They nod and swoop in a nose dive. They jam MARA between them. They push her with a powerful stroke of their wings. MARA loses her balance and goes down out of control. MARA tries to recover and get back to me to continue the race. We have obstacles to cross and we must do it as a duo. Those are the orders as decreed by the Gods."

“MARA and I, wonder what kind of game they are playing. It looks as though they want to swoop us over to disqualify us. As you know, every obstacle must be met as a duo. MARA then suggests, she will approach them from the flanks of the biggest dragon, we want to know what their intentions are towards us. Do they want to remove us from the race, eliminate us at all costs? Or what? She is to approach increasingly closer, and I must be ready to intervene if they try to strike her again with their wings. As we were moving to execute our plan, Taurarok and Draco both go skyrocketing. They are moving away from us. We believe the danger is over. So, we decide to fly towards the first obstacle: a cloud filled with bad and risky lightning.”

“MARA and I think they simply sought to intimidate us. Without further ado, we accelerate our flight to regain the time lost. Suddenly a huge force crashes down on us both at the same time. We lose our momentum and we both topple into total emptiness. Personally never before had I felt such force strike me. We barely regain our balance when we are again struck with great force. It’s at this moment that we see the huge black dragon sweeping down on us once again. The second dragon has disappeared from the race. We wonder where the other one is. We certainly don’t want any more unpleasant surprises. This is not part of the race. I don’t appreciate this kind of jostling. At this point, Taurarok is alone and we remain very cautious. We’re on our guards. He is flying above us.”

“Then Taurarok attacks again in MARA’s direction. I shout ‘watch out’ to MARA. It’s obvious now that this is not intimidation. It is evident that he will try anything to stop us from winning the race. It’s as though a duel is taking between us. I say to MARA: ‘leave me! I’ll take care of him. Perhaps we will be disqualified, but we will not be the only ones. He will have some explaining to do later. For now, we will not let ourselves be destroyed by that huge black dragon that seems to have lost his senses’. Now I’m in the attack mode. I make an about-turn and sink my claws into Taurarok who is coming at full speed. I slip on his dripping black scales. I lose my balance. Taurarok takes this opportunity to destabilize me. I then flip around and confront him face to face or if you prefer, muzzle to muzzle. Taurarok spits fire he seems so angry."

"MARA shouts out to me at this point, 'But he's completely crazy that dragon'. It's at this moment that Draco joins us and indicates that he absolutely does not understand his companion's behaviour. He telepathically notifies MARA that he thinks Taurarok has lost the ultimate purpose of this race. He believes that Taurarok is making it a personal matter."

"Taurarok must certainly not have digested his defeat at the last race, the first time we introduced ourselves at an inter-dimensional festival," interjects MARA. LYKA continues : "Drago confirms that 'Taurarok is a dragon worshiped by his peers. He doesn't tolerate defeat. One day while we were practising our soaring techniques he told me that he ranks himself in a separate category.' Draco assures MARA, who is carefully listening to this new partner of fortune, that he has nothing to do with Taurarok's plans, that he doesn't understand what's going on. The blows that Taurarok inflicts to me are not those of a dragon who is playing fair. I defend myself as best I can. Again, I try to cling to his scales. I manage. I resist his violent shaking with all my might. I hang on for a while. His anger is so great that he projects me in every direction. He eventually succeeds in breaking me away, however, on slipping off; my claws rip through the membrane of his left wing. Taurarok roars in anger and, turning quickly, bites and tears out a large claw from my left hind leg. It's at this point that MARA and Draco pursue Taurarok, still in an uncontrollable anger."

"The other dragons have witnessed this inexplicable combat. They join us to encircle Taurarok and try to reason with him, if not control him. The forces involved are disproportionate. Taurarok struggles as only a huge dragon can struggle on such occasion. He is considered a troublemaker, a being who has no place amongst the entire community of dragons who have travelled for the event of this obstacle course. All the participants are outraged at his behaviour."

“Taurarok finally realizes something is wrong. He inquires as to what is going on, why he is surrounded by competitors. It’s as if he is waking up from a nightmare. He is astonished at his behaviour. He doesn’t know what got into him to rush headlong into me like that. The other dragons stare questioningly at him. They keep on pushing him and bringing him back to the starting point of the obstacle course. His shame is visible. He notices a loss of energy at the level of his wings such as he had never experienced before. ’What is happening, asks Taurarok? I can barely fly and steer myself. Would the Gods have dared to intervene by reducing me to partial inertness? »”

--- OOO ---

“The tension is enormous. A great gust swirls around the armada of dragons. Flashes of lightning resound everywhere in the environment of festivities. All the Gods and the celestial hierarchies present at the obstacle course are flabbergasted. For the first time in their millenary history they face insubordination from one of their loyal dragons. These dragons are at their service since their creation. A revolt amongst these protectors is non-acceptable. Such a precedent must not happen again.”

“The organization’s committee awaits the first dragons returning from the improvised battlefield. An intimidating silence prevails. The loud breath released by the god responsible for the festivities weigh down the atmosphere and intimidates all the dragons present. Prior, the god responsible for the insubordinate dragon, orders the assembly to make space. He orders Taurarok to look him in the eye and says: ‘What were you attempting to do by attacking LYKA, the yellow dragon? What did you want to prove by standing alone against those two dragons that came to participate in this friendly event? There is nothing more humiliating than to see one of our own failings in his duty to show courtesy and chivalry to a visiting dragon. Besides, the race had just begun. You need to have a very good reason for your unacceptable behaviour.’ Taurarok looks the God Prior, in the eye. He doesn’t drop his horned head. He is very aware of his actions towards me. He has no explanation to give him. ‘I have nothing to say in my defence’, admits Taurarok to the God Prior.

Then he adds: 'I accept your decision and your punishment, if any. For the first time in all my celestial dragon life, tell me what you expect of me. I will accept your decision'. Taurarok never sought any favours from anyone. He is ready to take responsibility for his actions. He is at fault, he knows it. His life amongst his own only hangs by a thread."

"Taurarok waits, head high, without flinching, without moving a scale. His powerful wings, somewhat scraped, are lowered along his dripping body. MARA and I and all the other dragons are suspended to God Prior's decision. The God Prior, addresses the entire crowd of dragons, mentions loudly and clearly that he has the approval of all the other Gods present. He declares authoritatively: 'Taurarok, I announce you that, because of your unacceptable behaviour, you are banished from our environment, our celestial energy. You will be a stray dragon from this day forward'. The silence is deafening. Never, ever, had a cutlass been dropped so severely on the head of a dragon. The greatest, the most beloved by all, the most revered by his peers, the most rewarded by the Gods have just fallen so low that he would never be able to recover and redeem himself. There is no turning back. Pride did it! The Gods can't ever tolerate such conduct nor such offence."

"Taurarok is raging from the judgment of the Gods. He shakes out his wings, sniffs and smells the celestial essence around him one last time. He casts a last look at Draco, his racing companion. Then he turns towards all the assistance his face of stone, his eyes cold, menacing. His eyes lock with God Prior's unflinching stare. Finally, in this astounding silence he brings a hard and fiery look on MARA and me. I knew from that moment, from that look, that the confrontation between us would remain. I remember the insolent tone of his voice when he said: 'I leave this celestial space with the limited power I have left with no regret. I retain from my long stays amongst you only ingratitude, lack of recognition and lack of judgment on your part, God Prior. I shall know how to sell my services to one that can appreciate. I'm still qualified for the combat, don't ever forget that'."

"Before leaving, Taurarok stares at me intently and in a low rumble, spits out these threatening words: 'I will find you at some point, LYKA. This is only a postponement. I make you this promise.' All the dragons are silent. The race is cancelled. All those present remember Taurarok's promise."

--- OOO ---

"Well, that's the end of that historical saga. You were so attentive that I didn't see the need for a pause." "It's as if we had read a novel in a flash. It all happened in minutes. I absolutely understood everything," says William, shaken by the story. "Why did the Gods not give him another chance?" LYKA answers Cedric's question: "It is an implacable law that governs us. We are not allowed any such inclination. We don't have a choice to choose between good and evil as you earthlings. The law is the law. One infraction to any law by which we are governed and we are banished forever. Taurarok knew. He played with fire. He burned his wings. His vanity made a fool of him."

Once the emotions have subsided, the three dragons depart and let the children catch their breath in the company of their grandparents.

Louise hides her concern. She knows that these children will experience many battles spaced out all through their current existence. They will face many difficulties scheduled to come their way.

Brahima's Lair

Brahima walks to and fro in his magnificent lair, a giant cave on the side of the "Piton de la Fournaise»[15] volcano in the Reunion Island. The space was excavated and moulded by molten rock over the centuries. Dissimulated, inaccessible to the common mortal, this cave has continued to be the home of the wizard of sorcerers for centuries.

All kinds of skeletons adorn the walls. Alcoves with multiple shelves contain numerous terracotta or transparent pots of various sizes and from different eras. Some round flasks, other square, interspersed with bowls containing coloured powders, or unusual herbs, decorate a wall in the main room. Facing this wall, an ancient and a modern library completes the decor; ancient because of the ancient manuscripts, books of spells and artifacts, including slate stones, and modern because of the books of science and treaties of every kind. Rustic and rectangular chests line the hallway walls and the adjoining rooms. The different containers bear witness to experiences and lugubrious research as the ambient lighting in the hallways is nebulous.

---

[15] The Piton-de-la-Fournaise, culminates at 2632 metres of altitude and is the active volcano of the island of La Reunion. It corresponds to the summit and the eastern flank of the massif of the Piton-de-la-Fournaise, a shield volcano which constitutes 40% of the island in its southeastern part. This volcano is one of the most active on the planet. Wikipedia

A strong smell of sulfur curbs any animal and human curiosity.

In the centre of the main room, several tables, made of stone blocks, form a circle around a huge luminescent stone with magic powers. This stone reacts to the sorcerer's mood and energy impulses. It not only diffuses its dark light; it reacts to the sorcerer's questions. It communicates its answers in a codified language that only he can translate and understand. This cave bears no resemblance to anything one can imagine. It takes on the appearance of a space vessel from another world. The walls are living beings at the disposal of its sole master, the sorcerer Brahima.

Brahima does not walk; he slithers over the damp and hot rocks of his lair. Time presents no worth to his mind. He observes and manipulates the humans according to the needs and objectives of the moment. He exploits the inclinations and lusts of human beings. Nourishing inclinations and lust enables Brahima to enslave and place his power and that of his organization on all the continents and especially amongst the political and religious leaders. The organization he heads, dates to the time of antiquity. The shadow's power resides in the possession of matter and through its use. Brahima knows how to manipulate greed.

For a long time, his sorcerer brotherhood has been aware of the prophecy dealing with the opening of a portal on other dimensions, on the access to an incommensurable power for man. Patiently, the shadow's tentacles are on the lookout for any relevant clue. The books, books of spells, and manuscripts indicate that the coming is near. Political and social instability, chaos and public scandal scream the necessity to establish a new order. The secret society network of the Curretaras is present on every continent. Few organizations of global influence are yet to be penetrated. Currently, from a distance, he observes what is happening in the world around him. He carefully follows the news without recourse to the means of modern technology. He has his own perspective of events. His magic supports and satisfies him.

--- OOO ---

Brahima smiles at the thought of these covetous beings that serve the interests of his organization. He particularly appreciates the contribution of the mythical being that works and serves him unabated. He recalls, amongst other things, how the pride and vanity of a large black dragon caused its own downfall and banishment, how he himself could turn that errant dragon into one of his most loyal and efficient allies.

That dragon has suffered in his bruised body and spirit. Despite this, he remains nonetheless magnificent in his stature and his movements. "*I recovered this mythical animal for my personal needs and for the cause of our order, the Curretaras. For now, he responds sufficiently well to the orders I give him. As always, I keep some suspicion towards that dragon. One never knows... He is on his way back from an outing. He will be here soon.*"

Suddenly, a dark and violent energy penetrates an adjoining cavern. "*Taurarok returns. I have the impression he is frustrated. He is a beautiful animal, rebel yes, but true to my service.*"

"Master, I'm grateful to you for allowing my escapades across the terrestrial world." "Why do you say that to me today, Taurarok," questions Brahima, testing his loyalty.

Brahima waits patiently while moving towards his magic stone in the centre of his cave. "During my outing, today, I spotted, quite by chance, the energy of three yellow Huanlong dragons. They are messengers of the Gods I used to serve. I have fought with two of them a few times. These are the only existing dragons that defeated me in competitions. They are at the origin of my banishment, my wandering, until I met you..." "When I saw LYKA, the rage to fight him again came over me. I could not resist that desire to confront him."

Intrigued by the event and with no sympathy, Brahima questions authoritatively: "Where were you when this meeting occurred?" "I was possibly above a North American or Canadian countryside. It's hard to say. I would be able to go back, but why bother; they have gone off to another dimension."

Brahima remains pensive for a moment and encourages Taurarok to be on the lookout for those celestial dragon energies. "They are not there by chance, Taurarok. They surely have a reason; I would even say a mission to fulfill..." Then with authority he adds: "On every terrestrial day, you will patrol the environments where you are likely to find them again. I want to know their mission in this dimension and this period. That's an order."

Taurarok accepts the task and slips away while Brahima ponders: "*Why would Asian celestial dragons be back on this planet? Why was I not made aware of this coming?*"

Brahima leans towards his magic stone and questions it: "Is the presence of the yellow dragons connected with the prophecy?"

A powerful breath emerges from the centre of the room, an orange flame, flickering and powerful, comes out of the incandescent stone. A vibrational response is transmitted to him. "*What do you want to know that you do not know already? Do your own research on the subject that concerns you. The prophecy is there to be discovered and cleared.*"

The sound stops as suddenly as it appeared.

Brahima recalls Taurarok and orders him: "Go! And come back to me with answers. You know the world of dragons and their great ability to travel through time. Do not disappoint me, he says, in a calmness that gives one the creeps."

Taurarok remains impassive. He ignores the threat and flies away.

--- OOO ---

Meanwhile at grandpa and grandma's home, the children and Mimi, the cat are enjoying the last week of September. The nights are cooler and the foliage adorns magnificent autumn colours.

"They are already very busy with their school home work. My, how time flies!" Grandma is thinking while she observes them still playing like young children. *"A time will come when they will not want to play like this, with casualness and freedom. I hope they will take lessons from Ming and Patrick. For them, nothing is serious because, as they mention so well, life is a big play."*

Louise remembers LYKA's advice to Jocelyn: "*Why did LYKA caution* Jocelyn to be vigilant and especially three times? Dragons feel danger and in Jocelyn's case what is it? What is it I do not see or feel?" Louise says out loud to herself and to her surroundings: "Each one of us must be vigilant daily. The shadow will not stand idly! He has many tricks and resources! But so do we, Thomas, Ming, Patrick and I, we will be vigilant."

--- OOO ---

Louise has been living very special moments with her guide Pheas since the children's return to school. He discusses regularly with her on the continuous teachings of the triplets. He knows the sequence of the events. He encourages Louise to prepare Cedric, William and Sofia for the power over the elements. This will be the second step towards stimulating their crystal. "Soon the children will be taught by mages descendents from the Atlantis Tradition. I will guide you when the time comes. I support you in this mission that has been entrusted to you. Let this be a beneficial year for them."

Grandma Louise shares the message with Thomas who is prepared, once again, to meet the challenge. "Still, it's interesting that you should say that to me as, for quite some time, my morning reflections are pointing me to the regions of Central America. I recently caught William in the library, ferreting with the books we said they must not touch, the ones on the prohibited shelves." "Hu! Hu!" Agrees Louise looking at Thomas with interest. "Well, I let him be. I just kept watching from a distance.

He pulled out the old book, worn by time, the one with the engraving of the Aztec sun. He dared to open it. Then he froze, he was like petrified staring at the first page. I let him put the book back in its place and I quietly withdrew so as not to arouse suspicion. Do you remember that first page, Louise?" asks Thomas, sipping his morning coffee.

"Yes dear, and I understand why William would be stunned and remain frozen. He will surely talk about it with the other two. Let's await their reaction. The surprise will be enormous. The next trip will bring them exactly at that place."

To Note

This book is self-published. You understand that you can have an impact on its promotion.

Indeed, if you enjoyed it and wish to make it known to your friends and family, please do not hesitate to communicate your appreciation. This way, you will contribute to its publicity.

Marcelle Chapleau and Paul Corriveau

Marpa.productions@gmail.com

--- OOO ---

To be published:

The Triplet's Odyssey

- *Tome II: The Sacrificed...*
  Mexico, Cortez, the conquest, the dangers ... an inevitable journey...

Made in the USA
Middletown, DE
22 October 2022

13240147R00149